SKETCH MAP BY PATROL OFFICER F. SCULLY

PREPARED FOR CORONIAL ENQUIRY

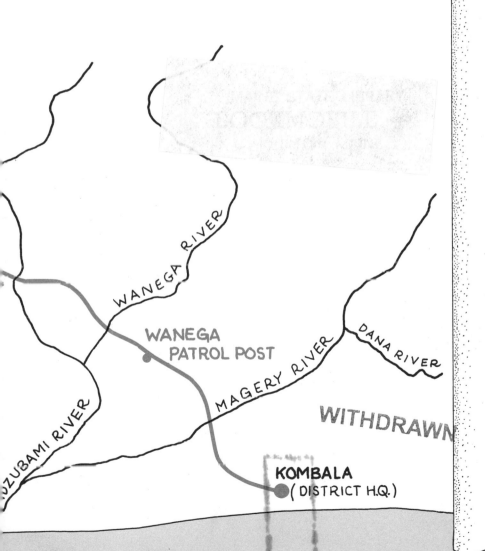

WANEGA RIVER

WANEGA
PATROL POST

MAGERY RIVER

DANA RIVER

UZUBAMI RIVER

KOMBALA
( DISTRICT H.Q. )

# THE FAR SIDE OF THE SKY

*Also by Maslyn Williams*

FIVE JOURNEYS FROM JAKARTA

STONE-AGE ISLAND: NEW GUINEA TODAY

# THE FAR SIDE
# OF THE SKY

A NOVEL BY

## Maslyn Williams

WILLIAM MORROW & COMPANY, INC.

NEW YORK

1967

For
Assistant District Officer James Sinclair
EMA Albert Speer and
Assistant District Officer Neil Grant
with affection and respect.

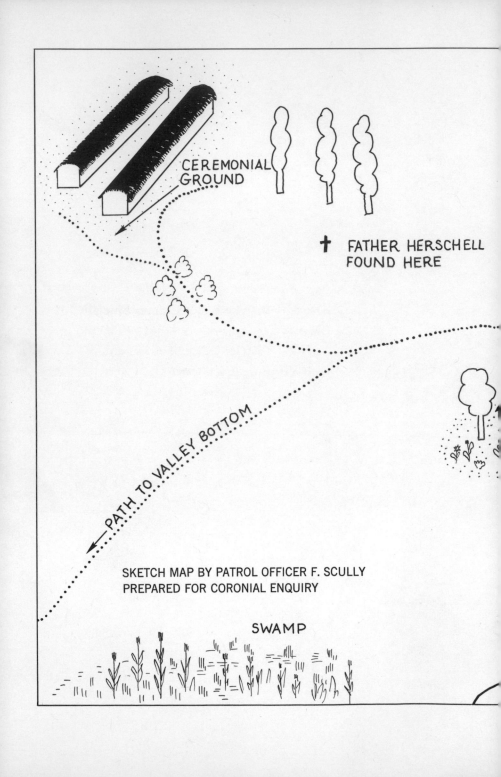

CEREMONIAL GROUND

✝ FATHER HERSCHELL FOUND HERE

PATH TO VALLEY BOTTOM

SKETCH MAP BY PATROL OFFICER F. SCULLY
PREPARED FOR CORONIAL ENQUIRY

SWAMP

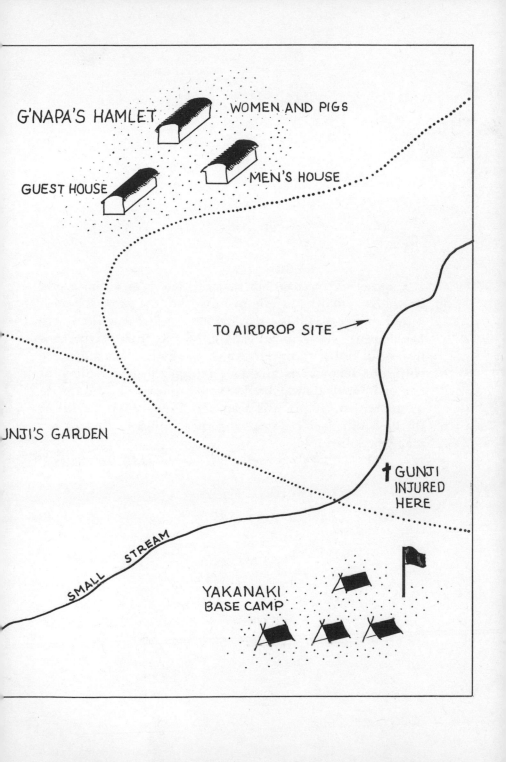

It is of no real moment whether this tale is taken for truth, or not. It would be as idle to insist that the work is one of pure fiction as to protest that everything that is written here has happened. Marshall is the most shadowy character, perhaps nearest in reality to myself, which is why my sympathies are with him. The others might be recognized, under different names, by anybody who knows New Guinea well. And we are all aware that the priest is dead. His obituary was published in the South Pacific *Times,* together with a picture of the man who killed him.

MASLYN WILLIAMS

# Prologue

The chain of events described herewith began on **May 7, 1965**, when the following memorandum was received at the Wanega Patrol Post, at which time Father Louis Herschell had been only a few days in New Guinea and was unknown to the other three men who were his companions on the ill-fated expedition into the Yakanaki Valley.

DEPARTMENT OF NATIVE AFFAIRS.

File No.  DHQ/10/98/65

> District Headquarters
> Kombala
> Northern Highlands
> Territory of Papua—New Guinea
> May 6, 1965

MEMORANDUM:

To:        Assistant District Officer K. P. F. Marshall, in charge of WANEGA Patrol Post
From:      District Commissioner J. McKerrow
Subject:   Visit of the Rev. L. H. Herschell

The above-mentioned Catholic priest has been given official permission to accompany a government patrol into Uncontrolled Highland Territory for the purpose of gathering data relevant to the structure and distribution of native languages and dialects in areas where there has been no known penetration of outside influences within living memory.

The Director of Native Affairs has decided that these researches shall be carried out in this District, and you are hereby instructed to make appropriate arrangements for the Reverend Herschell to accompany your forthcoming patrol into the Yakanaki Valley for the purpose specified.

I am informed that the Reverend Herschell is an internationally recognized expert in the field of linguistics and that his visit is sponsored by the United Nations Educational, Scientific, and Cultural Organization. You will realize, therefore, that in addition to the ordinary responsibility of seeing that he is given every facility and assistance, consistent with his own safety and that of other members of your patrol, to carry out his assignment, you should also ensure that every detail of the Yakanaki operation is carried out in such a manner as to avoid the slightest opportunity for criticism, particularly in such matters as the attitude of yourself and other white officers towards native staff, and your approach to any bush people you may encounter, especially in the case of first contacts.

Under no circumstances are you to employ firearms against tribesmen except in the case of a direct threat to the life of the Reverend Herschell or other personnel under your control.

He will bring with him a mission native from Madang to act as his personal servant. You will provide him, additionally, with two other carriers to handle his recording equipment and other technical gear.

Please advise me by radio as soon as you receive this memorandum, and state what arrangements you propose to put into train in order to receive, accommodate, and assist this gentleman to carry out his assignment.

Any uncategorized expenditure incurred in relation to this operation should be charged to FO/352/B/65 (sp.).

> (*signed*)  J. McKerrow—District Commissioner
> per Rosemary Mulholland (secretary)

"Bugger both of them," said Assistant District Officer Marshall reading through the memorandum a second time; and began to work himself into a state of irritation, being unready as yet to admit the pleasure he felt at being chosen to look after this visitor.

"Him and his bloody priests and linguists."

A Cessna had come over Wanega from Kombala soon after daybreak to drop the memorandum and other mail, and a few small parcels of medical supplies that would be needed on the patrol. Now, separate little heaps of letters, and packages of medicine, were spread about the floor of his hut.

He thrust the memorandum into the pocket of his shirt and stood frowning illogically, resenting all who, because of authority, could interfere in any way with the ordering of his little world. Especially the District Commissioner, who sent in visitors without prior advice or consultation or considerations of convenience.

It made him impatient.

What idiocy, to let an inexperienced, unknown, new chum come out here to piddle around linguistically among savages who would stave your head in with a stone club as soon as look at you. An academician. Worse than that, a priest, who would without doubt be useless in all practical matters. Absentminded, wearing spectacles, and when not in the way would always be sneaking off secretly to pray.

Yet underneath he was still pleased to have been chosen to look after the visitor. To have the measure of his reputation so recognized. Who else had the experience to lead an expedition into new, unknown territory and at the same time could look after visitors decently? Who else could be trusted to carry such an operation through without doubt of the outcome? Who else could they choose? Nobody else. Only himself, Marshall. But he must protest, on principle.

He shouted for the houseboy to come and take the packages of medicine down to Mr. Korbin at the medical center and while the boy's slow-moving, untutored, primitive mind wrestled tentatively with the problems of transferring these few articles from one bush hut to another, Marshall leaned down swiftly and gathered up the rest of the mail.

A few routine orders from headquarters. Replies to some of his own requests for equipment and information. Most of them stalling, putting him off, making vague and obtuse excuses in the pompous language of officialdom. There was notification of policy promotions in which he saw that Constable Garni was to be acting-lance corporal (second class). This would please Garni, whose wife was playing up again with Constable Palau and making Garni lose face. A circular from the Department of Health requested statistics (this could go to Korbin with the medical supplies). There was a private note for Patrol Officer Scully in an official envelope, direct from Kombala. This would be from Miss Mulholland, the District Commissioner's secretary who was also his niece. "Damned young fool," said Marshall out aloud, thinking of Scully. Getting mixed up with McKerrow's secretary was courting trouble, literally.

The houseboy, worried and uncertain, wondered if he was supposed to understand what the master was saying.

Otherwise there were only a few letters for each of them. Three others for Scully, all from his mother—a widow who lived alone in an upper-class suburb of Sydney, and wrote twice each week to her son though the mail came to Wanega only once in a while. There was a magazine for Korbin, from Germany. A few things for himself, including a list of releases from the World Record Club, the latest *Reader's Digest,* and a notice from the Pacific Islands Historical Society, advising members of the date of the annual meeting at Suva. Marshall regretted, briefly, that he would not be able to go.

There were some newspapers. And a thin letter from his wife which he would read sometime. He looked at his watch. In a little while he would go to the radio hut and call up District Headquarters to speak to the Commissioner about his linguistic priest.

Outside, the sun struck at him like a tiger.

He squared his shoulders and looked proudly around the station.

# PART 1

# Chapter 1

THE Government Station at Wanega * is no more than a cluster of huts, built native fashion of bush wood and plaited bamboo and thatched with a thick roof of kunai grass. It has been standing for six months, strung along both sides of a narrow red-earth ridge with a single steep way of approach out of a deep valley, so that if the tribesmen decide to attack they cannot come upon it suddenly or unseen.

Jungle slopes endlessly to the horizon, but behind the station the landscape rears up suddenly like a green wall thick with trees, which become sparse and spindly higher up and give way at last to thin, sharp-sided pinnacles of eroded limestone that stick up into the sky like a forest of stark white steeples.

Marshall had come to this upland country from the coast four years ago, with a reputation for being able to get along with natives of any kind. His assignment was to find and

* The following etymological note is taken from papers left by the late Father Herschell, all of which, fortunately, have been collected together and are now in the hands of his religious superiors: "WANEGA—pronounced to rhyme with Honegger with accent on first syllable. In each of the three main languages fo the area surveyed this or a similar word seems to refer to some landmark or common meeting place. Probably the name given to a territorial demarcation point or a neutral place for the holding of intertribal discussions."

pacify the Highland tribes and set up a sub-District Station and patrol posts among them, so that the Government could say that its influence was thoroughly established in every part of the Territory and among all of its two million people.

They had flown him in to Kombala, then newly established as District Headquarters and itself no more at that time than a cluster of rough huts, as Wanega is now.

The weather was bad and they had come cautiously, the pilot taking no chance of being trapped in the cloud-covered maze of mountain; but after several attempts he had slipped in through a slit between ridge and mist so thin that the draught from their slip stream had set the treetops swirling; and for one suddenly empty, terrifying second Marshall had been afraid.

So from the first he had learned to respect this uncompromising, hostile country, to accept and share its loneliness, its austerity. Even to admit a grudging love for the harshness that lay beneath its huge, breathtaking beauty. It offered no physical ease or comfort. Gave no promises of sensual pleasure. Declared itself an adversary from the beginning. Had nothing soft about it, no prettiness, no appeal to sentimentality. The only flowers to show among its sharp, metallic grasses were little, brittle everlastings and a few repellent insect-eating nepenthes.

Its people were primitives and killers, the men muscle-bound and squat, the women hideous and filthy. He had shuddered at the thought of touching one of them, even by chance, though it was not in him to think anything of women except in sudden, ugly moments of weakness; and he was glad that these female creatures were so repulsive that he could ignore them except as a technical element in his professional reckoning—a population statistic, and suppliers of garden produce with which to feed his police and carriers.

But the landscape, challenging his manliness, he tackled fiercely and with passion (as if seeking to subdue by sheer strength a lovely but stubborn woman). He rejoiced that it

18

made him fight every minute for its favours and gave nothing back, except a satisfying sense of his own strength and indestructibility.

McKerrow, the toughest District Commissioner in the Service, had set him deadlines, and for the first year he had fought this land, pushing himself each day to extreme limits of endurance as he clambered, panting, up its steep slopes or strode stick in hand along razor-edged ridges, always far ahead of the main body of carriers and police except in places where instinct told him that ambush was to be expected.

Month after month he had trampled and smashed a way through thickets of giant grass, more than head-high, that slashed and grabbed at him, leaving a network of stinging incisions on his arms and knees. At times, camped high at ten thousand feet and more above sea level, he had lain awake all night shivering with fever; and many mornings, before dawn, he had led his men floundering through swamps in the bottoms of high valleys never before seen by white men.

In little more than a year of walking he had worn out two junior patrol officers and a medical assistant, had gained reputation as an explorer that merited mention in the *Government Gazette,* and had made first contact with thirty thousand new people. Stone-age savages, said the pressmen who interviewed him when he went on leave. His photograph, appearing in newspapers and magazines, mostly showed him with a bow and arrow or a stone club, looking uncomfortable and vaguely troubled.

He married during that leave without telling anybody, so that none of his New Guinea friends were at the ceremony or attended any of the many receptions arranged by her friends and business connections. But it was soon rumoured around the Territory that she was an exceptionally beautiful woman, elegant and talented, and a well-known member of the fashionable set.

All of this, of course, was exaggerated. But even if it was half true it seemed that Marshall, the introspective, antisocial anchorite of the outback, had broken through in a big way. And there was much surmise and surprised lifting of eyebrows; and prurient curiosity. Especially when he appeared again in New Guinea weeks before his leave was due to finish, seeming keen to get back to work again.

"My wife's tied up and busy just now. Can't leave Sydney. She'll come up later when she's free and maybe we'll move around a bit then, so that she can meet a few people."

But she didn't come. And for two more years he ranged the high valleys on his own—traced rivers to their beginnings, made maps, estimated population densities. Then he chose the ridge at Wanega as the place for a subdistrict station. Established here, he could put down intertribal fighting, settle disputes of long standing and bring the whole area, in time, under the control of the Government.

Such was his function.

At his own request his next leave was deferred so that he could stay and build the station, train other officers to staff it, and then lead one more long patrol still farther out, to the last unknown valleys beyond the highest mountains.

So for the next six months he had stayed in this one place making friends with clan leaders, getting the nearby tribes accustomed to the continuing presence of white men, and gaining odds and ends of information about the last remaining pockets of population still isolated in the high heart of the island. And within a few days, he would set out to find them.

Now his voice came, complaining, from the radio hut perched on the highest point of the ridge. And loud, because transmission was bad and he was shouting, so that his voice could be heard all over the station. They could hear it down in the cargo compound where the carriers were sorting patrol gear and making rations into packs. They could hear it in the medical center at the far end of the ridge where Korbin's orderlies were shooting penicillin into children to heal, as if miraculously, the raw, suppurating sores which ate away the soft young flesh of so many of them. They could even hear him, though faintly, far down on the valley flat where Patrol Officer Scully and a hundred Wanega men, with digging sticks and a few steel spades, were levelling a patch of land long enough to make an emergency landing place for a light airplane.

He was saying resentfully, "Yes, I've read your memo. It's here in front of me. What's the idea of loading me with this priest? We're not going on a picnic." His voice had a sharp edge of petulance, an irritation not big enough to sound like anger (though the anger was there). You could tell that he was against the priest though he had never seen him; had never heard of him before this memorandum came.

It lay spread out between his elbows on the rough camp table, and he leaned over it, speaking into the two-way radio, a lean, sinewy man clean and smooth as a new-planed plank of cedarwood. And as hard. With blue eyes and thin brown hair. He was tensed now, impatient, and restless with unspent energy, speaking fiercely to his invisible superior.

"We'll be out for a month or more and it will be tough, and maybe a bit edgy. The people on the other side of the mountain have a bad reputation and we could get into a fight or two. I don't want to be handicapped with passengers on a first contact."

The answer crackled back at him from fifty miles away, and acting-Lance Corporal Garni, standing at the door, instinctively stiffened to attention. He had trained at the main station as a raw recruit and his insides still went wild with worry when he heard the voice of the District Commissioner.

"Who are you kidding, Mr. Marshall? The people on the other side of the mountain always have a bad reputation. It's been the stock excuse for beating up the neighbours for the past five thousand years."

Marshall had made his protest and was now prepared to give way gradually. But first he would have his say. "That may be so but we've got troubles enough without adding to them. The aerial surveys show that the country farther up is hungry.

**21**

There seem to be few native gardens and we'll run short of food. We don't want to take more people on this patrol than we have to, and if this priest comes with a servant and two carriers it means four extra people. In any case we can't get carriers enough for our own gear. The Wanega people believe that spirits haunt the passes into the Yakanaki Valley and they're frightened to sign on for the trip. That's why there's been no contact with the valley for as far back as anybody can remember."

There was a moment of silence. Then the District Commissioner's voice, richly cynical, came again. "If you have finished with the bedtime stories, Mr. Marshall, I will tell you what I want and what I expect of you."

Marshall began to answer but changed his mind. There was nothing to be gained by provoking the old man.

"The Reverend Herschell will leave here at dawn the day after tomorrow with his personal boy, six carriers and three police. I want you to send young Scully to meet them and escort them across the Dana country to Wanega. You may keep the three police and extra carriers to supplement your strength out there until this assignment is completed.

"Now, let us be quite clear about this. The priest is your responsibility and your guest until he is returned intact to me here. If you let him get hurt, or give him occasion to complain about the way in which he has been looked after and assisted, I will walk out to Wanega and personally shoot you. He's a UN expert, a priest, and an American. In my book that ranks him a little ahead of the Holy Trinity. And he's in my district as a guest of the Government. I hope I make myself clear. You've been too long in the bush if you can't face strangers."

When they had finished speaking to each other Marshall sent Garni, with a note for Patrol Officer Scully, down to where they were levelling land for an airstrip. Then he locked the radio hut and went striding along the red-earth bridge, through the station, towards the medical center.

Before he got there he could see Korbin crouched on the

22

bare ground in front of the aid post, busy with some unseen business, while a few curious New Guineans stood watching. One of them, wearing the red-edged khaki lap-lap of a medical attendant, stood beside him holding a glass flask. A group of elderly tribesmen, all naked but for string aprons, stood uncertainly to one side watching. Marshall strode past them and they shrank back. He stopped beside the white man.

Medical Assistant (Grade 1) George Vasyl Korbin, short, thickset, olive-skinned and bald, looked up. He spoke correct English with the merest trace of a middle-European accent. "These stupid old bastards have kept me awake for three nights in a row, mumbling and bumbling over this spirit hole, holding discussions with their bloody ancestors. I am now going to muck it up on them."

He shook a thumb in the direction of the tribesmen, then took the flask and poured a pint of benzine into the hole in the ground. Stepping back he laid a trail for twenty feet, then turning to the tribesmen made a speech.

"My friends. We have brought civilization to you and you must learn that from now on nothing is sacred unless we say so. You have used this piece of land for many generations as a place where you can meet and speak with the spirits of your ancestors, whose voices come to you from under the ground, up through that spirit hole. Every night, when the moon is full, you speak to them about your problems and get answers from them, get assurances, gain some benefit from their wisdom and the godlike knowledge that lies on the other side of death. But by chance, or by the design of whatever demons play their games with us, we white men have come and have built our station here on this ground, and your superstitious mumblings and bumblings keep me awake. And because my magic is more powerful than your magic, and my gun, if you object, more deadly than your bows and arrows, I am going to suggest to your ancestors that they move on, find some other hole farther away. For whatever they have to say to you now is obsolete, of no account, out of date. We can give you

**23**

more than they. Mr. Marshall and his police will protect you from each other. My penicillin will heal your children's sores. And when Mr. Scully has finished his landing strip the airplanes will bring you more and more of the white man's goods. So your ancestors must give way. I, Korbin, needing sleep, mark the beginning of a new age for the people of Wanega."

Marshall fidgeted, impatient and frowning. "Why do you make speeches? You know they can't understand a word you say."

Korbin nodded reflectively. "True, they have no idea what I am talking about but I must make the speech just the same. Not for them to understand but to convince myself that we are justified in coming here and doing what we do."

He flicked a cigarette lighter and lit the end of the benzine trail. The tribesmen gasped as the fuel took light, then cringed and hid their faces as it licked along the red earth like a live thing. There was a flash and roar, and a rush of thick black smoke and blood-red flame shot up out of the hole.

The tribesmen looked stunned, emptied of awareness and understanding, crouching almost to the ground with fear, moaning and making strange inarticulate sounds of horror, fear and shame.

"You shouldn't have done that." Marshall looked annoyed and uncertain.

Korbin observed him seriously, and when he spoke he sounded almost sad. "I know, but they must suffer as we do in order to understand that we are all caught up in history and must go along with it, or drop out and die quietly." He made a sign to his orderlies to get back to work. "You cannot apply civilized ethics to this uncivilized age. That way lies confusion and lunacy. We must insist, all the time, that we are right, whatever we do, however obviously wrong it is. As soon as we admit to doubts, or to any truth but our own, this civilization must collapse. And once we begin to wonder what right we have to be here in New Guinea, and what our objectives are, we are done."

Marshall shrugged, flustered, not wishing to argue but wanting to show that he had the ultimate authority on the station and that government instructions to all officers were to respect native custom and do nothing to offend against "acceptable" traditions. Then remembering why he had come he caught up with Korbin, who was already walking towards the medical center.

"I've been speaking to the District Commissioner. He's sending some linguistic priest to go with us on this Yakanaki patrol, and we have to put up with it. He'll be a nuisance. Probably won't be able to go more than a couple of hours a day without wanting a rest, and will get us into all sorts of trouble with the people if he starts meddling in their affairs, asking the wrong questions and breaking speech tabus." He fretted. "Why should we be stuck with a bloody priest for a month or more, wanting to talk religion, mentally criticizing everything we do, how we act or speak, or what we think even?"

Korbin said, "Come, and I'll make coffee." He called out, giving instructions to an orderly, then walked towards his own house with Marshall following. "Don't start worrying too soon, he might turn out to be good company. Priests can be quite sensible and pleasant fellows and this linguistic business could be interesting. If not, I'll keep him occupied with argument, and when he gets sick of me young Scully can take him over. He's a Catholic and they can pray together."

# Chapter 2

"In nomine Patris et Filii et Spiritus Sancti," said Father Herschell to himself three days later, mentally making the sign of the Cross and offering the pain in his own hands and feet and side to Christ crucified.

He shifted the grip on the staff that Constable Ki had cut for him some thirty-six hours previously, soon after they had left Kombala to walk through the bush to Wanega. Then he began to say the rosary again, counting the decades on ten little nicks which he had cut in the top part of the staff to help him indulge, discreetly, this pious exercise he had devised to remind himself that he was first a priest and only secondly an authority on lingustics engaged in fieldwork for UNESCO with the permission of his superiors.

Theoretically, repetitious mental prayer should have blunted the edge of pain and helped a man sustain more than normal effort (Brother Tom had taught him that at college) while the nicks in the top of the staff ought to have made it easier to grip. But the way was rough, often steep and slippery, and the friction of his skin against the green wood had worn raw patches on his fingers, so that now he held the staff awkwardly. And his feet were sore, though it was the pain in his side that made him wonder how much longer he could continue.

It seemed silly, almost shameful, that a man not yet near forty and in fair physical condition could not walk fifteen miles a day along a bush track, rough as it might be, without cracking up. The carriers, going barefoot with loads of fifty pounds, sang most of the time and played sly jokes on each other, even ran, sometimes, down steep slopes shouting with sheer pleasure like children, as if to use up excess energy. The three policemen, disciplined to exhibit greater dignity, strolled at lazy pace, each holding his rifle on his shoulder by the barrel: Constable Tau protecting the tail of the line, Ki in the middle with the priest, and Pahun up front with a local guide and Patrol Officer Scully, who had come to meet them.

They were all going slowly, adjusting with discreet sympathy to his unpracticed pace, and he was aware that without him they could have made the trip easily in half the time. The knowledge quite unreasonably discouraged him, made him feel inadequate and a little afraid that he would not be able to face the next month or more, to do the job he had come to do. If this was only an easy beginning.

Before leaving Kombala the District Commissioner had said, "The track to Wanega is no trouble and will give you time to get into trim for the big walk with Marshall. Don't overdo it to begin with. It takes a little time for limbs and muscles, accustomed to city living, to adjust to primitive conditions. In the first two days you'll discover parts of your body you never knew you had, and you'll hate it, and wish you'd never come to New Guinea. But after that you'll toughen up and take it in your stride. Then, when the four or five weeks are finished and you have to come back, you'll wish you could stay longer out there with Marshall, the eager beaver."

They came to a place in the narrow track where a tree had fallen. Stepping over it he stumbled awkwardly, fatigue dulling the edge of judgment, but before his mind could register resentment he felt his servant's hand steady him, then withdraw discreetly as he regained balance. He nodded thanks dumbly without looking round, and resumed the recitation of the rosary, keeping time to the stilted rhythm of walking he had devised to make most progress with least pain. The gentle, sensitive anxiety of Didimus his servant made the misery of his situation more difficult to contain, so that with little inducement he could have surrendered all dignity and cried out in protest like a child against the pain and punishment inflicted on his body.

The Bishop had sent Didimus to be his servant. "He is a good boy, a catechist, and maybe one day he will be a priest. That's why I'm sending him with you. He can serve Mass for you in the Latin, and perhaps out there in the bush he will find his vocation. Here, in the town, there are too many distractions for young men."

The Bishop had been a missionary for thirty years; had seen hundreds of boys like Didimus come up through the mission schools, learning as children to love the little white Jesus and wish to serve him. Then their parents came, took them back to the villages, and contracted marriages for them with related families according to tradition, binding them thus by customary ties and obligations to tribal life even though later many of them, who were in any way educated, would take jobs in government offices, or take to driving trucks and taxis, and would spend their spare time hanging around the towns in bars and cinemas, never going to church and losing touch with their own people.

He wished better for Didimus, who seemed truly to be walking in the way of grace. A sensitive lad, diligent in the practice of his religion, seeking always to come closer to holy things, to understand and share more fully in the substance of God's love (though one could never, really, get inside the native mind, even in confession). And humble. He could be trusted not to pilfer little things or forget the jobs he had to do.

Didimus walked almost at Father Herschell's elbow, ready at any moment to offer help, to check any slip or stumble, to go ahead and cut or hold back hanging vines which the priest could not see because he walked with his eyes down, watching the narrow track that zigzagged between high, untidy trees, got lost in bogs, crossed rivers and streams on wet, slippery logs and led farther and farther away from all that was familiar, safe, comfortable and comprehensible. Perspiration had fogged his glasses, and it was no good trying to wipe them with a wet handkerchief, anyway.

Two carriers from Kombala had his clothes, books and Mass kit in a tin trunk, lashed tight with bush vines and slung between them on a long pole. Didimus, in addition to his own pack, carried the priest's recorder and camera on his back, and on one shoulder a haversack in which were breviary, notebooks, pens, spare film, sunburn cream, repellents, cigarettes and candy bars. On the other shoulder, hanging on a loop of cord, in a canvas sack, he had his own guitar (made in Japan) with a bright red plastic back.

With all this he walked without effort as if strolling at leisure through his own village, listening to the soft plopping sounds of moisture dropping from the trees onto fallen leaves, and the raucous, ratchety cries of birds of paradise far down in the gully. Didimus was sorry for this priest, fresh from America, stumbling through the jungle.

They could not see Scully at the head of the line and obscured by bush, though he was no more than thirty yards in front of them, but suddenly they knew that he had stopped walking. The carriers, already aware, began to bunch together and hesitate, like bush creatures conscious of some strangeness or danger. Ki and Tau, the constables, being trained to face danger, separated and held their rifles ready.

They were no longer now a dozen separate and unique individuals, each living with his own thoughts, but had become, in a single instant, an entity, each equally part of a single completeness: Scully and the priest, the policemen and Didimus, the guide and the half-dozen near-primitive carriers. Together they were strangers, invaders, a corporate and alien element in this patch of bushland and jungle belonging to a group of stone-age savages.

Ki spoke quietly, "Dana people—it will be all right." But he moved closer to the priest while making a motion to Didimus that he should go ahead. They moved forward again and came into a little clearing on a hillside where Scully, Pahun and the guide stood in bright sunlight with five tribesmen, talking. A little higher up the hill there was a group of forty or more men and boys, watching.

The smaller group with Scully seemed in high good humour, and held on to him, stroking his arms and face with rough affection, laughing, their lips and tongues grotesquely scarlet from chewing betel nut and lime. But those in the bigger group, standing apart, were unsmiling.

None of them carried bows and arrows, so they were not looking for a fight, but their weapons would almost certainly be hidden in the long grass within quick reach, to be taken up if the meeting should lead to argument or dispute. But with young boys among them it seemed that the encounter, if planned, was intended peacefully, though each man had a stone ax in his hand and carried a dagger of bone in the cane girdle at his waist.

Each of them wore a wig, shaped like Napoleon's hat and faced with parrot wings and small dry flowers; and some young men of courting age had their faces painted with black wood ash and red and yellow clays. The small boys had their heads cropped close (when they came of age each would have a wig, like the men, made from these clippings, and from the hair of their womenfolk). Men and boys all wore a long apron of woven grass fibers in front, and a tail piece of green leaves behind.

They watched Constable Tau emerge from the bush and lead the carriers, now quiet, in a wide arc away from them, to sit them down a little apart on a piece of high ground, to wait. They saw, also, that he placed himself where he could keep both groups of tribesmen covered with his rifle, though

**30**

nothing in his movements or expression showed that he was either threatening or afraid. All, except the priest, understood quite clearly that in this situation the little cavalcade might expect to be attacked; that the Dana warriors would be within their rights to kill them all without hesitation or scruple, if they could. Or take their possessions. For they were trespassers and strangers with rich goods, and greatly outnumbered.

Ki and Didimus came with the priest to where Scully stood speaking with the leader. Scully seemed at ease and as the priest came up to him said, turning, "This is Parmi of the Dana people, a clan leader."

Parmi grinned widely and pressed Scully's hand in friendship against the inside of his naked thigh. But Scully withdrew his fingers gently and with his other hand pulled at Parmi's sparse beard, laughing. But he was watchful, moving all the time like a boxer to keep balance and be ready to strike or retire at any sign of treachery.

Scully kept on talking loudly, as if to Parmi, but his words were for the priest. "Don't get too near those other fellows, but don't show fright either. Parmi and his men ambushed us when Marshall and I came through here the first time, and two of our carriers copped arrow wounds. We had to fire a few shots to frighten them off but we've had no trouble since. In fact he's been very friendly—probably hopes that we will help him in the next fight against his neighbours." Scully touched a spent cartridge case that hung like a pendant on Parmi's chest. "That's one of the shots we fired at him when we first met. His introduction to civilization. The first piece of metal he ever saw. He's quite proud of it."

Father Herschell was alert now, his pains forgotten, and he moved as though to take the tape recorder from Didimus but hesitated, with his hand out, and asked Scully doubtfully, "Have I time to get down a bit of this language? It won't take long."

Parmi and those with him stopped their talk and looked at the priest and Didimus, sensing some new element, some other undefined authority that had come among them. They were immediately suspicious.

Scully, with evident reservation, said, "If you like, but it's best not to stop too long in a situation like this. Parmi is friendly at the moment but we are few, and far from help, and a temptation to these people. It's always a risk to hang around when you're heavily outnumbered and they can see steel knives and axes and guns and other things that they would like to own. If some of them decide to do us over Parmi will go along with them."

There was a pause, and the priest could feel that the situation was already changed. Goodwill had given way to uncertainty and suspicion. Fear was already whispering like wind in the grass. And when he looked round everybody was watching him silently.

"Go and sit over there with Tau and the carriers until they all get used to you." Scully now spoke quietly, without inflection, tiding over the tension. Then as the priest moved away he turned once more to Parmi and spoke directly at him, as one leader to another, using pidgin, which the guide turned into Dana bit by bit while all listened. And those on the hillside looked at each other and nodded, rolled their eyes or made grave faces indicating approval, doubt or disagreement.

He said that the clan should send some of its young men into Wanega to enlist as carriers for the big patrol into the Yakanaki Valley. "They will become famous," he said. "Big men, known all over the mountains for their courage. Mr. Marshall will give them each a blanket, and a shirt to wear like all the other carriers, and a bush knife. And after two moons, when the patrol is finished, each man will have a steel ax to bring home and a handful of shell money and twelve sticks of tobacco with which to buy a wife."

Parmi watched Scully's face, and when he had done speaking turned to the guide to know what had been said at the end. At the mention of steel axes his eyes opened wide and he spoke himself. The guide, scraping the ground shyly with his big toe, said, "He would like to have an ax for himself."

Scully said, "Tell him that we will camp tonight at the rest house beyond the river, and if he brings three strong young men to me in the morning to come with us to Wanega I will give him an ax." He turned away then and walked over to the priest. "We will camp soon, about an hour from here, where we have a rest house. Some of these Dana people will follow us and you can do your recording there if you want to. But we are outnumbered here and vulnerable, and the carriers will get nervous and panic if we stay much longer. So we should get moving and make camp before dark."

He called across to Parmi, laughing again now, and said, "Remember, an ax for you if you bring three carriers." Then without fuss, but quickly, he ushered his small cavalcade into line and let it back into the jungle.

They camped that night in the rest house, a hut of bamboo and bark built on a hilltop from which the grass had been cut for fifty yards around, so that an attack against it would have to be made uphill and across open ground. The three policemen, between them, would keep watch through the night. Didimus shared their tent, and the carriers made themselves a shelter of sticks and branches covered with grass. Before dark Constable Tau took some of them to fetch water from the river and wood from the bush, and afterwards fires were lit around the camp.

As Scully had said, some Dana men followed them, but only a few whose ways lay in the same direction, and these stayed around the rest house for a while and watched, twittering with curiosity, while Didimus boiled water so that the priest could bathe, and took clean clothes for him from the tin trunk, and opened cans of food to make a meal.

While it was still light the priest sat outside in a canvas chair, relaxed, writing in his diary that he was pleased to have made the distance without breaking down or begging for a rest, though many times it had been on the tip of his tongue

**33**

to cry out. Now, rested, though still aching from the waist down, he felt more confident of completing the whole assignment without shame.

A Dana man with a small boy stood unselfconsciously beside him, looking over his shoulder, watching the writing come upon the paper as if by magic. Man and boy spoke quietly together, knowing nothing of the greater magic of the tape recorder set up alongside to take in all they were saying —the boy's timid, hesitant questions and the man's reticent, uncertain answers overlaid with shame because here was something that he could not explain to his son. Soon they both became silent; and in a little while, because the sun had already gone behind the mountain, they went away down the hill, the boy looking up into the man's face, asking, and the man shrugging his shoulders, having given up groping for answers. They disappeared into the jungle.

Father Herschell switched off the recorder, then got up and fetched his camera to take a picture of the great landscape in late light—a blue, green and gold tapestry. Scully came. He said, "It gets you, Father, doesn't it? You wonder how a country so tough can be so lovely." Side by side they stood, watching.

In the valley a white cockatoo swung in slow loops, catching, as it curved, the last brassy light of the sun on its stiff wings. Dana men called distantly to each other on the opposite hills, and here and there they could see thin ropes of wood smoke rising in slow spirals to show where men were meeting in their garden huts to talk over the coming of the new white man.

Scully said, "They haven't quite made up their minds about us. The tribes hereabouts seem to agree that we white people are ghosts of some kind, wandering in a limbo between this world and the next. They're not sure yet whether we are their own dead ancestors wanting help to get settled into the spirit world—they sacrifice pigs for the repose of departed souls, as we say Masses for our dead—or if we are spirit-spies sent by an enemy tribe.

**34**

"They're undecided, but afraid that we might do them some great harm if they make us angry, so they're playing it safe, and so long as we're careful there's no need to be afraid. In any case they won't bother us tonight. They'll be too busy arguing whether or not to send their three men with us to join the big patrol."

They listened to the tribesmen calling from ridge to ridge, yodelling first to draw attention, then each in turn saying his piece in a long, high-pitched recitative that spent itself finally in echoes whispering sibilantly behind far hills.

"It's a big thing for them to decide, bigger than anything we can understand. To find a parallel in our own history you must go back to the time of Columbus when young men were asked to voyage in little ships to the edge of the earth, and beyond, to almost certain death, in search of some fabled land. Or coming to our own times, there's more uncertainty and fear in the minds of these people in the thought of crossing the mountains beyond Wanega, than there would be in the minds of three young men of our civilization faced with the idea of going in a spaceship to the moon."

The priest said, "How will they decide?"

Scully thought before answering. "Well, Father, Parmi will probably push for it. He's an enterprising fellow, naturally progressive and unafraid. He'll want one of his own relatives, a nephew or a son, to be in it for the sake of family prestige. The trouble is that these Dana people are old enemies of the Wanegas and it's doubtful if there is a single family on either side which doesn't have a debt of two or three killings to even up.

"Any young Dana who steps into Wanega country would be virtually committing suicide unless we are able to keep the peace and protect him. The question is, Are we strong enough to do this? Can we induce them, either by threats or gifts, to forget old scores and join forces in the cause of progress? You see, we have the same problems, in simplified form, as the

**35**

delegates to UN, or the President of the U.S.A., or any other of the world's leaders."

He smiled suddenly and said, "But you'll be able to discuss all this with Korbin. He's got some pretty forceful theories and opinions on this sort of thing."

Later, when they were eating the meal that Didimus had prepared, Scully went on. "It might take you a little time to figure out Ken Marshall and Korbin. They're as different as chalk and cheese and can both be a bit thorny, but they're good men to work with in wild country. Patient and safe with primitives but not soft. Confident without being careless. Once you get used to their ways you'll find them agreeable mates on a long walk, and they'll make things easy for you if you let them."

He was speaking judiciously, weighing his words, trying not to make too much of anything but conscious that he might seem to be making a case against the two men before the priest met them. So he changed face and said lightly, "We're all a little odd out here, and a man's peculiarities soon come to the top in this game. The thing is to give the other fellow as much scope for exercising his ego as you feel free to give your own."

The priest said, "Is there anything special about them that I should know, pet prejudices to be avoided, or particular interests that might make a point of contact?"

Scully was reluctant. "Well, most of us have problems that tend to become obsessive in this kind of isolation. It is said that Marshall doesn't make out too well with his wife so perhaps it's best not to ask about her. She's something quite important in the fashion world in Sydney and in spite of their difficulties I think he's quietly proud to have her as his wife. I don't know the whole story but she seems, maybe, just a bit too big for him and he gets mad with himself because he can't handle the situation. It's bad luck for both of them."

He was silent for a while, displeased with himself for lying, especially to this priest. But Marshall's affairs were private to

36

himself, and what he knew of the man's wife had come to him, in the beginning, quite by chance at a party on his last leave, no more than six weeks ago, and was not for telling. Not even to a discreet priest.

At least, not yet.

He remembered so well her astonishing loveliness. The almost unreal perfection of her face, her skin, her figure, even the cut of her clothes. Sitting alone on a rose-coloured settee, against a dark green wall, wearing a yellow linen dress and a brown, wide-brimmed forester's hat with a long feather in it. Straight and still, as if she were a painting. With an untouched drink in a wineglass beside her, on a small table. The room was filled with people talking and drinking, yet nobody spoke to her.

He had crossed the room self-consciously, through a group of elegant, sexless men and high-pitched women. A simple, brash young man on leave from New Guinea, carrying a drink in his hand, ready to be grateful to anyone who would speak pleasantly to him.

When he sat beside her she didn't move a muscle and, nonplussed, he waited several seconds before opening his mouth to speak. But before the words came he heard her say quietly though with meticulous enunciation, "Please go away. I am drunk."

He had got up and wandered about, confused, and found his host in the kitchen fixing drinks, and tentatively began to ask about her. But before he could phrase a discreet question his friend had said, "Sorry, I should have told you. That's Sandra Marshall. Her husband has left her. He's one of your mob, goes around taming savages in New Guinea, but apparently he couldn't manage Sandra and cleared out. What are you drinking?"

He saw her again a few days later, sitting alone in a hotel lounge, still beautiful, still immaculately dressed, this time wearing a cream-coloured sharkskin suit and red accessories.

**37**

He thought that she gave him a glance of recognition and risking a rebuff went across and introduced himself.

They went to dinner, at which she drank a single glass of wine and talked brilliantly and with wit about people they both knew, and of things that were happening, but made no mention of her husband. When she asked him to her apartment for coffee and a drink he was flattered, for she was older than he by several years (he thought her to be about thirty), more experienced and better equipped intellectually. He wondered, vaguely, why she should be wasting her time with him unless it was that she had some sentimental, mothering affection for young men from New Guinea.

She settled him in a deep armchair and poured a drink, then left him, saying that she wanted to change. He sat there wondering what Marshall would say if he knew that a junior patrol officer was having a night out with his wife. When, after a while, she did not come back he poured himself another drink and wondered if he might decently look for the lavatory. The telephone rang and she didn't answer, and after a while it stopped.

It must have been half an hour before he heard the sound of some small object fall and, listening, heard her call, faintly, as if she had been taken ill. When he went into her room the light was dim and she was in bed, her arms stretched out on the counterpane and her hair spread over the pillow. A glass lay on the bedside rug where it had fallen and spilt what had been left in it.

She was drunk and crying quietly, making soft, incoherent, moaning sounds. She turned her head with effort to look at him and he thought that he had never seen anything so sad.

The bottle was under the pillow, half empty, and when he moved her to take it, the bedclothes fell away, so that he saw the smooth translucent arching of her breast and the whiteness of her thighs. Her nakedness made him ache.

A photograph of Marshall looked at him from across the room. It showed him with his hand resting on the shoulder of a young Kombala man, who had a pig tusk through his nose and a tuft of fur through each of his earlobes. They were both laughing, and the expression on Marshall's face was one of genuine affection. It was a happy, friendly picture.

Father Herschell said, "And Korbin. What about him?"

Scully looked up. "I'm sorry, Father, I was far away. One gets a bit tired without realizing it, walking all day, and when you unwind, the mind seems to wander off."

He sent Sandra Marshall to the back of his mind.

"I think you'll like Korbin. He's a clever fellow, in a way a bit too big for the job he's doing, though it takes a good man to do it well. But he should have been a proper doctor, and I think he would have been if the war hadn't made a refugee of him when he was still at high school. His father, or an uncle, I forget which, was a surgeon or something in Lvov, but he doesn't talk much about it. In any case, as he says himself, he's one of many millions whose messed-up lives represent the price of progress in this century, and ordinary people in defense of their own sensitivities have stopped being sorry for DPs and refugees. There are too many of them and not enough tears to go round. That's the sort of thing he says. Things that might seem cynical if you didn't know that it's just an act with him, and that underneath he's as soft as a woman."

Scully was looking down at the table, speaking slowly, working out words carefully so that he could be sure of them, and of himself. "Korbin doesn't have much time for religion and maybe you'll feel a bit offended by some of the things he says, but he's not just a smart aleck or a man with a chip on his shoulder making cracks at everybody and everything. He's bigger than that, and decent. I like him quite a bit.

"He wanted to go to America but the Americans wouldn't have him. In some way or other his record wasn't straight. Maybe he had fought with the Communist partisans as a kid and someone had put him in with the U.S. Security. There were thousands like that in the DP camps after the war. They

**39**

wanted to go to America—the land of opportunity and political freedom and high living standards, but America wouldn't let them in. Fair enough. That's America's business."

He looked at Father Herschell apologetically.

"But many of these refugees didn't particularly want to come to Australia to live among the kangaroos. For a lot of them it was the only alternative to staying in the camps in Germany and going rotten on international charity. They had to get out, so they came here to the ends of the earth and made the best of it.

"Korbin came on an immigrant ship as a sick-bay attendant, then got a job as a male nurse in a hospital in Sydney until he qualified to come to New Guinea as a medical assistant. It's as near as anyone can get to being a doctor without going through a proper medical college, and the patients don't know enough to complain. In any case, not many regular doctors will come to New Guinea to work in isolation under these primitive conditions. In the Highlands, here, we've got only one fully qualified doctor for a hundred thousand people, and he comes from Budapest."

When the priest was in his bunk Scully took a writing pad out of his patrol box and added a page of scrawl to the serial letter that he wrote regularly to his mother. Then having checked that Constable Ki was on watch, and his own rifle and flashlight within reach, he turned off the benzine lamp and lay down on his bunk to think about Rosemary Mulholland, who was not as beautiful as Mrs. Marshall but less complicated and much safer to play with in spite of her being the District Commissioner's niece as well as his secretary.

He had composed some lines for her during the day to while away the tedium of the slow rate of their progress, paying lip service at least to discontent and the regret of separation, though still eager underneath to be going on Marshall's monthlong patrol with the priest. For he fancied himself, a little, as a poet, having been published several times in his college magazine and twice in a mission monthly.

> Now is all my life one winter long
> Of endless, empty days laid one on one.

He moved his lips silently, trying to memorize the lines but could hear Didimus, in the policemen's tent, strumming his guitar and singing some lugubrious, tuneless hymn that tripped the rhythm of his own thinking, making the meter stumble. He gave it up and settled down to sleep, trying to fix on the emulsion of his mind a tender, sentimental image of clean and decent Rosemary.

But tiredness let slip his disciplines, and the idealized image of one woman faded, to give way to a vivid, pricking vision of the other, so that suddenly—on the edge of sleep—each fiber of his body twitched, and a shiver ran through him, bringing wakefulness again. He turned over in bed, restless, impatient, ashamed and ill at ease to be thinking lasciviously of a friend's wife.

With a priest lying almost alongside him.

# Chapter 3

EXTRACT from the Daily Diary kept by Assistant District Officer Marshall, officer-in-charge of the Wanega Patrol Post.

11.5.65

THE Reverend L. H. Herschell arrived yesterday (May 10) at 1745 hours having been accompanied from the Mageri River crossing by Patrol Officer Scully and Constables Tau, Ki and Pahun, together with six carriers from Kombala and a mission native (servant) from Madang, Ngo Ningin known as Didimus. The escort also brought in three young men of the Dana people who have volunteered to join the Yakanaki patrol as carriers.*

Patrol Officer Scully is to be commended for achieving this breakthrough with the Dana people who have hitherto proved friendly but conservative and unresponsive to our overtures. This young officer continues to show enthusiasm and initiative in the best traditions of the administration and with the added experience of the forthcoming patrol should quickly develop into a first-class member of the field staff with many years of useful service ahead of him, especially in these forward areas.

* It should be noted that these diary entries are little more than notes, hastily written in spare moments, with no pretense to literary finesse. There has been no attempt to edit, punctuate or paraphrase this or later entries.

42

Our clerical visitor is a Catholic priest but I am pleased to observe that he is not of the Bible-thumping variety but more of a scholar and academic type. Although he was pretty tired last night after what was (for him) a long walk he gave us an outline of what he hopes to do and accomplish on this patrol which is to tabulate and differentiate the local languages and to establish the percentage of cognates between them so that a plan can be made to carry out further and more detailed study when the area is more fully under control. It is gratifying to know that he seems prepared to do the job properly and not become merely a tourist on this trip.

We have not had the advantage of observing this type of scientific research in forward areas before and it should be interesting and educational to see him at work as well as advantageous to the advancement of the various local people and the development of the area.

I was glad to note that Mr. Korbin (medical assistant) has offered to collaborate with him in every possible way and am sure that this will be beneficial to all concerned and help to establish good relations all round. This will give a pleasant but workmanlike aspect to the expedition.

I have set Friday 14th as the date of departure even though we have not yet recruited our full complement of carriers. The local headman, Tangaraga, has done what he can to encourage the young bucks to sign on and says that he is ashamed at the lack of response which he puts down to stories circulated by the old women of the tribe who say that the passes into the Yakanaki Valley are guarded by masalai (evil spirits) and that powerful devils live in the big river in the Yakanaki Valley (noted during our aerial surveys) waiting to drag down and drown strangers who try to cross over or navigate upon it. This kind of old wives talk undermines morale and could cause trouble later on.

Tangaraga has taken this very much to heart and feels a sense of personal disgrace. Yesterday he came to the station and put on a great display. First he walked the length of the station stopped at every vantage point and shouting across the valleys to tell the clan leaders to bring in all the young men. But although most of the elders came during the morning the young men were mostly conspicuous by their absence. These people, although savages, are very democratic and will not be forced into anything by their leaders unless they can see something in it for themselves.

The old man made a great speech saying that the people of Wanega would lose face because of the cowardice of the young men and capped it by throwing his wig on the ground and beating it with his ax to show that his shame was so great he might as well be dead. Then he lay on the ground plucking at his pubic hair and calling upon his ancestors to witness that he was the last man left in Wanega and that the tribe could now only produce women.

The other old men just sat around saying nothing but passing a bamboo smoking pipe around. In the end an ancient got up and opened his mouth pointing to the broken stumps of his remaining teeth then pulled at the few grey hairs of his beard and said that if the young men wouldn't go he would and show them that there were still men left in the tribe.

By afternoon we had collected a dozen more volunteers but later two of them went bush and another gashed his leg with an ax so that he wouldn't have to go. I feel that we should patch him up and make him stick to his contract but Mr. Korbin says that he would be a liability and he could not pass him on medical grounds. I am reluctant to accept this ruling but must defer to my colleague in matters of this nature. He put eight stitches into the man's leg.

An amusing incident this morning although I was annoyed at having to spend valuable time holding a court while there are so many pressing things to be done before we can get away. And all over a misunderstanding.

Cleaning my pistol at 1005 hours when I heard great excitement shouting etc. in the bush below the station and shortly afterwards a man running as if for his life through the station followed by thirty or forty Wanegas waving their axes and shouting threats. I sprang up and called to Constable Ki and old Sergeant Sosu who were checking the tentage for leaks or mildew on the parade ground and they ran to intercept the man and take him into protective custody while the Wanegas, foiled of their prey, danced around them with rage and became threatening until Patrol Officer Scully came running up and cuffed a few of them. He is a handy man with his fists.

As usual a woman was at the bottom of it!

When order was restored and the fellow hauled into court it transpired that he was an Adzubami man from across the river (the Adzubamis trade with the Wanegas and supply them with a type of tung oil which they use for shining up brides etc. and other special occasions for which they receive pigs in exchange).

One of the Wanega headmen alleged that the man, a stranger, had encountered the woman in her garden and without as much as a "by-your-leave" had tweaked her breasts and pushed her over and was about to commit an offense (take his will of her) when her cries of protest brought her menfolk running to the scene. The defendant (I charged him under the Women's Protection Ordnance 1951 Section D) ran off intending to seek protection on the station which is gratifying as it shows that we have made good progress in establishing the fact that a government station is neutral territory and a sanctuary where protection and justice may be obtained.

As usual there was a long and garbled rigmarole of conflicting evidence out of which it transpired that the man was under some interdict by his own tribe and had decided to take advantage of the custom whereby intertribal trading partners are allowed the use of each other's wives when visiting on business and had come brazenly into the district with this in mind.

He says that when he saw the woman in the garden he had no thought of molesting her until she gave him what he took

**45**

to be a sign of recognition. Then believing her to be one of the wives of his trading partner he went into the garden thinking himself invited and made the customary overtures at which she called out saying that she was being attacked. This he misconstrued as a conventional sign of modesty until the men of her clan came running and it is clear that if any of them had been armed with bow and arrows the visitor would have suffered some serious bodily harm if not killed.

There were some flaws in his story especially as this is not the usual trading season but there are reasonable grounds for accepting his plea that it was a genuine case of mistaken identity as his trading partner has three wives and was divorced from a sister of the plaintiff a little while ago. I shall keep him in protective custody until his relatives bring a pig with which to pay compensation to the woman's family otherwise the incident will start a tribal feud which will go on for years.

The Reverend Herschell was able to make a recording of the whole of the court proceedings and expressed great satisfaction with the degree of cooperation received from Interpreter Heli. I am not quite clear as to the correctness or otherwise of permitting a recorded transcript of court evidence for other than legal purposes and will be glad to have a ruling from the District Legal Officer in this matter.

I have expressed these doubts to the Reverend Herschell and am pleased to say that he has agreed that the recording should be kept in my custody until the position is made clear by the Crown Law Office as to the legality or otherwise of its being used for the purposes specified.

A little trouble in the police lines at the moment. Constable (first class) Gerua is down with dengue fever aggravated by syphilis which he must have picked up on the coast as he is just back from leave and was okay medically when he left here. So already the worst aspects of our civilization are making themselves felt here in the Highlands. I have applied for a transfer for Constable Gerua and will arrange for him to go out to Kombala under escort as soon as possible. It is this sort

46

of thoughtless conduct that makes one wonder if one is not wasting one's time trying to do something for these people.

Also I have decided to take both acting-Lance Corporal Garni and Constable Palau on the patrol as they are both good men so long as they are away from the influence of Garni's wife who is something of a w——e to say the least which reputation is enjoyed (?) by a great many women of the Trobriand Islands who seem to be overdeveloped in this regard.

It is a pity to see a loyal servant of the administration like Garni saddled with an unsatisfactory wife and a keen young policeman like Palau caught up in her sexual web to the likely detriment of his career as a government officer which gives him a position of respect among his people. I have therefore decided that it is best to take them both on the patrol for if I leave one behind the other will not be able to keep his mind on the job wondering what she is up to with the other. No doubt she will find other consolation while they are both away.

The priest's boy Didimus kept me awake half the night playing a guitar until all hours so that in the end I had to send the constable on watch (Tau Epi) to put a stop to it which he did pretty smartly. It seems that this Didimus comes from the same village as acting-Lance Corporal Garni and spends most of his spare time in Garni's house. I can only hope that the psalm singing and Bible talk will have some beneficial effect on Garni's wife and make her mend her ways.

Squatting in the kitchen of their hut, Maileeta, Garni's wife, poked at sweet potatoes baking by the fire, then, licking her fingers with a pink tongue, turned them over. Smoke and fine white wood ash fluttered up into her face making her frown and draw her head back, muttering.

She was not much more than twenty, lush with sullen sensuality, though lean and spare of flesh and long-boned like a lad, as many women of the Trobriand Islands are; her hair

**47**

close-cropped and curly, and her face tattooed with a clan pattern that flowed down neck and chest, arms, sides, thighs and biceps, but was covered now with a cotton frock.

She hated it here in the mountains, so far from her home; loathed the grotesque, green, ugly world that shut her in—this shapeless place without horizons or edges of sand or sea or sky, and nowhere for the eye to rest or find pleasure.

She felt lonely, alien, cut off from all things familiar to her since infancy (remembering the play of palm shadows on fine white sand; the movement of canoes slipping swiftly over the sea's soft skin; and children singing on the beach). Here the children never smiled, sang no songs, were silent, afraid of strangers, taught to be cautious and never to stray or make a sound that might betray them to marauders.

When she was newborn her great-aunt Miah had taken her to the water's edge to be washed; a shiny, light brown thing born to her father's third wife, and named Maileeta. Each day as a baby she had been bathed there, as a girl had played, gathered shellfish, swum, discovered herself, been coy with village boys, played love games on the edges of the beach when the elders were asleep. Each memory in her mind was framed and overlaid with the scent, sight, sound and feel of the sea, its regular rise and fall seeming to be the steady breathing of her universe.

Now, married to a policeman and squatting by his fire with her eyes shut, she saw herself again a girl, thigh-deep in the sea in front of her mother's house, felt the warm, caressing ebb and flow of water lapping against her legs, the intimacy, and the soft shock of its touch when, with cupped hands she used to fling it up over her face and shoulders, so that it ran back over her breasts and stomach, touching her like a lover. And as she thought like this her insides lit up and her arms tightened around the image of Constable (first class) Palau, who was also an islander and understood these things.

But Highland streams are rough and buffeting and so cold that the touch of mountain water makes the skin flinch and

48

shrivel. So she seldom washed her body now, except on Sundays in the privacy of the house, in water heated in a bucket on the fire. (Mr. Korbin, observing from time to time her eager, feverish look, suspected tuberculosis—common among sea-level people—and took a sputum test which he sent to the coast, having no X ray. Though she did not understand all this.)

Now she sighed and opened her eyes and, putting out her hand, poured coconut oil into a pan to moisten a mess of canned meat, rice and onion (the same every day) which she then set on the fire. In her mother's house there would be fish, papaya, bananas, fresh coconut, yams, sago and maybe a piece of pig or chicken. And the village would be busy with the evening intercourse of men strolling to and fro talking of tides and winds, plans for fishing or fetching logs, or cutting copra. Women would be calling to each other, gossiping, making vulgar jokes and laughing, the children chasing and playing games. The sea would be purple, and flat to the horizon, and the sky a gold and crimson backdrop.

Here, among these Highland primitives, there were no villages, no place where people could be together and at ease in the evening. Each family lived alone, isolated and separate in a tiny hamlet or single hut built close to the ground, concealed alike from neighbours and strangers; hidden away, secret and afraid, in places difficult to approach. Only in the daytime could women of the same clan meet together in their gardens to gather or plant sweet potatoes while the men kept guard. Then in the evenings, before dark, each family, with its dogs and pigs, would go inside to hide from the night like wild creatures, and seal themselves in with slabs of wood jammed in the doorways of their hovels, remaining so from dusk until daylight.

Now Garni was bringing this man Didimus to eat with them again (she could see the two men coming across the station from Mr. Marshall's house, where the priest was staying). A Madang man like her husband. They would talk their own

**49**

language all night and she would not understand, but would sit silent as she had when her father sent for her, five years ago, and gave her to the Constable in exchange for fifty dollars, two pigs, three gold-lipped pearl shells, an alarm clock and a benzine lamp. Three years and two babies later (one already dead and the other with her mother) her husband had been transferred to the mainland; first to the coast, which was not so bad, then here to the Highlands.

The two men were speaking of her as they came.

Garni was saying, "My wife is a harlot, as most Trobriand Island women are. It is their nature, and the way they have out there in the islands where old men have too many wives to satisfy, and the young men have none but must bargain with the women in their gardens for what a man must have when he cannot contain his own strength. And so the women get rich and the men get into debt."

Didimus said, "You should get rid of her. Send her back to her father. There are plenty of women in our own villages around Madang who would make you a proper wife. Good Christian girls who have been to school and would be glad to marry a corporal of police."

"Acting-lance corporal," said Garni diffidently.

"It's all the same thing. You wear the stripe and get the pay, and will soon get more promotion. These are things a sensible woman understands."

They were silent a while. Then Garni said, "If I send her back to the island her father will be angry, and because he is a big man he will go to the Government and make trouble for me and they will take away my stripe."

Didimus shook his head impatiently. "No, this is not so. A bishop is a bigger man and more important than a village chief, and the Bishop at Madang is my father. If I tell him that you are my friend and wish to marry a Christian girl from his church, he will not let them take away your stripe."

"The Bishop is your father?"

"Yes, he is my father, and the father of my father and my

**50**

mother, and of all the faithful in Madang. And I am like his son. When I was a baby he baptized me with water, and afterwards, when I was at school, he put his hand on my head and made the mark of the Holy Spirit which no one can see. Only God. I tell him all my sins and he speaks to Jesus for me and I am forgiven. Every day, when he changes bread and wine into the body and blood of Our Saviour, I help him. When I die I will go to heaven and be with him forever."

"How do you know all these things?"

"They are in the Book."

"Ah," said Garni, and knew that he had come to the edge of his capacity to comprehend; could go no further, but must be satisfied to accept, without understanding, what Didimus had said, knowing that beyond the limits of his own awareness lay a wider world of knowledge and understanding, the key to which was contained in books, that it was the ability to read these books that gave any rubbishing white man more mastery than the biggest tribal chiefs, and made such a one in many ways wiser than an old man or a witch doctor.

Words written in government books gave Mr. Marshall unearned power over tens of thousands of tribesmen. Other books told Mr. Korbin what made people sick and how they could be cured. It was in a book that missionaries like Didimus' bishop found wisdom and knowledge so secret and profound that they were able to speak with the great spirits who live on the far side of the sky, beyond the stars; who make the moon and the sun move; who take the breath of life out of the bodies of old people and put it back into the bellies of young women to be born again; who give to all white men unlimited riches while New Guinea people continue to eat sweet potato, and sago, and sometimes a little piece of pig.

Father Herschell was saying, "The problem is, of course, one of communication, and every intelligent person understands this."

He was in Scully's house, visiting for dinner, sitting com-

51

fortably in an easy chair talking to Korbin while their host moved between them and the kitchen giving instructions to the cook boy, then coming back continuously to listen.

"It's no good you asking me what semiliterate New Guineans like my Didimus, or your doctor boys and police, are able to understand by 'the sacrifice of the Mass' or 'redemption through the blood of Christ crucified'; the real question is, What do we, ourselves, understand by these phrases?" He sipped at a glass of sherry and went on.

"In our sophisticated, catchpenny civilization many words have ceased to have clear meaning. Most of the important ones have been forcibly divorced from their philological origins and let run loose, to be taken up and used with ignorant innocence by salesmen peddling spurious truths in every field of human activity, including politics and religion. We belong to a civilization which is losing all its meaning because the language we use, the language of this twentieth century, has abandoned reality and has itself become meaningless, so that there is no longer a common currency of communication."

Scully, coming again from the kitchen, proffered a bottle and, when the priest held out his glass, filled it. Then he opened a can of beer for Korbin, who sat watching, while the priest continued to speak.

"Words like *chivalry, honour, truth,* which once were symbols of civilization and a way of life, have become obsolete. Others like *democracy, freedom, liberty* and *justice,* that were part of our own historical evolution and not so long ago defined clear and honorable concepts, now belong exclusively to the mock-language of politics. And *God,* no longer held in awe, or loved as a nice old man with whiskers, is what? No more than a word. That's all. A word with no meaning."

Korbin looked surprised. "Do I detect overtones of heresy in that speech? A tendency to schism in this linguistic philosophy? Can we be sure, we simple bush folk, that you are, indeed, an ordained priest of the true church, in good standing with your superiors in religion?"

52

The priest grinned. "I'm not so sure about the last part, but I'll hear your confession any time, and get you ready for heaven when the call comes. Because the active and practical truth of the sacraments remains the same, yesterday, today and forever, whether we know what the words mean or not."

Korbin flipped an olive stone into the fireplace and leaned forward. "Well, you're a linguist as well as a priest, and definitions are your business in both vocations. So tell me, if you can, how you square continuously changing meanings with a fixed infallibility?"

The priest looked at him with affection and respect. "George, I believe that I am going to enjoy this walk into the Yakanaki Valley in spite of any blisters I might acquire. But, I warn you, this is the open season for souls and you're vulnerable, for you still seem to believe that there is a truth worth seeking. Watch out, or you may catch up with it, and if you do you'll have to submit, or quit."

There were firm footsteps on the gravel path outside, and Scully cocked his head. "Here's the boss. Now we can eat."

The door banged open and Marshall came in.

"Right on time," said Scully. "Dinner is about to be served. Sit down, gentlemen, and have the last decent meal you'll have for a month or more."

They moved to the table and when they were all seated Marshall said, pleasantly, "Well, Father, perhaps you'd care to say a grace?"

"Bless, Oh Lord, these thy gifts to our use. . . ." said Father Herschell.

Scully poured the wine; and Marshall remembered that he had not yet read the letter from his wife.

# Chapter 4

By nine o'clock on the morning of the third day they were ready to leave.

Father Herschell had said Mass, before dawn, in a corner of the bulk store, where Didimus, with Garni's help, had cleared a space and built a small altar with cases of canned meat, among the bags of rice and bundles of shovels and pickaxes. Didimus served for him, and Scully was there as well and one of Korbin's doctor boys. And Maileeta, who watched Didimus most of the time as he moved about behind the priest.

"Accept these gifts, these offerings, these pure and holy sacrifices," whispered Father Herschell and, holding God fearfully in his fingers, offered the Mass for Marshall and for all who would go with him on the patrol.

Yesterday they had worked out a rough timetable together, basing their calculations on a map made by Marshall from aerial observation. It showed the big rivers, and mountains that stood above the rest to make landmarks from which they could take bearings. Patches of extensive garden land were crosshatched to indicate areas of concentrated population.

"We'll stay in these parts for one or two days to give you a chance to do some work. For the rest of the time we must keep to a routine of solid walking, otherwise we'll be out for months." Marshall traced the route with his finger. "We'll follow the high ridges for a week until we come to this big river, which we'll probably have to bridge or raft over, depending on how fast it's flowing. Then we'll climb the next high range and come into this valley and work along it until we meet up with new people. When we do we'll stay long enough to establish a contact with the headmen, then move on to repeat the process until we get into the Yakanaki Valley, where we expect to find the last of the undiscovered tribes of any size.

"We'll spend, maybe, a week with them and build a rest house to show that we intend to come again, and if possible we'll bring a lad or two back with us to train with George Korbin as doctor boys."

Now the carriers were coming into line with their loads.

Scully had weighed and allocated each man's pack, and Korbin had distributed medical stores in tin trunks among his doctor boys. Marshall, keen to get going, inspected the police contingent, examined their rifles and issued to each man three rounds of ammunition.

He found a live cockerel in Constable Palau's knapsack (a farewell present from Maileeta) and, grabbing it by the feet, threw it out, shouting impatiently that they were going on a patrol and not a Sunday outing. The bird ran squawking between his feet, making him skip clumsily, and swear, and he heard Maileeta laugh loudly from the doorway of her kitchen; then Garni, ashamed, shouting at her to be silent and go inside.

There was quiet all over the station as he walked to the head of the line where his houseboy waited, hung about with the paraphernalia of the master's travelling: camera, map case, compass, binoculars, altimeter and water bottle. And beside the boy, big Constable Ki and Heli the interpreter. Marshall, followed by these three, would lead, with Korbin and his medical crew in the middle of the carrier line for protection. Then Scully at the tail with the priest and Didimus, and acting-Lance Corporal Garni and Sergeant Sosu to guard them.

Marshall looked at his watch, glanced at the sun, then slowly looked all round the station as if saying a private good-bye. He saw the thin, ribby, old men with tatty wigs and wispy beards who sat in little groups smoking green tobacco in bamboo tubes. Then the women, dirty and dusty from their garden work, standing pigeon-toed in a cluster, dully regarding sons who were going away with him. He caught a glimpse of the young lad who had gashed himself, sneaking about in the background, underneath the houses, and saw another man standing beside one of the carriers, holding his hand and crying. Police wives stood quietly with wide-eyed children clinging to their skirts, and those of the police who were staying behind to mind the station were drawn up in line, smartly, their rifles held ready for a ceremonial salute.

"Up 'im cargo!"

Marshall, lifting his head high, called the command like a battle cry, an apostrophe to freedom; then, gripping his stick, strode quickly along the red-earth road between the station buildings and disappeared down into the creek bed, anxious to escape, to rid himself of the ties imposed by paper—the reports, orders, instructions, memoranda, and requests for information that had tied him to the station for the past six months.

The carriers, as glad as he to get away, began to chant a marching song, and as the tail end of the line dropped down into the creek, out of sight, a group of Wanega men led by the old chief Tangaraga followed them, skipping with excitement, and then a few lads too young to be carriers (one of them with Maileeta's cockerel dangling by its legs from his belt, its yellow eyes blinking with bewilderment).

They went along, these older men, with intent to take advantage of Marshall and his armed policemen; to make of them a safe and unpaid escort into neighbouring territory where they might face old foes with advantage, to bargain and argue old scores with Marshall's little army to support them.

They saw in this expedition a golden opportunity to collect debts and settle delicate questions of reparation for deaths met in recent tribal fighting, or for women taken in raids.

"Jesus, Mary and Joseph pray for us," said Father Herschell to himself, stepping out bravely. But he was already afraid.

They came, soon, to a knee-deep stream no more than ten feet wide through which a barefoot child would have waded with delight. But a narrow log lay as a bridge over it to let a man cross without wetting his feet, and this he found formidable, and eased his way over cautiously with a hand on Sosu's shoulder to steady himself, while Didimus kept close behind to hold him if he should slip.

Scully, watching, said quietly, "Take it easy, Father, there's plenty of time and in a few days you'll be as used to it as any of us." But the priest was embarrassed and ashamed to seem already so awkward and incompetent, conscious of being the best educated but least adequate person in this company of illiterate and semiprimitive New Guineans and a few adventurous white men.

But when, a little later, they came to a wider river with no bridge of any kind, he waded through it with the rest of them, wet to the waist, and would not let Didimus and Garni carry him across as they wanted to, but was one with all of them. Coming to the other side, soaked to the skin, he felt equal, and began to whistle.

Some of the carriers beat upon the water with their fists, or bunches of twigs ripped from trees, while wading through it, and kept up a continuous shouting to fend off water spirits. But when they had all reached the other side one of Scully's three Dana men collapsed, chattering with fright, and lay stiffly on his back with eyes staring to the sky and his breath coming in gasps. His two friends fell on their knees, keening over him, crying out that he was likely to die.

Korbin, standing at the riverbank watching everybody cross (in case of accident), came and stood over him and soon said that it was nothing but fear intensified by cramps in the thighs brought about by the coldness of the water. But the man's companions, and other carriers standing around watching, were sure that the river spirits had picked on him to pay the toll for everybody's trespassing, and that he would surely die.

Two doctor boys were told to rub his legs while another made hot coffee, which Korbin gave him to drink, sitting on the ground with the man's head cradled against his chest. Then with much mystery and mumbo jumbo he seemed to produce a pebble from the frightened man's thigh, and a sigh went up among those watching, and they were satisfied that Korbin had met magic with magic and that the man was saved. So in five minutes they were able to go on again.

Korbin, catching the priest's eye on him, could see that he was dubious of the subterfuge, so dropped back for a while to the tail of the line to talk to him as they walked.

"You seem surprised by my little trick. Perhaps you are thinking that it is unethical and very wrong to substitute illusion for reality in medicine, even under these primitive conditions. But you have to remember that for all of us reality lies not only in what we know but also in what we believe, and this is mainly a matter of custom and environment.

"For the next few weeks the safety of us all may depend on some primitive person's concept of reality, and not on yours or mine. So what am I to do? Should I ask Marshall to halt the patrol for two or three days while I treat that carrier with drugs, which I don't have, and psychotherapy, for which I'm not qualified? Should I admit helplessness and let him die of fright as he almost certainly will if I can't convince him that my magic is able to keep him safe until we get him back to his own people? Or should we simply get rid of him? Send him back to Wanega right away, before his evident tendency to hysteria gets us all into trouble?

"My own solution would be the last of these three, but young Scully here would not agree with me because he has been clever in getting the Dana men to come along, and if we send one of them back the other two will insist on going with him, and this will set back our efforts to close the gap between the Dana people, the Wanegas and these others we are going to find on this patrol.

"Also, if we send this fellow back, still sick with the magic of the river spirits, I will lose face, admitting that I am not able to defend any of us from bad magic. And through the next few weeks uncertainty will seep deeper and deeper into everybody on this patrol, including you and me and even Marshall, because whatever we say we are all afraid of wicked spirits (excepting young Scully who is protected by love): and instead of being a confident band of explorers we will become a bunch of vulnerable individuals, mistrusting, and ready to blame and hate each other if things go wrong.

"So there it is. With my magic, which is clearly greater than that of the river spirits and those who guard the mountain passes, I have taken a stone out of a man's thigh and everybody is amazed, made confident, given faith because they know now that one among them can make magic, another has charge of many guns, and a third loves them like a brother."

He looked mischievously at the priest. "And you too, Reverend Father, have a status that might surprise you, thinking yourself a stranger amongst us, and believing the ignorance of these people to be so abysmal that they have not yet heard of America. Yet the talk among the carriers is that you are a great fighter in your own country, and have killed ten men, each of them represented by a notch cut in your walking stick. So be careful how you face up to danger when it comes. Our lives might equally depend upon you as upon any of us."

Early in the afternoon they crossed the borders of Wanega country and made camp on an open hillside among people calling themselves the Ongi, who, although they had seen Marshall come through once before, knew little or nothing of the Government except that it had since established itself on the ridge at Wanega. These people came now and stood about the hills overlooking the camp, safely out of arrow range, watching, and calling to their neighbours to come, too, and see what the white men and their followers were doing.

They kept out of sight, a little below the skyline, staying for safety mainly within the dappled shadow patterns thrown by trees and shrubs, camouflaged; and from that distance could make only general sense of what they saw. But they sucked at their teeth and made sounds of astonishment and envy to see trees going down with a crash after only a few blows from axes that flashed in the sunlight. This amazed them, making them think how long it took even the strongest of them to cut through such timber with their own stone tools. And the way that great swathes of kunai grass (used for thatching) fell flat to the ground as the carriers moved in on it with bush knives.

They saw a line of five men leave the camp and go down to the stream with buckets without knowing what the metal things were, and their instincts said that they should swoop down and ambush these few while they were separated from the rest of the patrol: but they saw, also, that two more men wearing government clothing went with the five and that these men carried the sticks which, when pointed at a man made a great noise and knocked him down, sometimes killing him. Or such was the story going round. So they stayed quiet, waiting to find out more about these people before deciding what to do.

In any case there was much more to see from where they watched: men swarming about in small groups out of which sprang whole houses, complete in a matter of moments and men going in and out of them—these being the tents for Marshall and the others, and the medical center.

Then Heli the interpreter, a proud, fat man with a fringe of beard, came and stood apart on the edge of this activity (each man having his own work) and began to throw his voice up onto the ridges all around, giving out Marshall's message, with his hands cupped behind his ears and his head bent back to give power to his shouting.

"Men of Ongi, listen. We are the government. We come in peace to sit with you this night. We will not touch your women or take your food or kill your pigs. We have come to talk with you and tell you what we will do in the time to come." He used the trading language of the area, a lingua franca understood by the tribes round about which engaged in a regular, traditional exchange of goods or women.

Korbin, getting ready to treat any of the Ongi brave enough to come and try the white man's sorcery, was speaking to the priest, who sat in a canvas chair close to the medical tent, setting up his tape recorder to make a list of local words and terms. "Listen to Heli, making history—if only he knew it— uttering the first words, the first double-tongued attempt to open the gates of a new age to these people. Hark at him. 'We come in peace,' he says, as some Phoenician or Spanish serf, working for the Romans, must have shouted to a bunch of primitive Britons huddled on the edge of a forest in the South of England, watching Caesar's galleys come. Listen to him telling them that we have come to put an end to tribal fighting. That we will protect them from their neighbours and stop all wars.

"We believe this. You and me and Marshall, and District Commissioner McKerrow, and the politicians who send us to bring these people 'under control.' We who kill more people in one day of our own wars, more barbarously, with less discrimination and for less logical reasons, than these people kill in a generation of tribal fighting." He was laying out swabs and syringes, and capsules of penicillin which he would shoot into anyone who came to him suffering with yaws. Then he broke open a carton and took out powdered drugs to be used on ulcers and arrow wounds, for these would be the main ailments of his patients.

Heli was now calling upon the Ongi clan leaders to come down to meet Marshall, saying that he would exchange a steel ax for the first pig brought in as food for the carriers. Then he spoke of Korbin, saying that the white man had great

**61**

magic and could cure ulcers, sores, pains and toothache, and was waiting for people to visit him.

They came cautiously, a few at first, mostly men of middle age with their hands resting ready on stone axes, hesitant and apprehensive, triggered to fly or to strike at the first sign of treachery. Those who had wounds of any kind wore pads of damp leaves held in place by grasses twisted into string, and these were directed with gentle gestures and smiles towards Korbin. Others, not sick but simply curious, stood looking at things strange to them: the tents, the metal tools and implements, kitchen equipment used by the cooks. Some came and stood beside Didimus, watching him wash the priest's socks and scrape the mud from his boots, and wondered what these things were.

A man brought a small boy to Korbin, the child's body a mass of raw rosettes of flesh with hardly a patch of clean skin showing, the man himself limping with the pain of a huge, nauseous sore on his shin, so eaten away that the bone was almost exposed. And after them a young man came with four inches of arrowhead embedded in his back, which Korbin pulled out under local anaesthetic, pumping antibiotics into the cavity and plugging it with cotton.

"The problem, of course," said Korbin, "is that they each need at least two or three treatments and tomorrow we go on, leaving the job unfinished. But what I've done will do no harm, and will give them something to talk about until we can come back and set up a patrol post in the area."

As more men came Heli gathered them together, telling them that if they sent their women to the gardens for sweet potato Marshall would buy it all and pay with shell money, salt or coloured face powders. And soon a dozen men or more were standing around the edges of the camp calling to their women, out of sight, to go fetch food from the gardens. When it came, Garni collected it in a heap, giving to each woman a few small seashells or as much salt or coloured powder as would rest on the end of a small spatula.

**62**

Constable Ki appeared surreptitiously among the cooks to beg from them the higly coloured paper labels from meat cans and tobacco cartons and, having collected two such, went a little way apart with an Ongi man to make some quiet exchange. Later, the man came parading through the camp self-consciously displaying one of the labels worn as decoration on his wig, replacing the parrot feathers that had been there when he came. Ki, for his part, had the whole skin of a superb bird of paradise, for which any white man would later pay him fifty dollars. This he wrapped in a soft green leaf and hid in his knapsack.

Sergeant Sosu, less adventurous, was content with a cluster of betel nuts, for which he paid a grey-bearded old man four small seashells, and later sold singly among the carriers for one shell each, though few paid him, having no such money. But he noted down each debt, hoping to collect at the end of the patrol when the men would be paid off.

And the priest, seeing all this for the first time thought, So have men travelled over the earth for thousands of years: tribes in tents, immigrant clans, traders and pilgrim bands, crusaders in troops and cavalcades, carrying their own worlds with them, bringing change but seldom bringing peace.

And he wondered, watching Korbin at work taking out a man's tooth; What proportion of good can we give these people, even the best of us like this man who pretends to be so acidulous and unsentimental but is as gentle as a young mother towards most men, and especially toward these uncouth savages? What can we offer that can compensate for the innocence which we take away from them? Will a tenuous extension of their general knowledge, and the promise of longer life, with steel instead of stone to work with, blankets instead of bark cloth to keep out the cold, guns instead of bows and arrows to kill with; will these outweigh the doubtful gain of refined intellectual enlightenment, and heightened sensitivity to spiritual pain and shame? God told Adam and

Eve that knowledge would bring sorrow. No other simple legend contains so much of cruel truth.

Korbin, straddled across the man's shoulders, took the forcept from between his patient's jaws and showed him the extracted tooth, then dropped it into his hand, gave him aspirin and set him upon his feet, where he stood bewildered, wondering how it had been done (feeling no pain), waiting like a child being dressed for school while Korbin pushed a pig tusk back through the septum of his nose and, having him now fully dressed, patted his shoulder and sent him away. But the man went only a few feet and stood still again, gazing at the tooth in his hand, then felt inside his mouth to make sure that it was his own, and no trick; and smiled suddenly and went whooping and leaping away, released from the ache, to tell his friends while Korbin cleaned his fingers.

"When they do it themselves they cut along the gum of the infected tooth with a sharp stone or piece of kunai grass to expose the root. Then take the pig tusk from their own nose and, using one hand as a fulcrum, lever the tooth out with the tusk while two other men bear down on the patient's shoulders to act as counterweights." He screwed up his face. "It makes me sick to contemplate the pain, especially if the tooth is ulcerated, as it usually is." He sent a doctor boy for more dressings and knelt down to look at a small boy's foot, burned when the child had rolled into a fire in his sleep.

There were, by now, fifty or sixty clansmen in the camp and more coming in, some of them sitting about with the carriers and police or mixing with the old men from Wanega, discussing the visit, finding out about Marshall and the other white men, where they had come from, and why. Others were still wandering about, whispering like yokels at a country fair, discovering strange things never before seen, nudging each other, pouncing swiftly upon discarded cartons, cans and pieces of string, each man stowing these things quickly into the net bag that he carried.

Then Marshall, gathering them all together, made them sit

**64**

in a semicircle so that he could face them, with Heli by his side and two policemen discreetly placed on guard a little apart, and the Wanega men separate and closer to the camp (Marshall always precise, working everything out on the basis of safety, seeing each element separately as in a lecture-room exercise).

He asked, then, that the headman stand up, and when he did (a tall, thin, vicious-looking man) he went and shook him by the hand to show that he acknowledged this man's status and authority. Words were passed, and Heli said that two other men had been sent to fetch a pig and would bring it soon, a gift to Marshall from this headman.

Marshall then began to question them through Heli, asking how many clans and families they called Ongi; what were the boundaries to their land; who were their neighbours; with whom they traded, exchanged wives or made war. What names did they give to their landmarks, the mountains and big rivers; which was the best track westward through their land; and who among them would earn a new bush knife by being a guide?

There was much whispering at this and then the headman said that his brother would go, and two other men, but only to the river that ran on the other side of the range, three days' walk away; for the people beyond the river were quarrelsome and not to be trusted, and no Ongi man would cross over to their side for fear of being killed by them.

Then the two men came carrying a pig on a pole, and the headman, having received his ax in exchange, made a speech, which Heli turned into pidgin, saying that the Ongi were glad to have this visit from the Government but had many reasons to distrust the people of Wanega and so were afraid to come to the station; but they would be pleased if a white man would come and live among them to explain the Government and give each man a steel ax and some of the other things that they could see about the camp.

The Wanegas murmured among themselves when he said

this, resenting the suggestion that they were in any way treacherous and not to be trusted, or that these Ongi people could think themselves of so much consequence that they, too, should have the Government set up its house among them. A few men got to their feet and began to speak out, but Marshall turned and motioned them sharply to sit down and be silent.

But they were restless now, unsettled; and the muttering among the Wanegas seemed as threatening as coming thunder.

"What is it? What do they say?" Marshall spoke impatiently and tugged at Heli's tunic. "Tell me what's bothering them."

But Heli seemed confused.

Then a young Wanega man stood up, his painted face fearful, and, pointing at one of the Ongi, spoke in a loud, accusing voice though seeming half-afraid.

Immediately there was uproar, men leaping to their feet, waving axes and screaming at each other, Wanegas and Ongi; some thrusting their friends forward to attack, others holding back but shouting insults and threats, while on the edges of the riot old men with thin, spindly shanks danced and pranced like maddened marionettes, urging the young men to kill, to spill each other's blood.

Marshall, in the middle of this melee, stayed unafraid and calm, demanding of Heli what had triggered off the frenzy. Then watchful, he saw a Wanega man run in among the Ongi, striking blindly with his ax, and quickly, before damage could be done, he pulled his pistol from its holster and fired a shot into the sky.

There was a wild, terrified cry and the Ongi men, like panic-stricken animals flying from a bushfire, stampeded through the camp, among the tents, shouting sounds without sense until breathless and a safe distance from danger they stopped in a mob, then turned together and stared back baffled, because they could not see what had made them so afraid. What was the noise and how was it made? And why had the Wanega people not run away but were still there, standing a little

66

apart from Marshall? And the carriers splitting their sides with laughter?

"Call them back," said Marshall. "Tell them not to be afraid. I will show them what made the noise and what a pistol can do to a pig."

Heli began to shout, and Marshall turned, looking for the priest, thinking that he should witness these things, but could see only Korbin going about his business and Scully talking to the cooks. He was a little displeased that Father Herschell should show no interest in what was going on, this, the primary business of the patrol and the fruitful functioning of his leadership—this business of making contacts with headmen, laying foundations of understanding and future friendship. But he could not be worried much about the priest at this moment, and so turned back to his work, calling to Constable Palau.

When Palau came he told him to tie the headman's pig by the foot and tether it to a pole. Then when the Ongi came back, slowly and still a little afraid, though fearing more the scorn of the Wanegas and the carriers' ridicule if they should refuse, Marshall showed them the pistol and explained it to them as best he could (though skeptical of Heli's ability to turn this kind of talk). Then to demonstrate its power he shot the pig cleanly through the head, firing twice to make sure it died quickly and quietly.

The Ongi men flinched at this, but stayed staring at the pig as it twitched and coughed blood convulsively, until at a sign from Marshall the boss boys of the carrier line dived on it with bush knives and, having carved it, carried the pieces to their lean-to, laughing and chanting praise of Marshall and the headman's gift, leaving, as they passed, drips of blood on the green grass.

Father Herschell, sitting on the edge of the bed in the tent which he shared with Scully, said, "The word for *blood* is apparently the same as the word for *red* in this Ongi language."

He turned off the tape recorder, and taking the receiver piece from his ear laid it down. "It's what we call a collective. An associative relationship, common in most simple languages. For example, the Wanega word for human hair seems to serve, as well, for animal fur."

But he was talking at random, afraid that if he stayed silent Scully might ask where he had been when the Ongi went racing through the camp, shouting as if violently insane.

This would have been embarrassing: because he had been caught at that moment alone, between the medical tent and his own, and, taking fright, had slipped swiftly into Marshall's tent to stand petrified and silent, except that his heart beat so wildly that he could hear it thumping like a drum. And his hand had been shaking so much that when he took up Marshall's rifle to defend himself, if necessary, against Ongi axes, it had banged against the bed poles.

Some of the Ongi had brushed the tent in their mad rush through the camp, almost falling over the ropes. But not until they had gone, and he could hear the Wanega carriers laughing uproariously and Heli calling upon the Ongi to come back, had he realized that there was no need to be afraid.

He had felt stupid, then, and humiliated by the thought that Marshall might come at any moment and find him standing there with the rifle in his hands. He had put it down where he found it. Then, keeping hidden, he had looked out and, seeing Marshall talking to Palau and not watching, he had slipped away quickly to his own tent.

The excitement was over now. Marshall had done his work with the Ongi; had established, with a pistol, his right to arbitrate in disputes between them and the Wanegas. And, to press the advantage, he had pointed to the policemen's rifles, asking the Ongi to consider how much bigger these were than his pistol (which had killed a pig). He told them to count the rifles. To estimate, if they could, the damage they might do. But the Ongi were afraid and had nothing to say. For this was a new thing, beyond their understanding.

Afterwards he sought for the cause of the afternoon's fracas, and found that the young Wanega man had claimed to recognize among the Ongi the man who had killed his father in a recent tribal fight. After much discussion Marshall had settled the matter, binding the Ongi to the promise of pigs in payment, to be taken to Wanega when the patrol returned. This would bring the Ongi people to the station, and with them any who had grievances against the Wanega on account of old scores unsettled.

Scully said, "It's a good day's work, though we don't know the half of what goes on. Heli and the old men of Wanega have probably put it across the Ongi, telling them that our police will take them all away to jail if they don't do as they're told. Heli will pretend that he is acting for Marshall and will collect a pig or two as commission for any deal he pulls off for the Wanega, and on the other hand will promise the Ongi headman that, in exchange for a consideration of some kind, he'll make things good for him with the Government. It's the old story of the unjust steward."

A bugle call cut across their talk and brought them to the doorway of the tent, where they stood quietly, in the twilight, to watch the lowering of the camp flag. Policemen held their rifles rigidly. Marshall stood stiffly at the salute. And long, sonorous notes leapt after each other, far into the dark mountains.

Later, at the evening meal, Marshall seemed irritable and, when they had eaten, called for Sergeant Sosu and asked if he had seen anybody hanging about near his tent, because his rifle had been handled and the safety catch slipped. When Sosu looked troubled and puzzled Marshall spoke sharply, telling him to keep a better watch about the camp or it might be thought that he was too old to go on patrol, and in future would be left behind at Wanega to look after the women and children.

Afterwards he asked the priest, plainly, how he had spent the afternoon, and the priest said that he had been busy re-

69

cording anatomical words and terms, and was pleased with what he had been able to achieve.

But Marshall, frowning, seemed to be thinking of something else and said, "I'd be glad if you would speak to that boy of yours, Didimus. He's keeping my policemen up half the night listening to that damned guitar of his, and they're getting too tired to do their work efficiently. If you can't keep him disciplined I may have to take some action. I'm responsible for everybody's safety on this patrol, including yours."

He turned away and went to his own tent, calling for acting-Lance Corporal Garni.

# Chapter 5

For three days more they kept climbing, each day reaching deeper into the heart of the upland country, and higher, until a week after leaving Wanega they broke out of rain forest into an open landscape among sharp-sided, giant mountains that were naked except for a thin covering of sickly, undernourished grass.

And Scully was troubled. He was beginning to worry and to wonder how long he could go on living alongside the priest.

As the tail end of the carrier line left the forest he stood awhile (having held back purposely for the last hour to be by himself) and stood, now, alone, looking at the massive peaks and the long, clifflike walls of limestone scarred white by landslides. The thin thread of the patrol climbed diagonally onto a plateau where Marshall would pitch camp for the night.

He wished that the priest had not come; that he could lie in his tent at night by himself, without the priest alongside (though he liked him as a person very much). But the pleasure was going out of everything and there was hardly a moment now when he didn't feel uncomfortable because Father Herschell had come and, having come, had set up judgment.

He felt certain that without the priest he could have maintained a natural and unstrained relationship with Marshall;

could have rationalized, for himself, the strange association with Sandra and written it off as an incident, an experience in a young man's life. Morally wrong, perhaps, but worthwhile. No, much more than merely worthwhile. Touching, lovely, creative in a natural, pure, almost childlike way.

But the priest, simply by being here, seemed to make sin of it; something filthy and despicable, to be ashamed of, so that there could never be a relationship between himself and any future woman, even a wife, that wouldn't somehow be contaminated and cheapened by this experience: this act of being suddenly complete, and knowing what God was. It had become an obsession with him, this daily scarifying of his conscience. Because the priest was there, all the time reminding him of it.

He hitched the rifle higher onto his shoulder and moved on after the patrol, seeing the priest ahead of him labouring on the steep slope and stabbing the pockmarked rock with his stick to drag himself upward. He was sorry for him, knowing that he would be aching after six continuous hours of hard climbing, though he was toughening up well and not holding them back.

But he shouldn't have come on such a patrol as this. It was too hard. The three of them, Marshall, George Korbin and Scully himself, were too tough a team to keep up with, physically and psychologically.

Sometimes in the night he could hear the priest sigh in his sleep, and turn, trying to ease the ache in his limbs. And he pitied him.

Then Sandra would come to Scully and take possession of him; would insinuate herself into his skin and become one with him so that he could literally feel the warmth of her body lying on him, and inside him, and the softness of her. The smell of her neck and shoulders and her hair. The smoothness of the inside of her thighs. The quiet, contented, childlike sounds she made when they embraced and she nibbled at him with her lips.

72

"Sweet Jesus!"

He stumbled over a stone, not looking where he was walking, and, recovering, blasphemed and began to jog-trot up the track to discipline his body back to a conscious awareness of where he was and what he was doing, here and now, on the way to the Yakanaki Valley, in the middle of New Guinea.

In Sydney it had seemed so simple and uncomplicated—as real and unreal as the night sky; as magical and natural as the unfolding of a flower. Something to be done without pain or shame or payment, now or later. Except, perhaps, in the end when it would be all over. And even then the pain would be tender and gentle as their loving had been. There would be a little emptiness somewhere inside him, and a small, sad memory would lodge forever in his head or his heart.

Except, of course, that it wasn't like that, ever.

"Scully, my son, you're a bloody nut. You've made a mess of everything and sooner or later you will pay. Or somebody else will pay for you. For the law is unchanging—you get nothing for nothing, and for every pleasure someone must suffer."

Sergeant Sosu turned round, wondering why Mr. Scully was talking to himself. There seemed to be something very funny about this patrol. Everybody was on edge.

When they came onto the plateau Marshall was waiting, sitting on a patrol box and studying his map.

Scully went straight to him. "Will we camp here?"

Marshall looked up. "Yes, the Ongi guides say that there's a spring close by where we can get good water, and this seems as reasonable a place as any to pitch the tents. They say that it's rocky farther on, with lots of landslides." He turned back to his map. "They won't come any farther, but according to my reckoning we should be close to the big river. I'd like you to take Garni and a couple of the others and go on a bit, maybe for an hour, and see what's round the corner. Get me the lie of the land, and if the river is there see what water is in it. Whether we can swim or bridge it, or will have to go looking for timber to make rafts."

Scully went with Garni, Constable Ki, and two boss boys from the carrier line, and, climbing a high peak, saw the river a long way off, with the sun flashing on it so that it seemed like a shining silver snake.

Looking at the policemen he asked, "How far?"

They were thinking. Then Garni said tentatively, "Four hours, maybe five."

Scully, noting the lie of the land, nodded and stood silently for some seconds, fixing the picture in his mind. Then he felt the earth tremble as if, far down inside, something had moved.

The carriers began to fidget and he knew that they were afraid, believing that spirits living on the mountain were watching them, angry at the trespassing and warning them to stay down in the valleys where men were meant to live and make gardens, and marry women to plant them and to bear their children.

But Scully was thinking that this little tremor was one of many and explained the great scars on the mountain sides, the gashes and tracks of landslides where the surface of the earth had cracked and slipped because of subterranean shifts. He waited a while in case there was another, then led them down the other side a little way, looking for a track that might take them back more easily to the camp.

They found one and followed it across the face of a vast rock wall until it became little more than a ledge just wide enough to walk on, with a steep drop, almost sheer for five hundred feet, into the valley below.

Ki went first, the carriers, then Garni, and Scully at the back. They were forced here and there to clamber a little way up the slope to negotiate an overhang of jumbled rubble left by a minor landslip. It was dangerous but less so than turning back, so they went on carefully and came again onto the track. But they were no sooner on it than a rumble above them made them look up to see a slice of rock face crumble

74

and fall towards them in an avalanche of earth and huge stones.

Scully, shouting, saw Ki drop to the ground, and Garni flail with his fists to make the carriers do the same. Then he, too, went down, covering his head with his hands as the rubble roared over them. In the middle of the thunder of it he heard a shriek and knew that one of the carriers had been hit.

When the dust cleared he saw the man lying a little below them on the slope, and went down to get him, with Garni and Ki making a chain with their rifles, while the other carrier crouched back against the mountain face, afraid to move.

The man was shaken though not much hurt, apart from a bruised arm and abrasions on his face, and Garni swore at him, saying that if he had kept his head down the rocks would have flown over him, doing no harm, but he had tried to get up and run and had only himself to blame for the pains he would carry about for the next few days.

When they came back to camp Korbin examined the carrier carefully and, having treated his cuts and bruises, put him and his friend to sleep in the medical tent to keep them from spreading panic through the camp with their superstitious chatter.

Marshall said to Scully, "We felt the tremor down here and heard the rockfall. It might have been worse but it's bad to have a thing like this happen at this stage. They'll all be as nervous as cats about crossing the river tomorrow. We'll need to keep our wits about us or we'll have trouble."

He was thinking of the priest and the possibility that his timidity would be contagious.

"I think I'll take off pretty early in the morning with a small team so that I can move quickly and get things started at the river before the rest of you reach it. If it's as wide and as full of water as you think it is we may have to build a couple of rafts to take the gear across. You and George break camp and get everybody on the way by daylight, which means

75

that you should reach the river by midmorning. I'll have the crossing organized by that time. Then we can get them over before they have time to get worried about water spirits."

Scully watched Marshall go, long before dawn, with a dozen men led by Sergeant Sosu, who, though slowing down with age, was still the best bushman among them. He could say which trees were most buoyant and would make the best rafts; could judge the currents, choose the safest crossing place and go first, with Marshall, to show that there was no danger.

Two hours later Scully followed them, taking the lead with Garni beside him, the priest in the middle of the line and Korbin at the tail.

It was harsh limestone country and hard going—sharp underfoot and barren except for the thin, sickly grass. There was no sign of life and no shade. No cloud in the white sky. No breath of wind.

One of the carriers began to sing but the others stopped him. And for three hours nobody spoke, until they came round the shoulder of a bare mountain and saw the river a long way below.

When they came to it Marshall was waiting with two rafts ready at the water's edge, each able to take six men and their packs, and some general gear.

He looked up, watching Scully walk towards him, and spoke with an edge of complacency. "They're big enough to be efficient, and light enough to handle without much trouble." He was unwinding a nylon fishline, laying it out on a patch of bare ground, in coils, so that it would run freely.

Scully admired the facility with which he planned and carried out all that he did. He and Sosu had chosen a place where the river curved and the current would carry any floating thing diagonally downstream and land it on the opposite bank. Scully saw, also, that the current turned back upon itself on the downstream end of the bend and made a whirlpool, but this was too far away to be dangerous unless someone blundered badly.

Marshall came and stood beside him. "Yes, that whirlpool could be a nuisance but we can take care of that. I'll go across first with Sosu and Ki and take one end of this nylon, leaving the other end with you. When we get across you can tie a manila line to it and I'll haul it over and make fast to something on the other side. Fifty yards should be enough. That will give us a lifeline so that the rafts can be maneuvered back and forth hand over hand, instead of simply drifting with the stream. We can use a second rope as a towline to steady the downstream trip and help haul the empty rafts back to this side. Sosu will captain one raft and Palau the other, with you and Garni on this side to look after the loading and me and Ki on the other to unload. Two hours should see everything across."

He looked round for Sosu, Ki and his personal boy and, finding them waiting together close by, said briefly, "Okay, let's go."

Three policemen stood in the river holding the raft steady while Marshall settled himself in the center, sitting on a patrol box with the boy at his feet, frightened. Sosu and Ki stripped down to their briefs, ready to swim if necessary, and wrapped their rifles in their tunics. Then they squatted, one at each end of the raft, facing outward. Marshall took one end of the nylon line and held it above his head to keep it from tangling.

He nodded, and the three policemen pushed the raft out into the stream, gently, while everybody watched.

The carriers, excited, whispered like children; then gasped and cried out in sudden alarm as the current caught the raft, spun it round once, and carried it downstream so swiftly that it seemed that nothing could stop it from going on forever, down to the sea.

But the crossing place had been well chosen, and in a few seconds the raft swung sweetly into the opposite shore. They saw Ki lower himself over the edge, into the water, to catch and hold the raft fast while Sosu reached at an overhanging tree and hauled his end in to the bank.

Then the carriers began to chatter all at once until Scully put them to work, separating the camp gear into loads, while the manila rope was passed across the river to Marshall and made fast.

Sosu brought the first raft back and Palau went across with the other, taking six carriers. When he returned Sosu went, taking more carriers, police and the priest. Then Korbin and two of his orderlies with the medical gear. Everything was going well.

Didimus went with the next load, and four more carriers, taking the priest's equipment and his own gear, and the guitar. Sosu supervised. The policemen pushed them out into the stream.

Five hornbills, coming from the west, flew over them in formation, their wings creaking.

Korbin, on the other side, making himself comfortable on a medical box in a shady place above the riverbank, was first to sense that something was wrong. He ran down to the water's edge shouting and pointing at the raft. "Watch him, Didimus, watch him. Don't let him stand up." He went past Marshall, muttering. "Oh what a fool I am, what a fool."

Marshall, looking up sharply, grabbed at his arm. "What is it? What's wrong?"

But already they could see what was happening. Didimus, still sitting, was struggling with one of the carriers, and Sosu, keeping the raft on course with the help of the lifeline, was looking down over his shoulder and shouting.

They saw a patrol box go over the side with a splash and drift away, then get caught in the current and go sliding off in a wide sweep, nodding and bobbing until it sank.

Korbin was angry with himself. "It's that carrier who had the scare with Scully yesterday. The one who got knocked over in the landslide."

"Christ," said Marshall, "he's gone mad." He stood, tense and anxious, knowing that now there was nothing he could do; that to start shouting instructions to Sosu would only confuse things and make the danger greater. In a few seconds the raft would be beyond the critical point of the crossing, out of the mainstream's swift rip and into the slower flow along the river's edge. If the other carriers kept their heads they would soon be out of danger even if they got a wetting.

Korbin was saying, "I should have doped him. Should have stayed alongside him. What a fool I am, what a bloody fool."

The man on the raft was standing up now, struggling, but Didimus seemed to have him anchored by the leg, and the other carriers were keeping still, with Sosu watching them.

Scully was already running along the other bank, downstream, and Marshall knew that he had in mind to be ready to go in after anybody who might fall off the raft. He shook his head. Scully was a very fit young man with a lot of courage, but he couldn't do much good from that side of the river.

The man had fallen down now and Didimus was grabbing at him, trying to drag him back into the middle of the raft. Then he seemed to break free and bend to pick up something. A food pack went into the river with a splash and sank almost immediately.

They saw the man stand and Didimus grab at him again, then stand up too and begin to wrestle.

Marshall turned away instinctively, then looked back again, muttering, "The idiot, why does he do that? Why, why, why. . .?" Then he broke off, knowing why, and knowing now what was going to happen. He ran down to the riverbank to watch.

They could all see that the man had hold of the guitar and that Didimus was trying to pull it away from him. They saw it fall and both men bend and claw at it. Then Didimus began to pound at the man's back with his fists, trying to distract him. They saw the man slip and Didimus kick at him. They saw him clutch his stomach and roll to the edge of the raft and rock there for a moment, then drop into the river. And Didimus stand, staring, afraid of what he had done.

Marshall ran downstream, reckoning as he went, guessing where the man might be carried closest to the bank so that he could grab him as he swept past or, if necessary, swim in and get him. He could hear Ki coming behind, calling, but took no notice until it seemed that everybody gave one single shout of surprise. Then there was silence, followed by a low moan.

He stopped and, looking back, saw that the raft was close inshore with Didimus still standing. One of the other carriers had control and was holding onto the lifeline. He wondered, irritably, where Sosu was. Then Ki caught up with him and pointed, wide-eyed, out into the middle of the river.

Extract from the daily diary kept by Assistant District Officer Marshall, on patrol west of Wanega, on the borders of the Ongi country.                                      18.5.1965.

A calamitous day. One of the worst in my career as an officer of the New Guinea service for today I lost a man who was under my command. One who in spite of his colour race and creed I am proud to call a friend. I refer to Sergeant Sosu the senior member of police on this patrol who lost his life today because of someone's stupidity.

I will not blame any particular person because as is usually the case in this kind of thing many factors contributed to the final act of the drama. It is the old story of wars being lost for want of a horseshoe or ships for a haporth of tar as I am always telling those under me. If only people would pay attention to details there would be fewer things go wrong.

At the same time I must point out that if I had not been carrying passengers on this patrol tragedy would not have struck and Sergeant Sosu would be alive at this moment for it was the crass stupidity and inexperience of Father Herschell's boy Ngo Ningin (Didimus) which was directly responsible for the untimely death of this old and valued servant of the Territory Administration (Sergeant Sosu had only fourteen months to go before honourable retirement on a full pension).

I am not blaming this boy Didimus for being ignorant of elementary bushcraft though a child of five would knew better than to stand up and engage in a bout of fisticuffs on a raft in midstream. I merely venture to suggest that more care should be taken in choosing people to take part in expeditions of this kind. The additional fact that this lad was prepared to engage in a life and death struggle over a gimcrack guitar worth a few dollars at most makes it all the harder to find excuses for what has happened. . . .

He got to his feet to grapple with the demented carrier for possession of the instrument with the result that the man fell or was pushed overboard (no charges can or ought to be made until the whole matter has been considered legally).

Both Patrol Officer Scully and myself anticipating some such consequence were already heading downstream on either bank to effect rescue or rescues should this be necessary and being engaged in these maneuvers were not in a position to see what took place next. Therefore I have to rely on the eyewitness account given by Mr. Korbin as to the order of events (I have of course asked Mr. Korbin to prepare a statement for presentation to the coronial court which will be convened to consider the death of Sergeant Sosu as soon as this patrol returns to Wanega).

Meanwhile the facts as described by Mr. Korbin are that when Sergeant Sosu saw the injured carrier being carried downstream unable to help himself he seemed to think for a moment and then hand over control of the raft to one of the carriers (Goro of the Penda tribe) after which Sosu took off his service belt and cap and put his hands together as if to say a prayer before diving into the river by which time the carrier was already some twenty or thirty yards ahead of him downstream.

It seems that Sergeant Sosu misjudged the depth and direction of his dive and surfaced too far out in the center of the stream so that instead of being able to swim strongly with the run of the current to catch up with the carrier he found himself struggling for his own life in the main ripstream and being carried swiftly downriver towards a whirlpool at a speed which outstripped Patrol Officer Scully's capacity to intercept him. As for me I was busy fishing the carrier out of the river as the current brought him close to the bank and so I did not see Sergeant Sosu being carried away to his tragic end in the whirlpool.

Patrol Officer Scully with a medical orderly, four police and a few reliable carriers is now searching downriver for the body in order to get evidence of death or to be able to presume death with reasonable certainty as per regulations appertaining to Family Compensation. Meanwhile I have made camp some two miles from the river so that the police and carriers will not be worried by the possibility of Sergeant Sosu's ghost coming among them in the night to look for company which is what they are now frightened of.

To make matters worse we are in rough and inhospitable country devoid of population and so have had no fresh food for several days and the carriers do not take kindly to rice but I will ask Mr. Korbin to issue vitamin tablets to everybody this evening and to have a general medical inspection which will keep all hands occupied for a couple of hours.

I cannot get it out of my mind that there is more in this incident than meets the eye. Sergeant Sosu is (was) a first class bushman, none better, and should have been able to judge accurately what course to take when he decided to go in after the drowning carrier and although well up in years was still a skilful swimmer.

Thinking back, I begin to remember little things that now make me wonder if in fact he was feeling his usual self. For instance, he seemed to have lost touch a little in recent days and was not quite as alert as was his wont (I am thinking of the incident of somebody getting into my tent and tampering with my rifle the other day), but now we will never know.

Towards evening Marshall heard the faint echo of rifle fire —a single shot or volley—and knew that they had found Sosu, had buried him, and were firing a salute over his grave. He thought sentimentally, ·The old fellow will be lonely down there by the river, in this desolate place so far away from his own people and the village where his grandchildren run about. But he dismissed the idea quickly as silly superstition. The dead had no memory, no feelings.

But he called the camp together, and acting-Lance Corporal Garni (now the senior policeman) lowered the flag to half mast while the trumpeter sounded the Last Post.

Marshall spoke briefly, saying that Sosu had been a good comrade; that he had given his life that another might live; and that the Government would like all men to be unselfish like Sergeant Sosu, and work together for the good of the country even to the extent of giving their lives. If everybody did his job properly, however, accidents would not happen.

Having said this he hesitated, thinking that he should, perhaps, ask Father Herschell to say a prayer for Sosu. But he suddenly felt that the priest was an interloper and had no business to be there. So he turned and walked away from the parade.

Later, when Father Herschell was in his tent resting and reading his breviary, Didimus came asking if he might go to confession, for he was troubled by his part in Sosu's death and in need of sacramental consolation and an assurance that he was not wholly to blame.

When he had given him absolution the priest said, "Didimus, you must understand that true humility, which is the perfect state of grace, requires that we share our weakness as well as our strength. Only Christ was big enough to take upon his own shoulders the whole weight of the world's woe. The rest of us can only carry a tiny share of the evil that we help to do, and of the sins we help to commit."

He said that other members of the patrol could perhaps feel as guilty as Didimus about Sosu's death. Mr. Scully, for example, might say that he was responsible in the first place for leading the carrier into danger and letting him get hurt, and mentally upset. Or Mr. Korbin could think that he should have watched the carrier more closely and could have done more to help him keep calm. And even Mr. Marshall would no doubt be sorry that he had spoken a little harshly to Sosu in recent days. As for himself, a priest, he might also feel ashamed because he had not done enough to help all those around him in many evident ways.

But he did not tell Didimus of the shame that he himself carried inside him because he had let Sosu take the blame when Marshall complained that someone had gone into his tent and tampered with his rifle. And now Sosu was dead, and it was too late to say, "It was me. I hid in your tent because I was afraid." Nothing could be gained by saying it now.

Scully came back and, when he had eaten, went to the tent he shared with Father Herschell and scribbled a few lines to his mother, telling her that everything was going well with the patrol; that a carrier had fallen into the river but Ken Marshall (he was mother's hero) had rescued him at the risk of his own life. Otherwise nothing very exciting had been happening. In fact he was getting tired of this patrol work and had it in mind that he ought to get married and settle down. There was a girl named Rosemary, the District Commissioner's niece, who might make a fellow a good wife.

They heard the guitar, heard it, all of them, at the same time. Together. The priest and Scully in one tent. Korbin and Marshall in the other. They listened, sitting quite still. Then Marshall got up and went out and walked through

the camp, following the sound until he came to the policemen's tent, where Didimus was singing softly:

> O let me be like Jesus
> The lamb of Galilee
> O let me be like Jesus
> Who died to set me free.

He looked up, surprised, when Marshall walked in.

The policemen scrambled to their feet and stood to attention, half-dressed. Some of them held cigarettes or partly eaten
food in their hands. Acting-Lance Corporal Garni was embarrassed to be discovered in his underpants.

Marshall didn't look at them. He merely moved his right
hand impatiently in a gesture of dismissal and stood looking
down at Didimus, who had stopped singing and playing the
guitar. It was like a film that had frozen—a tableau. Then
Marshall moved forward and snatched the guitar away from
Didimus viciously, and stepped towards the tent pole.

Korbin in one tent, and Scully and the priest in the other,
heard the cringing, crushing sound of wood smashing, and
the jangle and tangle of twanging strings. And were shocked.

But they understood. And they said nothing to each other.
Or to Marshall.

# Chapter 6

In the dark of morning they broke camp quickly and quietly, with no joking among the carriers or sly switching of uncomfortable loads for light ones. Then at dawnlight they moved off soberly in a long line, silently, not chanting as they usually did at the start of a new day.

As they left camp each carrier passed smartly between Scully and Ki to have his load looked at, felt, and given a perfunctory check for heaviness (the sharper boss boys made it a practice, whenever they could, to get through with blankets stuffed into their packs, loading the most awkward and angular pieces of gear onto the simpletons).

Now they were all anxious to get away, to leave Sosu with the river spirits who had taken him because they had trespassed—had entered into a place belonging to the dead. They knew that if they stayed longer others would be taken. And some among them had been embarrassed, too, by the wild violence of Marshall's reaction to the tragedy.

They saw him, already racing ahead, escaping as they were: not from river spirits but from a shame which they shared with him because, needing somebody to blame for Sosu's death, their leader had put his finger on Didimus the outsider, the least protected, to be the scapegoat for all of them.

The priest was speaking as they walked. "I understand very

well how you feel, Didimus. All of us must go through these times of discouragement and doubt, when we feel that everybody is against us, and it seems that even God has turned his back upon us and has walked away, leaving us alone with our troubles."

They were going easily, down a long ridge, Didimus ahead of the priest, carrying his equipment. Of the guitar he had saved only the strings, now hidden in the bottom of his haversack.

"Christ Jesus, Our Lord, had to suffer this loneliness too, even though he was God's own son; otherwise he would not have known what it is to be human.

"So you must not feel bitterness or anger against Mr. Marshall. Like Christ crucified you must forgive those who seem to do you the most harm. You must see that this is a trial of your strength and your courage. Of your faith in God and your love for Our Lord, whose sufferings we must all share willingly if we are to be his disciples. Because to be like him we must suffer like him; otherwise we cannot expect to share equally his wonderful resurrection and his everlasting glory in heaven. It is the suffering that we share that makes us all equal in and with Jesus.

"And you must compare your own suffering with his. The loss of your guitar against the pain he suffered hanging on the cross. The agony in his hands and feet and side. Which is the greater? How much more must we all suffer before we can equal the suffering of Jesus?"

The priest, anxious both to comfort and convince Didimus, was running out of breath, but he went on.

"Perhaps Mr. Marshall is suffering just as much as you are. Perhaps God chose him to be the cause of your trouble. Perhaps in this way he may prove to be the cause of your salvation. This is the mystery of God's ways, that out of evil comes good. Out of sorrow comes joy. Out of death comes life everlasting."

For a fleeting second he wondered how much of this he

believed himself, and swiftly made a mental act of faith. Then with an encouraging smile he handed Didimus fifteen dollars, saying, "Mr. Marshall is sorry and gives you this to pay for a new guitar."

But Marshall had already absolved himself and was making pace, planning to reach within an hour some high point where he could set up the radio and establish contact with District Commissioner McKerrow at Kombala.

Garni went with him, Palau and Heli, his own boy, and three carriers with the radio gear split into light loads so that they could move quickly.

The District Commissioner would be upset about Sosu. They were agemates and had joined the service almost at the same time more than thirty years ago—McKerrow as a cadet and Sosu as a police recruit new from the village.

He would be angry and would call for a full report, complete to the last detail. Well, when the patrol was done he would have it, and maybe he would remember, then, what Marshall had said when last they spoke together on the radio. "We are not going on a picnic." That's what he had said. Already he had been proved right, though he had no wish to underline this yet.

He made straight for the mountains, going against the grain of the land, aiming to get away as quickly as he could from this barren, arid valley; back into forest country where there would be shade and living things and, in a day or two, people. The sooner they could get among new things and be busy, the better for everybody.

After two hours he came to a high place with an open aspect looking eastward, and here he told Garni to get the radio set up and going, ready to break in when the District Commissioner came on the air for his daily talk to the substations.

As soon as they found the wave length and could hear that McKerrow was on the air, Marshall broke in. "Yakanaki patrol calling Kombala. Yakanaki patrol calling Kombala. Do you read me? Over."

McKerrow was telling the Assistant District Officer at Lake Timbudu that the Regional Education Officer would be coming in by floatplane during the afternoon, to discuss with him the siting of the proposed new school. There were details to be settled—of making access roads, and of finding temporary accommodation for teachers until such time as budget allocations would allow for new houses.

Marshall contained himself until the discussion was done, then broke in again. "Yakanaki patrol calling Kombala. Yakanaki calling Kombala. I have an important message for the District Commissioner. Yakanaki patrol calling Kombala. Do you read me? Please acknowledge."

But McKerrow, refusing to be flustered, called in the Patrol Officer at Yelaki instead, asking for a progress report on the clearing of ground for a new airstrip, and when would it be ready for inspection.

The Patrol Officer was vague and complained of rain and the laziness of the local people, who seemed to lack interest in the project and had failed to show up when rostered to work on the strip, saying that they were busy making new gardens. And the surveyors sent out by the aviation department had done a botched job, marking the site out so badly that he would have to shift a whole lot of rocky outcrops, and had no explosive.

Marshall made impatient noises, scoffing at the lad for his inefficiency. "Bloody little nitwit. He ought to be doing some office job back in Port Moresby." He began to fret, suspecting that the District Commissioner was deliberately making him wait. Then without preamble he was called in.

"Kombala to Yakanaki patrol. Come in, Yakanaki patrol. We are ready to receive you. Over."

Marshall was formal. "Good morning, Kombala. Good morning, Mr. McKerrow. Marshall talking. Sorry that I have to report bad news repeat bad news. Do you receive me do you receive me? Over."

The answer came back straightaway. "Kombala hearing you at strength ten. What's your trouble?"

Marshall coughed respectfully, thinking of Sosu, dead and himself at a disadvantage. "We've lost Sergeant Sosu. He was drowned in a river-crossing accident yesterday."

There was a burst of sudden chatter at the other end, cut short as McKerrow told somebody to keep quiet. Then in the ensuing silence McKerrow spoke again. "How did it happen?"

Back and forth they talked for ten minutes, Marshall giving his news, McKerrow questioning, not missing a trick—seeing past the stated facts to the whole unspoken complex of contributory causes and probable consequences; clearly seeing the possible effects of this disaster so early in the patrol, but confident that Marshall would deal with the situation sanely. Knowing his man, his strengths and his weaknesses, McKerrow was gentle with him, though mainly for Father Herschell's sake.

"Bad luck, but it could have happened to anyone. I'll want a full report, of course, to put to the coronial inquiry when you come back. Meantime, keep everybody fully occupied for the next day or two with anything you can think up. If there's nothing special you can do right now, tire them all out with walking."

Marshall said, "We have to keep moving whether we like it or not. There's no fresh food to be had around here and we'll be running low on rice and canned meat before long. If you could organize an airdrop for tomorrow it would provide a diversion as well as serve a purpose."

There was no hesitation from the other end. "Will do. Where will you be?"

He gave a probable, approximate position for noon next day and a list of things needed, including medical supplies and replacements for the stores lost in the river crossing.

"How's Father Herschell getting along?" The question was casual, inviting no real reply.

"He seems to be happy enough and is fitting in. We've no

particular complaints, and he makes none. There hasn't been much opportunity for him to get thoroughly stuck into his job so far, but I think he's satisfied with the way things are going."

McKerrow noted the ambiguities but let the subject drop, having no mind to encourage an open discussion at this stage.

"What about the sick carrier?"

"Korbin has him under close observation and says that he can deal with him. If we have real trouble he'll put him under heavy sedation and have him carried on a stretcher until we find a place where we can camp decently for a few days, and get everybody rested and well fed."

"Call me up when you've had your airdrop, and ask Korbin to be standing by for consultation with Dr. Hovas about this case."

Marshall heard McKerrow dictate a note to his secretary, then come back to the radio. "That's all from this end. Do you have any more?"

Marshall hesitated, wondering if he should mention Didimus. But McKerrow had already gone. They could hear him tuning his set again, reaching out to another station.

"Kombala calling Pindaro, Kombala calling Pindaro." There was a faint response, and McKerrow's voice again, "Come in, Pindaro. I'm waiting." A pause, then McKerrow once again. "What's this I hear about more tribal fighting in your area?" He sounded professionally testy.

They dismantled the radio and moved downhill to intercept Scully and the others, and after a short rest regrouped and kept walking for five more hours, monotonously crossing range after range, waist-high in uncomfortable kunai grass, aiming to get as far away as they could from this vicious stretch of land before making camp again.

In the afternoon they crossed a swamp and began to climb once more towards high forest, but turned at the timberline and followed laterally for a while without climbing, thus resting everybody's legs. Father Herschell fell back to the end of the line and walked for a while with Scully. After a time he asked, "How far will we go today?"

Scully, seeing that he was tired, said, "It's tough, Father, I know, this dull slogging up and down in dead country, not seeming to get anywhere, but we can't let up until we find a site that will do for an airdrop tomorrow, as well as for a camping place tonight. It means looking for a spot that is fairly well exposed, so that the pilot can find us without having to comb every ridge and gully between here and Yakanaki. And it should have open approaches so that when he comes he can run in on us at low level and have room to turn at the other end without smacking into a mountain. And there has to be a flattish patch for the cargo to drop on; otherwise it gets scattered all over the landscape and we lose a lot of it. So we must keep going now, and hope that we'll see something suitable before dark."

They came upon the place when the light was golden, the sun getting low, and the horizon cluttered with a stormy red and black pastiche. A rainbow hung across the end of a long valley that was filled with trees, so that once more there was a multigreen vista as far as they could see, and the promise of shade for tomorrow.

The priest fingered his scarlet, sunburned face, and was grateful, remembering wryly that in the first days of this patrol he had hated walking in thick forest; had found each aching step painful—the tripping over hidden roots and slipping on sticks covered with wet leaves; the awkward clambering across rotten logs slimy with moss and fungus. He had hated the long loops of hanging vine with little hooks that caught at his clothes and left catlike scratches on his arms and face; and the leeches that squeezed through the eyelets of his boots, or dropped inside his shirt to suck blood and leave ugly, ulcerous slits in his skin.

But now, seeing the forest again he was glad—glad to be away from the brittle bareness, the harsh cruelty of dry, sharp, limestone country; to see once more an unbroken ocean of green, untouched, untilled and stretching, many days' walk distant, to the feet of mountains much higher than any they had so far seen or crossed over. The great range that lay between them and the Yakanaki Valley.

The red and black sky of evening brought rain by night, and dawn came grey and damp, with drab clouds dragging back and forth across the camp like tired old washwomen.

Marshall, standing in the doorway of his tent and looking at the sky, began to argue with himself the sense of staying for an airdrop that might not come or of moving on, since weather like this in the Highlands might last for days and they would gain nothing but misery and the danger of more madness by waiting. Better to walk in the rain and make capital of any extra effort than to sit around getting wet without achieving anything. But the trouble with such weather was that one could never tell what was happening over the hill, and in Kombala it might be fine for flying and everybody ready and anxious to help poor Marshall out there in the western mountains, having bad luck and needing the diversion of an airdrop.

But it was dull in Kombala too, though not yet raining, and there was discussion in the District Office about the airdrop, whether to give it a go or wait until tomorrow.

"It's Francy's birthday," said Rosemary, "and it would be nice if he got his mail today, and the parcel from his mother."

District Commissioner McKerrow wondered for a moment what his niece was talking about. Who was this "Francy" and what had he to do with the weather, and the airdrop to Marshall and his men?

"Francis," she said impatiently. "Patrol Officer Francis Scully." And wondered how a man so dull could have everybody in the district scared. "He's out with Mr. Marshall and it's his birthday today, and if there is to be an airdrop we could send his mail out to him. And the parcel from his mother which is most probably a birthday gift. It's been sit-

93

ting here for a week waiting to go out to Wanega." She didn't mention her own birthday letter, in the mailbag, ready since yesterday.

"Ah," said McKerrow absentmindedly. "Yes, of course, Scully. A good lad though inclined to act the part of everybody's aunt. If he ever toughens up he could go places." Then, catching his niece's eye, he asked, as though not knowing, "And how long have you been so chummy with young Scully as to call him pet names, and know what mail he gets from his mother?"

But she was not to be caught so simply and, twisting a sheet of paper into her typewriter, went sternly on with her work, though smiling quietly inside at the thought that "Rosemary Scully" was as good a name as any, and if Mother was anything like Francy it might work quite well. Hong Kong would be nice for a honeymoon, and afterwards they could live in Sydney.

McKerrow stopped watching her and called an orderly. "Get me the weather report and see who's flying this morning."

The orderly saluted, said, "Yes, sir," and went.

Marshall, deciding to wait, picked a drop site well clear of the camp and put carriers to work under Ki to cut the scrub and high grass, while Scully set smokefires nearby, ready to light at the first sound of an aircraft.

Garni unrolled long strips of white calico and made a cross with them to mark the middle of the target area. After that, said the priest humourously, there was nothing to do but to watch and pray.

By midday Marshall was doubtful if the plane would come and, if it did, if it would find them. There was still thick cloud cover on the mountains between them and Kombala, and patches of thin rain in the valley, so that even if the rendezvous had been clearly defined and pinpointed on a proper map it would still be difficult for the pilot to catch sight of them.

94

In weather like this he could not get high enough to pick out tents from the general background, and without sunshine would not be able to catch stray flashes of light that might reflect from metal things about the camp; or cans discarded by the cooks, which sometimes gave pilots their first fix.

The pilot's only chance in this weather would be to make a low approach, following along the edge of an escarpment like a man feeling his way through fog by keeping to a wall. But this was chancy business, hardly justified; not worth the risk except in real emergency. Marshall was already resigned to wait out another day, though hating the idea of staying in this place with the aftertaste of ill-luck and fatality.

Then Constable Ki heard it, and sang out excitedly, relieved for Marshall's sake, "Balus i kam"—the pigeon comes.

Though they couldn't see it yet.

One of Scully's Dana men caught a quick glimpse of it flittering through a fringe of cloud, though being shy stayed silent, but nudged one of his mates and turned his eyes in the right direction. Then others picked it up, a grey shape no bigger than a bird, a pigeon, keeping to the wall of the escarpment, but too far over for the pilot to sight them.

Marshall was shouting. "Light the bloody fires, you fools, light the fires."

But they stood gaping until Ki came bustling among them and snatched at the matches. Then Scully came running with benzine to get things going quickly.

One fire flared, then another. Smoke and flame shot up with a rush. And in another minute four thick sticks of white smoke were climbing into the wet, heavy air.

They saw the wings of the airplane dip to signify a sighting, then watched while the pilot changed course and circled round, working out a way of approach that would give him a getaway clear of cloud.

Now Marshall was shouting at Heli and the police, telling them to shift the carriers out of the way and so leave a lane for the aircraft to fly through without the danger of cargo falling among men. For this could happen and, with luck running the way it was, might easily do so. Then there would be another disaster, more death or injury, with the longest and most difficult part of the patrol still ahead of them.

So he screamed at the police to lay about them with fists and sticks if necessary to get the carriers back safely right inside the camp, and to hold them there until the airdrop was over and the airplane away. For he was beginning to feel uncertain, afraid that a hoodoo was hanging over this patrol, though he didn't believe in this kind of thing.

The pilot crisscrossed the valley, seeming to search for room in which to maneuver, and they knew that, being hedged about by cloud in a narrow and unknown valley, he was working within thin limits of safety. They would not have blamed him, or have been surprised, if he had turned away.

But suddenly he came again, out of cloud, aiming straight at them, sending the carriers down to ground with arms bent protectively above their heads as he swept over them. Only the white men watched, and the police, knowing that the pilot was making a dummy run to test his judgment, to see if he had room to climb and turn with safety inside the curtain of cloud that hid mountains all around.

They saw him make the turn, seeming to scrape the inside rim of visibility, then circle back to begin again; and this time he came thundering down across the tents to drop a clutch of cargo cleanly into the clear patch marked with the cross, where the bags skipped and jumped and rolled to rest while he pulled the nose of the airplane up and round, and seemed to hang stationary on the edge of an arc as he turned for another run.

Three times he dropped and each time cleanly, coming in so low that they could see the freight crew working in the open hatchway kicking out cargo, then quickly stacking more bags for the next run.

It was exciting, everyone looking up, heads turning all at

**96**

once as though a common spell had hold of them while they followed the airplane's parabola. And it was strange how the sounds they made matched the mathematics of the act—silence at the orbital extremities when the airplane was almost out of sight; then sibilant whisperings beginning as it turned to run in at them, building quickly with the thunder of its coming, increasing as it slanted down across the camp until the sound of the engines' pounding was smothered and completely covered by a loud, primal, orgasmic shout of exultation as the wings swept over them: and a swift, satisfying sigh as the cargo fell beyond them from the belly of the big bird. The release was almost sexual in its completeness.

And they were grateful, all of them, that the pilot had persevered and found them, had taken more than normal risk to free them from the grip of their discouragement. No longer were they disparate, fragmented, negative. The linked mechanism of their minds was set going again. Once more they were collectively aware, alive, moving onward in unison.

When the pilot made his final run to signify completion of his mission they all waved up at him, carriers, police and white men, and watched in silence until he went, and the beat of his engine was a whisper in the wind. Then the Dana lads began to laugh (for this was all new to them) and the sick carrier raced with the others to pick up cargo. Only Didimus and the priest remained withdrawn.

They spoke again to Kombala on the radio, and the doctor asked Korbin about the carrier. Then before they signed off McKerrow said, "My niece wanted to send a birthday greeting to Mr. Scully, but it's against regulations to use official radio time for personal messages. Please let him know this."

"The old man's getting soft," said Marshall.

Then keen to be busy again, he took a party hunting and, having flushed a hillside with fire, came back in two hours with a python, eight feet long, together with some bush rats and parrots. The carriers were singing, pleased that there would be at least a taste of fresh meat with their meal.

In the evening one of the Wanega men, a wizard, blew away the rain, standing on a little ridge facing the wind, flickering his fingers in front of his face, and making soft whiffling sounds with his lips.

Korbin, talking to the priest, said that the man was also a healer and that there were several Wanega men among the carriers who were specialists in some branch or other of the tribal culture structure. The little man with the bent back, who usually walked near the tail of the line by himself, was a ritual killer and had seven murders to his credit though between jobs (like any Western executioner) he was a gentle and peace-loving person.

The wizard's magic was effective and before sunset the cloud cover broke into pieces and blew away, leaving the night sky black and shiny.

Garni, looking up, saw the new star travelling fast and pointed it out to Didimus, who watched it for a while (all around the world scientists were tracking this satellite which carried two officers of the United States Marines). Then Didimus said, "It is a holy star sent by God to tell us that he knows about our suffering. Now a prophet will come, the same as Jesus, to save all men from their sins."

He stood, following its flight across the sky. Then he excused himself from Garni and went a little way into the forest to pray:

"Papa in heaven, I am alone: like a man who is far from his own village, living with strangers. I speak and no one understands. There is no woman to get my food and to lie beside me in the night. No children to play outside my house in the evening when the day is finished and the night not yet begun and people sit under the houses to talk.

"I talk to you all day but you don't talk back to me. Do you listen to me, God? Do you hear what I say? Don't you know that I cry in the night because there is nobody? Can

**98**

you see me now kneeling among the high trees trying to talk to you? Do you hear what I say? Papa, I have seen the star. Talk to me now so that I will know that you are up there too.

"The priest says that you love me. Did you tell him? If you talk to him why don't you talk to me? Why don't you speak into my ear secretly, as the wind speaks, 'Didimus, you are my son and I love you'? That is all I ask. Talk to me, once in a while.

"You don't have to give me the things that you give the white people. Not money or a big house and plenty of meat and beer. Just speak once in my ear, 'Didimus, I can see you. Believe in me always, Didimus, and when you die you will be with me forever in heaven.'

"I looked at the woman, Maileeta, who is the wife of Garni though she likes better to lie with Palau. She is lonely like me. Give me Maileeta and we will go to church every day and put flowers on the posts, and on Sunday we will lead the people in praying and singing the hymns, even though I don't have a guitar any more. I will still sing the hymns without my guitar because I don't ask for anything. Only that you speak to me. Then I will know."

# Chapter 7

THEY walked all next day almost gaily, in sunlight tempered with a little wind, and passed through gardens again (the carriers eying mounds of sweet potato and muttering to each other covetously), but saw no people—only a net bag such as women use to carry food and babies in, left on the ground.

Garni, seeing the disturbed earth still damp where it had been turned with digging sticks, guessed that women had been there gathering food and, hearing the patrol, had run away.

He could see no one, but higher up the hill a pair of long-tailed blackbirds were flapping peevishly from tree to tree complaining; and he knew that the patrol was being watched.

They skirted a great swamp where Scully shot six ducks, climbed another ridge, and made camp in a pleasant place, open in front with a valley view and sheltered at the back by a forest of tall trees.

Korbin, taking his boots off and rubbing his feet with spirit, talked to Marshall in their tent. "You know, we ought to have a little party to mark young Scully's birthday. We have six ducks, and in yesterday's airdrop there was a small bag of carrots and onions from Dr. Hovas, who has pet theories about the therapeutic qualities of root vegetables, which he wishes me to test on suitable subjects and occasions. This is one of them. And there was a parcel smuggled in from Scully's

**100**

mother, hidden in the middle of a bag of rice and put there, I imagine, by Miss Mulholland, who has designs on the lad. According to our priest, who has seen the loot, this parcel contains two pairs of hand-knitted socks, six handkerchiefs, some chocolate, and a bottle of fine French brandy which might easily become a troublesome source of temptation to everybody if left intact. . . . So I suggest we give ourselves a fresh beginning. Make a new start with a modest dinner party this evening. As medical adviser to this patrol I can recommend this in all honesty."

Marshall fidgeted, uncertain whether Korbin was being serious or was just playing games with him. He opened his mouth to argue but was too late.

"It will be quite simple. I will cook the ducks, Scully will give us a drink, and afterwards Father Herschell will dig into his liberty bag and produce the coffee and cigars he keeps for feast days. It will bring us together pleasantly in a relaxed and amiable state of mind and do us all a great deal of good." He stood up. "I'll go to the medical center for a while and dispense aspirin and malaria tablets, and then I'll get the dinner ready."

Later, when they were all together in the store tent, which doubled for a dining room, he lifted his cup. "Here's to Scully's mother and her favourite son."

Father Herschell, looking up, added, "Perhaps we should include Miss Mulholland in this context since she played no inconsiderable part in making the occasion possible." He had helped Korbin prepare the dinner and had carried it to the table. Sitting among them now, he was quietly glad, feeling almost equal again. He bent his head over the food. "Boy, does this look good! Bless, O Lord, this food, and the work that we men do together." He glanced at Marshall almost shyly, wanting to please him, to be accepted again, without reservation.

Constable Palau, being on watch, walked past in the dark and could hear them laughing. The tent flap bulged and Marshall's boy came backing out with dishes. Palau could see briefly the four men at table, a hanging lamp drenching them with incandescent light. The tent flap closed again, cutting them off, leaving only a thin white, upright scar in the darkness. He looked at his watch by flashlight, impatient for his shift to finish so that he could get back and sit with Garni and Didimus to talk about Maileeta, and what they were going to do with her.

There had been a big change in Didimus since Mr. Marshall had come and smashed his guitar against the tent pole. The shock seemed to have unsettled him, made him strange, made him anxious to settle something that involved them all in some uncertain way: Palau, Garni, Maileeta, Mr. Marshall, and Didimus himself.

It was difficult to follow his thoughts now, or to understand all that he was saying, especially when he spoke about the star and Mr. Marshall, and sinners and the Bishop, and the blood of the Lamb.

But it was almost definite that Garni would give up Maileeta if Didimus' Bishop could find him a new young wife who had been to school. And in the discussion that had taken place between them on this matter Garni seemed ready to be reasonable about payment for Maileeta, asking only sixty dollars in cash, a bicycle, a pig big enough for a wedding feast, and a bag of sweet potato.

Some people would think this too much for a woman already married once, and the mother of two children, but when Palau thought of her lying alongside him on his mat, so great was his desire he had no doubts about the worth of her and could hardly wait.

Inside the store tent Father Herschell was saying, "But, Francis, you musn't trifle with Miss Mulholland's affections. It's clear that she regards you as a favourable catch and you must, in decency, declare yourself. It's the only honourable thing to do."

They were teasing Scully, and he was playing along.

102

"Well, I suppose you're right, Father. A fellow ought to marry and have done with the worry of who to choose. But any fish will fight when it feels the hook." He picked up the brandy bottle and looked at it, measuring what was left. "Pass your cup, Father. We haven't far to go."

Marshall said, "I've heard stories that you were playing the field a bit in Sydney on your last leave. You certainly seemed smug enough when you came back to Wanega. Maybe there are other starters in the Scully Marriage Stakes we haven't heard about yet." He spoke openly enough, partly smiling, with no suggestion of malice or of knowing more than he had said.

Scully looked at him seriously, waiting for a sign, but Marshall only held out his cup and watched while Scully tipped the bottle carefully.

"You must give the lad latitude," said Korbin. "He's a romantic from way back,—the lovelorn sheperd boy, the poet, the young cavalier, Galahad or every woman's comforter. The eternal sucker for love."

Scully wondered if Korbin knew how close he was to the truth; wondered how he would react if the story ever came out how a young patrol officer had sat up in a chair all night long, watching over his boss' beautiful drunken wife, without quite knowing why.

He remembered every second—how, after the first disturbance, when she had dropped the gin, she had been quiet until morning and then, hearing him stir, had called in a tired voice, "Is that you, Francis?"

While he was in the kitchen she took a shower and put on a wrap, and when he brought her coffee she was sitting up in bed looking fresh again, and lovely, and whimsically ashamed. But she was frank about her drunkenness.

"I don't know what's happening to me. Other women have learned to live with a cracked image, and I'm not really hysterical, or a weakling. Maybe I waited too long, rehearsed the big act so often in my mind that the pattern was fixed too

**103**

rigidly. I wasn't prepared for any variations in the script or surprise approaches to the big moment. And when they came I was embarrassed. Then shocked. I tried to help him but didn't quite know what to do. All I know is that it was horrible, and maybe I reacted the wrong way. I don't know. I haven't talked about it to anybody else."

He had stopped her, not wanting to know what had happened, unwilling to look into any mirror that would distort his own image of Marshall—the man he had to live with in an isolation and intimacy as sensitive in many ways as that of marriage.

One half of him had wanted to escape the situation, to give it away and forget Sandra. Let her work it out with Marshall, for it was their business. But the romantic element in him was reluctant and when he said, excusing himself, that he must go to Mass, and she had looked interested and asked if she might go with him, he waited for her to get dressed.

And again he stayed the night, just to keep her off the drink, making a bed for himself in the lounge and going to it feeling virtuous.

He had really tried to play it straight, the benevolent friend doing good turns all round and wanting nothing from it. But of course it didn't work.

During the week they went to dinners, to pictures and plays. On Saturday they went to the races, and on Sunday to Mass again, then borrowed Mrs. Scully's car and drove out into the country. They walked along bush pathways holding hands like children, quoting favourite poets and reading the psalms in Latin out of his Mass book.

Love divine all love excelling!

And on Sunday night they made love on Marshall's bed, then lay awake, empty of everything but content, talking about him and what a good, decent chap he was, dedicated to the people of New Guinea. What a pity it was that sex had him confused, for they might have been happy in a fashion!

Then she had suddenly clutched at Scully and sobbed, and

**104**

dragged him down, digging her fingers into his back and twisting her long legs around his until he gave way, ashamed of himself and her, while making love again.

Marshall was saying in a flat, detached voice, "I don't know what people mean when they talk about love. A man and woman getting together and having babies is a law of nature that applies to all people everywhere. It's the same with those who are civilized as with these primitives here in New Guinea. The love myth is some kind of gimmick that women have thought up to give themselves a mystique that sanctifies their sex, and makes them all a little more special than cats. It's a racket designed to confuse men and keep them tied unnaturally to one woman."

Father Herschell was thoughtful. "You're right, you know. Love is a gimmick. The mystique that makes a man a man and not an animal. The mystical thing that links him to God or whatever you care to call his creative origin. Love, in its purest and most creative form, is, I think, this urgent reaching up of the goodness that is in all of us, this climbing the spiritual heights, full of faith, hope and love, to meet with and embrace the descending grace of the Creator." He hesitated. "Sorry, I didn't mean to preach. But it does seem to me that if we could only take hold of these fundamental things the rest would be easy."

Marshall said almost diffidently, not wishing to offend, "Well, God is quite a problem for some of us. If the churches would show ordinary people like me an example of their God in action it might be easier for us to believe that he exists. As it is, I believe that in doing my own particular job as well as I can, with justice and the best of intentions, I'm nearer to doing God's work, whatever that may be, than a lot of people who go around singing hymns and looking down their noses at us sinners."

He got up to leave, knowing that very soon the priest and Korbin, however polite, would tear away and lose him in this kind of discussion. In any case he was feeling just a little bit

**105**

sick. Nothing much, but enough to make him wish that he had stuck to his rule of eating nothing but plain food and taking no alcohol on patrol. At the door of the tent he turned to the priest. "You understand there's nothing personal in that. I've got a lot of good friends among the missionaries and some of them do a damned good job here in New Guinea."

Then he looked at Scully. "Thanks for the drink, and good luck with your loving. If these fellows don't keep you up too late I'd like to get away soon after daylight, so that we can make camp again early in the afternoon. We ought to meet up with some people in this valley, before we get to the main range, and Father Herschell will get a chance to do some new work." He nodded, including all of them. "Goodnight."

They listened to him walk towards his tent, then stop for a few seconds to talk to the constable on watch, and go on again.

When he was out of earshot Korbin looked at the priest. "You know, Father, Marshall's argument is right as far as it goes, and there are lots like him. People who insulate themselves with a protective coating of efficient self-sufficiency, simply because they feel isolated, and nobody has the time or the desire to understand them and their needs."

Scully, interrupting, picked up the bottle and made a face. "We've had it! Mother always underestimates my friends." He shared the last drops between the two of them, then got up and excused himself, and went out to make the rounds.

Korbin watched him go and then, holding the cup between his hands, turned back to Father Herschell. "It would be nice to be as simple and uncomplicated as that lad, but you priests have made it too difficult for most of us.

"Your insistence on impossible rules and disciplines has broken up and scattered a great part of the human family. Has made spiritual orphans of millions of good, decent people who just simply cannot swallow your impossible definitions of God, or follow the complicated demands of dogma which agonize the honest mind, and confuse what ought to be a simple, elemental relationship with the mystical being you ask us to believe in.

"Instead of the Christian road to heaven being kept wide open, you clutter it up with cartloads of sanctified garbage and speculative gobbledegook, cooked up by a succession of saintly fanatics and pedants like Paul and Aquinas, who have built up barricades that people just can't climb over. The hungry ask for bread and you give them polemics. Instead of striving to defend and perpetuate the obstacles that men of this kind have set up between God and those who need him most, the churches should surely be busy day and night tearing them down, so that the way can be opened for those who are hungry for an understanding of God, who are ready and willing to run and fling themselves into his open arms if he will have them as they are.

"And you know, Father, as well as I do, that there are millions of us—the lost agnostics, atheists, schismatics, heretics, religious cranks, Communists—who can't or won't pay the price you demand for the right to be loved by your jealously guarded God."

He took the cigar proffered by the priest and when it was lit, drew on it, and slowly let the smoke out. He looked tired. "You see, people like me don't reject the idea of God. We're really no more self-sufficient than you are. But we find the concept of a scholarly or a magisterial god ridiculous and grotesque. Neither can we accept a blackmailing god who tabulates everybody's sins and dishes out purgatorial punishment on a sliding scale. And, for myself, I hate the horrible, disgusting image of a fatherly god who will condemn me to burn forever in hell because I cannot completely understand him. We had such gods at home, not so long ago."

He drained the cup and set it down.

"No, Father, it won't do. If there is a god who is the father of us all, then he is god of the whole human family. The family to which we all belong by birth, without exception. We

**107**

share, through him, the same miracle of combined mind and spirit and flesh. We are equally complete with the self-same capacities for love, for stubborn individuality, and a regrettable tendency to error, all of which must be accepted equally as natural, put up with, forgiven, as in a family; not as in an institution."

He stood up.

"Sorry. It's the brandy taking over. Scully's mother, good pious soul that she no doubt is, must share the blame for these heresies. Tomorrow I will probably be ashamed but will carry a headache around with me as a penance. And, of course, you are expected to pray for me."

# Chapter 8

THERE was an arrow tied to a thin sapling where two paths met, making a signpost to tell any who passed by that a battle was going on in the district, to be joined or avoided according to inclination.

A little later they marched through a garden that had been plundered and left empty, with plants rooted up and the earth scattered about. And on the edge of the garden a smoking patch of white wood ash that had been a men's meeting house. Casuarina trees that had been planted years ago to make shade for it were chopped down and still bleeding.

Marshall frowned and made impatient sounds, understanding by these signs that the whole valley would be in a turmoil of tribal unrest for months to come, until such damage as this, done all over the district, had been paid for by retaliation.

Fights and family feuds and private payback activities would go on, stopping normal tribal life, until there was no more food to keep the fighting men supplied. Then it would all stop while they made new gardens, and trading parties went visiting neighbouring tribes to buy breeding pigs, and to find wives so that decimated clans could be bred back to strength.

Now, the valley women would be hiding in the bush, finding what food they could and keeping clear of the fighting.

This meant that there would be no sweet potato to be bought for feeding carriers, and no pigs to give them a little fresh meat. And their spirits would droop again which would be a nuisance, in fact worse than a nuisance, coming on top of what had already happened.

They saw another sign of the fighting: stems of grass, growing by a path, knotted together to make a symbolic barrier, forbidding anyone to pass. Normally it would mean that a party of warriors lay waiting in ambush a little farther on, to shoot arrows at anyone coming. But Marshall broke through the knotted grass and passed on, knowing that no tribesmen would be so foolish as to tangle with a strange, unknown invader without closer scrutiny and some calculation of the consequences.

But when they came to a patch of country that was clear of ambush he called a halt and issued extra rounds of ammunition to the police, and gave instructions that the carrier line be tightened and an eye kept on stragglers. For there was every chance now that anyone separating from the company, even for a few moments, might be ambushed and killed.

They went on again, downhill for a while, and came to a river, and a place where there had been a bridge of vine strands stretched over it to make a high crossing. But on the far side the vines had been chopped through and the bridge made useless, the cut end hanging loose and swinging in the river.

They moved downstream and found a shallower place and spent an hour cutting down trees to make a firm footbridge with safety rails of jungle vine; and were watched from the opposite bank by a shrivelled old man with a patch on one eye, sitting with a small boy.

The broken bridge, and the old man seeming unconcerned, might have been a sign that fighting was confined to one side of the river. But Marshall was taking no chances; and when they had all crossed, and the old man offered to guide them to a good camping place among many people, he feared a trap

**110**

and said that they would choose their own way and pitch their tents where it seemed safest. However, before moving on he told Heli to thank the old man and say that if any of his friends had wounds, or were in pain, or had sick children, they should come to the camp to be treated. And if their gardens were flush and they had food to spare he would pay well for it. And to show that he was generous and full of goodwill he told Garni to give the man a spoonful of salt, and the boy two little shells.

They saw no other people until they were camped, and then only a few old men, some of whom brought little net bags of small, juiceless tubers to sell and sticks of wild, tough sugarcane and bundles of edible plants. The total would not have fed a dozen men, but Marshall bought all and was generous in payment, hoping to encourage others.

Heli spoke with them, then came to Marshall to say that every man of fighting age was away taking part in battles and would come back later. Meanwhile the women, being unprotected, would stay hidden and not go near the gardens. So, clearly, there would be no useful quantity of food to be had before morning, and few visitors to the camp unless they stayed at least another day, by which time the fighting men would be back, curious to come and visit.

Marshall thought; then said they would stay as the place might later prove suitable for a patrol post, and so should be roughly surveyed by Scully next day while he and Korbin made contacts with the people, and the priest worked at his linguistics.

Later, after dark, they heard the fighting men come back, singing and calling out excitedly. But afterwards, when the men had quietened down, an eerie sound of women and young girls wailing wandered aimlessly up and down the valley all night long on a drifting wind.

"Bloody fools," said Marshall in the morning. "They must have left a few dead men behind them, wherever they've been.

Why can't they stay home and do something useful instead of buying into fights all the time?" He forked a few beans onto his plate fastidiously, still feeling a little sick, but clinging to the discipline of eating breakfast in order to keep up his strength.

Korbin, leaving the table, went straight to the medical tent in case wounded men came, and found a tribesman already waiting with a woman and a baby. The woman, young and ugly, was a battle prize from another tribe, and had a broken forearm and a long knife wound in her thigh. Her child was dead, its skull dented.

He complained to his orderlies.

"Why do they bring this baby? Who do they think I am? Jesus Christ?" Seeing the man standing by, looking at him silently, he felt helpless and a fraud and hunched his shoulders, muttering, "I am not God. I can't work miracles."

But he dealt with the woman gently, setting her arm in a splint. Then he cleaned and stitched the wound in her thigh though she was filthy and stinking of rancid pig grease and stale urine.

Then he called for Heli to tell the man that if the patrol came back this way he would look at the woman again within ten days. Meanwhile she must do no heavy work in the bush or in the gardens.

He gave the man pain-killing tablets for her to take and said that if he did not return within the ten days he would come after one moon (having in mind that he would, by some means, make a follow-up medical patrol as soon as he could).

The man listened and made a brief reply, holding out the dead baby. But Korbin went inside the medical tent, saying that Heli must explain to them that it was too late; that the child was already dead and its spirit left behind in its own village, unable to find its way back into the body unless they went back to look for it.

He was angry with them for making him feel stupid. He knew that he might never be able to get back again to see the woman. Within two or three days, or sooner, she would be carrying wood or digging in the garden; and the women of the man's family would ill-treat her whenever they could. The man would take the splint off her arm and use the bandages himself, for decoration, and the bone would set by itself, crookedly. The wound in her thigh would go rotten and in the meantime the man would get her pregnant. But she would die before the baby could be born.

He shrugged his shoulders. He had done what he could.

Many more men came during the morning, some with broken arrowheads embedded in their flesh, others flushed with the excitement of fighting and the expectancy of more to come. The headmen among them, eyes flickering suspiciously, lips whispering, went through the camp in little groups, furtively searching about, anxious to discover and assess the strength of the patrol—this forerunner of the mysterious new influence called "the Government."

They were curious to prove or disprove the truth of rumours that had come through from Wanega and Kombala along the trade routes—fantastic stories that spoke of the white men being able to kill by pointing sticks at people; of being able to remove parts of their bodies and put them back again, eyes and teeth, and to peel the skin from their feet; of being able to talk to spirits who lived in the sky; of being fed by huge birds that brought food to them. But chiefly they wanted to see in what way, if any, the strangers were weak and could be overcome, for they had many marvellous things which, if possessed by this or any other tribe, would make them more powerful than all the others, so that they could overcome their neighbours and take their land, their gardens, their pigs and women and betel nut trees.

"Just like us," said Korbin, "except that they haven't yet learned to lie about these things, or to find fancy names for common or garden greed and avarice. But we'll teach them pretty soon."

He was standing with Scully watching them come and watching Ki and other constables direct them to leave their weapons outside the limits of the camp, keeping them on the move, sending some to the medical center for treatment, seeking out clan leaders and taking them to Marshall and Heli for questioning.

Scully said, "It looks as if we're staying here a day or two, so as soon as the boss can find out who owns this land we're camped on, and can shake him by the hand and pay him an ax as rental, I'll take a team of carriers and clear away some of the scrub in case we want room to maneuver. There are too many fighting men around here and they're in the mood for a bit of excitement. It wouldn't take much to start something." He was looking around all the time, assessing the defensive aspects of the situation and what should be done to make the camp safe. Seeing Father Herschell outside their tent, the center of a cluster of excited tribesmen, he frowned and shook his head doubtfully.

The priest and Didimus were busy making tapes, with a constable beside them, armed, to keep guard. But the two men were sitting on the ground with the eager, inquisitive tribesmen leaning over them, hedging them in so closely that the policeman could have done nothing to protect them from ax blows or knife stabs had anything provoked a sudden rumpus.

Father Herschell was not thinking of this. He seemed to have shed his timidity and was totally intent, accepting the circumstance and the men crowding around him as a normal and necessary part of his immediate being. He was, in fact, intrigued by what seemed to him to be something unusually interesting, perhaps unique, in the structure of the language of these people—a systematic tonal element in the syntax. It might be nothing more significant than a purely local and idiosyncratic system of pronunciation, but listening to them speak he thought that he could catch a grammatical dimension that took into account not only inflection plus the use

114

of digital and other physical gestures, but regular variants of basic tone in vowel sounds.

It was no more than a hunch, a professionally perceptive response to something linguistically novel. There had been a bit of speculative writing about it in one of the European anthropological journals some time back, and later in the day he would remember it. Meanwhile, for the first time on this trip he felt elated.

Holding the microphone to his lips he repeated words and phrases being spoken by the men around him, and terms common to the trading argot, learned from Heli. Then he played the tape to let them hear what he had said.

Immediately there were cries of surprise, men looking at the priest and his machine in astonishment, recognizing words and phrases they had themselves just spoken, and believing that this man had caught their very thoughts and put them in this box.

They drew breath, amazed, and some were a little afraid and moved back to let others push past them and get closer to the priest. They, too, leaned down, astounded, watching the tape turn and hearing the spirit in the box speak their own language and that of their neighbours.

Marshall, seeing Scully's worry, came and moved the tribesmen back and sat them on the ground in an arc facing the priest, but separated from him by a space of several feet. Then he set constables on each side to watch.

"I don't want to interrupt you, Father, or to interfere with what you're doing, but you're taking just a little more than normal risk by sitting too closely among these men with no real protection. They've got axes in their belts and if they take fright at something they don't understand, or feel insulted by some chance remark that you might make without knowing its implication, you could have a hole in your head before you knew what was happening."

The priest nodded, aware that Marshall was right but certain, too, that there was no immediate danger from this group.

They were interested in what he was doing, eager to see and hear more of these strange tricks and pleased that he seemed to know something of their language. So, having let them hear his own voice coming from the box, he recorded Didimus and played that back. Then he invited one of them to sit and face him and say the words he called for by pointing to his head, his hands, feet, teeth, eyes, ears and nose. He played these words to the men again, asking them with gestures to repeat them and point to each part of the body as they spoke.

He went closer to the man and sat facing him, knee to knee, and spoke the word for *head,* repeating it several times. Then he asked the man to do the same, and as he did the priest put a finger on the man's larynx to feel the mechanics of pronunciation, and on his nasal bones to gauge vibration. Then he measured the plosive strength of the man's breath with the back of his hand. Next, he attempted to repeat the word himself, exactly as the other had said it, and asked the man to speak it with him so that he could imitate precisely the movement of his tongue and lips. So they all sat for a long time, totally absorbed.

A man who said he was headman of the clan that owned the land came quietly from the bush, was presented with an ax, and having received it stood submissively while Marshall explained, with Heli's help, that this was how the Government always acted: never taking a man's land; never using anything without payment; never asking anything for itself but doing everything for the good of the people.

The man seemed too dull and unintelligent to be a clan leader by right, or anyone of consequence, and although his eyes glistened when he took the ax into his own hand he made no speech in answer to Marshall's rhetoric, but turned without speaking and went back into the bush.

Then a few women came with a little food, hardly enough to make one meal for the carriers. Marshall, looking at it, understood that it was no more than a token. Remembering the dull, unlikely headman he realized that the man had been an

**116**

understudy, an elected substitute, and that these people had not yet decided what to do about the patrol but were making, at this stage, only conventional gestures of acceptance.

By midday only the old men were still hanging about the camp, quietly scavenging.

In the afternoon Scully took a compact team of police and carriers to look about the countryside and find a place that might one day do for an airstrip. He made a rough map, took photographs and noted that garden land covered several hillsides and could support a considerable population.

They were watched wherever they went and could hear unseen men calling continuously from hill to hill. Circling back to the camp along a treeless ridge and coming near the top, they were stopped by a band of young bucks in war paint, waving spears and bows and arrows, dancing, and shouting insults.

Knowing that nothing would be gained, and perhaps much lost, by testing their strength in this situation he turned aside and went round them. Back at camp, he told Marshall, "They're stirred up all right, and ready to fight anybody who shows up. They're that cocky, I'll not be surprised if they have a go at us."

Yet the landscape seemed to deny such excitements. Green hills somnolent in the afternoon heat. The still, ovenlike air. No sound but of men calling, distantly, to each other. The only movement (except for a blue butterfly flapping antickally over shirts drying in the sun) that of men in the camp moving about their business slowly, at a tropical tempo, as in a deep, meaningless dream.

Korbin, calling discreetly to Scully, led him to the medical tent where they could talk unseen.

"I'm a little concerned about the boss. I've watched him these past few days and think he's sickening for something. He's not eating enough, and when he lets down his guard he has the look of a man in pain. If we can get away from here

**117**

tomorrow without clashing with these people we should do it, and camp for a few days in some other place where things are quiet, and we can get rest and plenty of fresh food, and come back some other time to deal with the fighting. But if I suggest this to him, and imply that he's sick before he's ready to admit it, he'll get cranky and stubborn and want to stay here to get things settled. So, see if you can find an opportunity to drop a hint along these lines, and maybe he'll make a sensible decision."

Scully took a shower under a bucket, then put on clean shorts and an undershirt and stretched out on his bed, wondering what Rosemary would be doing at that moment, and whether it would be sensible to think seriously, when this patrol was over, of talking to her about being married. The first lines of a new poem were running about in his head:

> You seemed so lovely standing there
> At the top of the stair,
> Looking down at me in the half light
> Suddenly aware.

But Father Herschell, sitting just outside, was playing tapes, back and forth over the same phrases, and making notes, then playing them again, industriously.

Korbin, filling in the daily report of treatments given and drugs dispensed, wondered about the woman with the broken arm and the stitches in her thigh.

Marshall, sitting at ease in a canvas chair, in the doorway of his tent, was writing in his diary.

. . . I must admit that I don't feel as well as I might and suspect duck and brandy the other night though cannot blame anybody but myself and in future must not let my own judgment be overcome by Korbin's subtle tongue. In fact am a bit annoyed with myself because we are in a situation where I need to keep my wits about me not that I'm expecting trouble but the tribes here are fighting and the people in such a state of high excitement that anything might happen. . . .

He rested a moment, looked up, and could see police and carriers in clannish little groups lighting fires to cook their evening meal. The thought passed through his mind that it must be almost time to lower the flag and sound the evening Retreat. He looked at his watch, stretched, and stood up.

With a tiny thud, an arrow struck the ground four feet in front of him and stood slantwise, quivering. For a second he looked at it as if academically fascinated.

Then he let out a shout. "The bastards!" Running into the tent he grabbed his rifle and came out calling, "Garni, Ki, Palau, where are you? We're being attacked!"

They came running, with other police, and gathered round him in the middle of the camp, struggling into bandoliers, boss boys too, wanting to be told what to do, though most of the other carriers were already scuttling into tents for shelter, or rushing about blindly like frightened fowls, crying and shying violently from arrows that were flying among them.

"Gerua, go get Mr. Scully. Tell him to keep the carriers quiet and spread them out a bit. Tau, tell Mr. Korbin to look after the priest." And as Tau hesitated, "Go on, son. Go quickly."

He turned back to Garni and the others, and in his mind measured the time left to them before dusk turned dark, and wondered how many tribesmen were in the scrub, working up the courage to attack. By the sound of their shouting there might be a hundred, maybe more, and all in one place, hidden on the high side of the hill, forty or fifty yards from the edge of the camp, looking into it.

They were darting out into the open in small groups only, four or five at a time, crouching as they came. As each man shot his arrow into the camp he backed away a little to watch its flight, then turned and ran back into the protection of the scrub while another came out to take his place.

Marshall, moving fast, spread the police out in a line, well spaced, and moved forward with them towards the edge of the camp.

What was it that McKerrow had said in his memorandum?

Under no circumstances are you to employ firearms against tribesmen except in case of a direct threat to the life of the Reverend Herschell or other personnel under your control.

Well, Father Herschell would be safe enough. He was the last person on this patrol to cultivate danger. But what about the "other personnel under your control"? What about Scully's three Dana men, or the mad carrier, or any of the others? Didn't they rate as much as the Reverend Herschell, SJ, UN, USA?

The arrows came more thickly, and straighter as the range closed in. He held up his hand, then motioned his men to go to ground. And standing alone he fired three rounds rapidly, high over the heads of the tribesmen, hearing one shot ricochet and whine away far into the forest.

There was a wild, excited shouting from the tribesmen, then a kind of chant or chorus of short, sharp, barking sounds compounding fear and anger: then more arrows flying in a flock.

Then a single warrior came scampering out from the scrub, bow flexed and arrow aimed straight at Marshall.

Marshall waited. A sharp crack lashed from behind him and the tribesman dropped in his tracks, surprised. Then, lying on the ground, he suddenly jack-knifed like a rabbit, coughed, and slowly stretched, shuddering, to accept death.

Marshall turned quickly and saw Palau on one knee, reloading, and was both grateful and dismayed: grateful because he had been saved the decision of whether or not to shoot at the man (and Palau's action carried with it overtones of a personal loyalty which pleased him); but still dismayed because he had not wanted to have any man killed, and Palau had no right to fire a shot of any kind without permission.

**120**

But he could not stop now to consider these things or to give speeches; for the tribesmen, made mad, came pouring from the scrub in scores and began moving implacably towards the camp, firing arrows as they came, screaming insults and obscenities against the white strangers and their servants.

A carrier, somewhere in the camp, cried out in pain and ran away.

Then Ki, beside him, dropped his rifle, spun half round, clutching at his side.

Marshall thought, I must do something now. Must lead. He looked around at the police. "One round only, over their heads. Fire!"

A crash of sound bounced round the mountains. Then there was silence as the tribesmen froze for a moment in fright. Were still. Then they came on again, screaming with rage and hate, craving to kill, to smash these people who trespassed on their land and slaughtered them.

"One round only, at their legs." He sounded calm. "Fire!"

Two tribesmen fell this time and the rest hesitated, uncertain, except for one who came on ahead, separate from the rest, advancing upon Marshall with high, eccentric steps, face thrust forward in a fury, hooting hate and waving his bow above his head.

Both sides waited, watching the two men, the two civilizations.

Marshall took aim carefully. Then, as the man came on, prancing, he fired at his shoulder, spinning him round so that he faced his friends, astonished, and dropped as if dead, and lay still.

The tribesmen stared at him, gaping, then at Marshall standing like a statue, expressionless, pale. And the police kneeling behind him with their rifles ready.

Suddenly they gave a frightened shout and fled—the two men who were wounded in the legs, dragging themselves away like injured animals.

Marshall seemed to shrink where he stood.

**121**

Then he walked across to look at Ki, then at the tribesman he had wounded, and the man whom Palau had killed. He kicked at the man's bow and arrows and called to Garni. "Look after these, and have Mr. Korbin look at Ki and this other fellow."

Then he was sick.

He went to his tent, and inside fell straight upon the bed.

# Chapter 9

Extract from Patrol Report (medical) submitted by Korbin, G. (Med. Asst.) to Regional M.O.          25.5.65 (Interim)
*Subject: Yakanaki Patrol—casualties.*

**O**UR camp was attacked yesterday (May 24) just before dark by an estimated 100 tribesmen who seem to have been on a rampage for the past few weeks all round the district, engaged in general destruction and in warfare with the neighbours. Bad luck for us to have arrived in the middle of the fighting season and so to start off on the wrong foot to teach these people the arts of civilization and the joy of living in the modern world. But sometimes a good argument clears the air of doubt and sentiment and leads to a mutual understanding based on common needs and the prospect of profit on both sides.

I was occupied in the medical tent and did not see anything of the fight but understand that it was exciting while it lasted (15–20 minutes) though in spite of all the noise and dramatics it passed off with little serious damage—total casualties being as follows:

| CASE: | COMMENT: |
| --- | --- |
| 1 Tribesman | Dead. Penetrating lung wound and fractured thoracic spine caused by .303 bullet fired by |

123

|              | Constable Palau (allegedly in defense of A.D.O. Marshall but my own opinion is that Palau was eager to have a potshot at somebody and this was his opportunity). |
| --- | --- |
| 1 Tribesman | Wounded. Shattered left shoulder, likely to deteriorate without further treatment which we cannot give. |
| 1 Tribesman | Wounded. Superficial thigh wound. Treated. Should recover. |
| 1 Tribesman | Wounded (presumably in the leg) but removed from the scene of battle by friends and relations before inspection became possible. |
| Constable Ki | Wounded. Ragged penetration of the chest. Evidence of early infection. Needs watching. |
| Carrier Bogui | One of Scully's Dana men. Missing, presumed dead. Deserted during the fracas and unlikely to survive among these people. Has a history of hysteria. |
| Carrier Wark | Wounded. Penetrated calf muscle (arrow). Stretcher case for some days. |
| Carrier Pak | Wounded, neck, superficial (arrow). |
| Carrier Goli | Wounded, buttock, superficial (arrow). |

All wounded available for treatment have been attended by me and should recover (for details of treatment see Daily Clinical Report).

In addition I have put Assistant District Officer Marshall under strict medical observation.

Mr. Marshall experienced a minor blackout after the engagement, and I am of the opinion that this was due to reaction aggravated by a morbid condition probably related to what appeared to be symptoms of an attack of scrub typhus or dengue. He has obviously been sick for some days and this morning admitted to having suffered intermittent but severe pains in the back and shoulder joints, nausea and some body

124

rash. His temperature this morning was 100 and this evening 102. At present he is passing through a period of depression.

Referring again to the attack on our camp. The facts, briefly, are that it began without warning and for no other clear reason than that the tribes around here are in a fighting mood and, having had no previous contact with the Government, lack experience of the consequences of matching bows and arrows with guns, which is something they all have to learn sooner or later.

I was in the medical tent when the affair began and took little notice until Constable Gerua came with our visitor, the Reverend Father Herschell, and a message from Mr. Marshall asking me to keep him out of harm's way during the fighting.

We stacked up medical boxes to make an armour-plate bunker in the tent in case of stray arrows, after which I prepared to deal with casualties.

Upon the withdrawal of the tribesmen Father Herschell accompanied me to the scene of battle and proved most helpful in interpreting between me and the two wounded tribesmen left behind by their friends. It seems that as a result of his researches on this trip he has quickly picked up a working knowledge of the trading language used in these parts, and with his help I was able to diagnose the extent of the tribesmen's injuries more quickly than would have been otherwise possible. It was an impressive performance seeing that he has been in the area less than two weeks. I will inform Mr. Marshall of this.

As it happened our official interpreter, Heli, was busy with Patrol Officer Scully all through the night, keeping watch on the tribesmen to make sure that they did not make another attack, and telling them that we would look after their wounded and that they could collect them in the morning.

Having dealt with the casualties I saw Mr. Marshall, who was in a feverish condition (temp. 103) and gave him 15 grains of aspirin and 3 grains of nembutal, which together brought his temperature down and allowed him to get a good night's

**125**

sleep instead of fussing and worrying about the camp and knocking himself about to no good purpose.

Early this morning, after some discussion, he agreed with Mr. Scully and me that there was nothing to gain at this stage by staying in the area while the people are in this unsettled condition. They probably lost other men in some foray yesterday and will be working themselves into a frenzy with death ceremonies for the next few days, and our own situation is complicated by Mr. Marshall's sickness and the fact that he is personally responsible for the safety of Father Herschell.

As a result of this discussion we broke camp at about ten o'clock this morning and after an easy walk of something under five hours (with wounded carrier Wark on a stretcher) came to this place where we are now camped.

Mr. Marshall and Constable Ki walked the whole distance but I have insisted that they must both take at least two days' rest before we move from here, for the sake of all of us and the success of the patrol. With that in mind I have moved Constable Ki into the medical tent where he can be kept under observation. Both patients are at present sleeping under sedation.

Under a big tree, on top of a hill, Father Herschell was saying the Mass for pilgrims and travellers, with a folding table for an altar.

. . . if I walk in the midst of the shadow of death I will fear no evil, for thou, my Lord, art with me. . . .

He looked at the dark sky, alive with a myriad sparkling stars, and shivered, still unaccustomed to the swift change from burning days to chilly nights at these equatorial altitudes. But he was grateful to be quiet again and at peace, away from fears that fluttered around him like black bats whenever the shouting began, the maniac threats of grotesque maiming or melodramatic death at the hands of savages.

**126**

It was no good saying, "I will fear no evil, for you, my Lord, are with me."

He did fear evil, hated to be within range of it. He was frightened all the time, even though the Lord was with him. For the Lord never showed any real concern with death, seeming always prepared to let nature or calamity take its course, even with His own son. And thought martyrs rather special people, to be encouraged rather than protected.

Turning outward, now, towards the night, Father Herschell said soundlessly, "Dominus vobiscum," and thought that perhaps he should be saying the Mass for a happy death, though it had the same psalm. Or the Mass for the conversion of the heathen, though there was no guarantee that making Christians of people made them any the less aggressive or liable to unspeakable violence.

Yet, being burned to a spoonful of ash by an exploding atomic bomb, or obliterated and transmogrified into a shadow on a wall, might in fact be less fearful than being pierced by a wooden arrow. At least, the man who triggered the bomb would most likely not feel personal hate against you. He would not make hideous faces or scream obscene insults like these savages; he might even feel sorry for you, not being entirely sure why he was killing you, except that it was for your own good and to free you from error. Primitives could never understand so detached an attitude to murder. He held his arms apart over the little table that was his altar.

. . . God hath given his angels charge over thee to keep thee in all thy ways . . . thou shalt walk upon the asp and the basilisk, and trample underfoot the lion and the dragon . . .

The words were rather wonderful but how much could one rely on them for practical encouragement?

Well, it would be over soon.

Two weeks had passed since the lovely, sunny day when he had first seen Patrol Officer Scully waiting for him at the Mageri River crossing, twelve hours out from Kombala.

**127**

Two weeks ago, and two more to go.

But how could one measure "being" in time? By what system of mensuration could one assess what had happened to him since he held out his hand to Scully and said, "I'm Father Herschell," and Scully had replied, smiling like an overgrown schoolboy, open and frank, and a little shy, "I'm Scully. I'm as low down the list as you can go"? How appraise, weigh or set to scale the links and ties that held him now to these people he had not even heard of fifteen days ago, but who were now and for ever part of his own personality, his totality of sense, mind, and understanding?

Even Didimus, this semiliterate New Guinean, kneeling beside him on the dark hillside, beating his breast and saying earnestly, "Lamb of god have mercy on us." How could he ever forget Didimus, or Marshall, or Korbin, or Scully? For they had all given him something of themselves without which he could not have existed in these two weeks, had protected and sheltered him, had been patient and generous of their deep-down charity. All of them.

. . . be mindful, O Lord, of thy servants . . . for whom we offer this sacrifice of praise and thanksgiving. . . .

He loved them and would remember them in every Mass he ever said, from now until the day of his death.

When he had done, Palau came from the shadows where he had been keeping watch, and helped Didimus to fold the table and take the Mass things back to Father Herschell's tent.

Scully was there, changing a crystal in the radio transmitter.

"We'll have to call up Mr. McKerrow in the morning and report the fight, seeing that people have been killed in it. There'll have to be some official explanation for Palau knocking that fellow off. And the boss will have to admit he's sick so that George can keep the record straight with the medical department. I tell you, Father, we've initiated enough strife in the past twenty-four hours to keep ten clerks busy for a

**128**

month or more. God knows what people did for a living before paper was invented."

But in the morning Marshall insisted on calling up Kombala himself, though he looked dreadful sitting in the canvas chair just outside the tent, huddled in a blanket with Korbin fussing over him, his face grey and thin, because he was really sick and had not been eating, had driven himself these past days, up and down the mountains, refusing to give in.

Korbin was sure now that it was dengue, which he could map with some certainty. Three or four days of pain and high temperatures. Then a break for a few days before it came on again, with more pain and sickness and vomiting. It would run its course but leave Marshall weak, and when they got back to Wanega he would insist on having him lifted out by helicopter to Kombala, for hospitalization.

Meanwhile Marshall, wrapped in his blanket, was calling McKerrow, peevishly, feeling very weak and ill. "Yakanaki patrol to Kombala . . . Yakanaki patrol to Kombala . . . do you read me?"

There was McKerrow's voice at last. "Come in Yakanaki patrol. . . . What's your trouble?" It seemed to come from a world elsewhere, a world remote and unrelated where people could walk into a house and switch on lights, get a drink, read a magazine, listen to music on the record player, relax, then go to bed more or less unworried.

"We've been having a bit of bother. Got jumped by a tough bunch of fighting men just before dark the night before last, a little way up the valley that leads into Yakanaki. We killed one of them, and lost a carrier. A Dana man. He took fright and shot through. I don't give him much chance of getting out of this area on his own."

As always with the District Commissioner, he felt it necessary to fight to be believed, and so spoke fiercely, leaning forward over the microphone

"There's fighting going on all over the place and it needs a patrol in here for a month or so to stop it. But we've got this priest and you mightn't get him back in one piece if we stay around here interfering in tribal fights."

"So?" McKerrow was waiting for him to say something that he could jump on.

"We'll just have to push on to Yakanaki, and maybe come back here some other time to deal with the fighting. Meanwhile we've got a bit of sickness and George Korbin thinks that we should sit around for a couple of days and get people fit."

"Who's sick?"

"Constable Ki stopped an arrow with his ribs and needs a little treatment, and three carriers have minor wounds, one of them in the calf of the leg, which means that we've had to carry him."

There was a pause, and McKerrow could sense that he was keeping something back. "What else?"

"Well, I've a touch of fever myself. Nothing much but George thinks that I should lay up for a day. I'll be all right again in twenty-four hours."

"Is Mr. Korbin there?"

"Yes." He handed over the microphone.

"What are the facts of the matter, Mr. Korbin?"

"He has a bit of dengue fever. It's unpleasant for him but if we nurse him along it shouldn't give him any real trouble."

"Hm. How's Scully?"

"As fit as ever. No problem there."

"Right. Call me up again in three days from now." Then, casually, "Who shot the tribesman?"

Korbin was about to answer but Marshall took the microphone. "I did."

"Why?"

"He was a suicide. It was either him or me and if I'd let myself be killed or badly wounded the whole patrol might have been in trouble." He spoke more calmly now. "I didn't do it without thinking. In fact it's the first time I've killed a man and it didn't make me feel that good. But I had the

**130**

priest in mind and played it the safe way, like the savages do. Kill, and pull out while the other side is wondering what to do about it."

"Were there any witnesses?"

"Police only. George and Scully and the priest were in other parts of the camp."

"Hm." They could tell that he was not completely satisfied, and waited for him to speak again. "Okay, we'll talk more about that later. Meanwhile you're under Mr. Korbin's orders for the next forty-eight hours as far as your own physical activities are concerned. That's all for now." They heard him move away from the radio, leaving them alone in their own isolated world, cut off again.

Marshall switched off and sank back, tired.

Korbin said, "You're crazy. What are you protecting Palau for? He had no right to fire at the man without your permission, and if McKerrow finds out that you lied to cover up for him, you're a goner. They'll pull you out of the bush and put you behind a desk down in Port Moresby for the rest of your days. What did you do it for? Why go to so much trouble to complicate your life?"

Marshall waved a tired hand. "Palau's in line for promotion and if he can stay out of trouble for a while he'll get it pretty soon. Anyway, he probably saved my skin and I'll punish him in my own way for disobeying standing orders. Nobody else saw him fire the shot so we can let it go at that. A man needs to be loyal to something even if it's only to savages." He tried a smile. "Anyway, I'm only under your orders as far as my physical activity is concerned, so tell me what I do next."

"Get back to bed and stay there until I take another look at you."

Korbin turned and went to the door of the tent, knowing that there was nothing more to say, nothing more to do but to go on loving in a vague, ineffectual way this stubborn, mud-dleheaded man who was loath to let go of his childhood; who, because he could not cope with the complex, creeping deceits and indecent demands of being grown up, stayed obstinately loyal to boyhood's too simple, impracticable decencies. He was the permanently upright, honourable, chivalrous lad who was true to his chums, right or wrong; the type that dies by its tens of thousands, generation after generation, for leaders who have long ago learned to compromise. To the politician, Korbin reflected, everything is politics but to decent people everything is a matter of morality.

Outside he saw Scully organizing everybody into jobs, so he turned back and put his head inside the tent again. "Scully is building a rest house to fill in time and keep the camp busy. He says that when we move on from here it will remain standing, a symbol of our continuing presence, of our being always among the people of this place in the spirit if not in the flesh. A sign that we will come back again in due time. Then, seeing the doubt in Marshall's eyes, he smiled. "If you don't believe that he said all that you can take a quick look at the new Patrol Officer's Manual, part 2, page 33. He quoted it at me this morning, over the baked beans."

He went out once more and stood watching for a while.

# Chapter 10

ALREADY it was taking shape. A scaffolding of tall saplings with thinner sticks lashed lengthways to make a latticed box. A framework to be faced with sheets of plaited cane and capped with sheaves of kunai grass. Fifteen feet high with pitched roof, a verandah, and a raised floor of flattened bamboo.

Men were spread along the ridge busily splitting cane, flattening it into strips, using billets of wood as mallets, or weaving wall sections while others bound grass into broomlike tiles. Garni, in charge of labour, sent Constable Gerua and other police to protect the men who went bush to cut saplings and gather sticks and lengths of vine for lashings. Other carriers were reaping kunai along the ridgeside and carrying it up on their shoulders in stooks, like peasant farmers bringing hay to the barn.

Constable Ki, miserable with sore ribs but reluctant to be left out of this collective creativity, sat in the shade watching those who were plaiting, telling them from time to time that they were clumsy or too slow. But when he tried to show them how much more neatly or quickly it could be done the pain caught him like a knife in the side, so that he had to stop, and stay silent.

Scully, architect and master builder, was on the site supervising while Garni moved among the craftsmen, sending forward materials as needed. No man was idle, none unemployed or uncommitted. Some sang, some vied with others to work more quickly, to complete one side or section before another, to build better or faster.

And the priest was pleased again, finding in this communal activity a whole new area of communication to explore, record and compare—dialogues of instruction, opinion, criticism and technique.

Scully was saying to him, "Well, it gives everybody a sense of unity as well as being something to do. It's instructive as well as constructive, and even if the local people burn it down, as they probably will as soon as we move on, this effort will have served a purpose and will not be wasted.

"Before we came to Wanega none of the carriers had seen any building bigger than the sties they live in. All built low to the ground, no more than three feet high, well below the level of surrounding grass and scrub, hidden from enemies who might be prowling around.

"But a thing of this size stands out as a skyscraper must have once stood out among the ordinary buildings of New York. As a sign that the times were changing. That a new age was about to begin. An age that was not afraid of anything, then or in the foreseeable future.

"It's the same here with us. This bit of a rest house made of sticks and grass and bush vine, made without nails or iron or tools of any kind, is to these people a monumental work. A fabulous piece of architecture. An eye-opener. Something which says, 'My God, what have we been doing all these years? What can't we do if we have a bit of courage and put our minds to it?' "

Scully, unaccustomed to such uncovering, was suddenly self-conscious, stubbing the toe of his boot in the loose earth; but having come so far, he continued.

"These people are human, like we are, and have exactly the same capacities. If we can break down their fear and free their minds from the terror of life lived under a continuous threat of sudden death, they will begin to live creatively. To see, even if dimly, the endless perspectives of possible development that stretch away from mankind in all directions like railway lines leading into infinity, if only we stop fighting and arguing and get going together."

Father Herschell was surprised. It had not occurred to him before that Scully was ever actuated by other than physical and sensual instincts. But he saw now that this young man's seeming simplicity was in fact the reflection of an unusual maturity, a sureness of perception that accepted certain postulates and measured the rest by them. It was limited, perhaps, but aware of its limitations and prepared to work to capacity within them.

He said, "Why, that's interesting and quite profound. I didn't know that you thought and felt so deeply about your job."

Scully answered cautiously, without looking at the priest. "Well, it doesn't seem to me to be enough just to take on a job because you need something congenial to do. Nor is it enough, I think, to just want to be useful, although this helps a lot. I feel that unless there's an element of actual and activating love for people in what one does with, and for them, there can be no real creativity, and no confidence that one is aiming in the right direction.

"Perhaps that's why three such people as Marshall, George Korbin and me, each so different, can get along together in this kind of situation. It's not because we share a firm faith in the kind of civilization that we're bringing to these people, or that we have the same proselytising spirit or sense of adventure: it's that each of us wants to give, without stinting, whatever limited talent we have, together with some share of whatever love is in us, to people who can use it." To cover his embarrassment he kept his back to the priest and seemed to be busy testing lashings on the scaffolding while he spoke. "This, I think, is the whole point. That as individuals we can

**135**

only grow in proportion to what we give of ourselves, freely, in a genuine nonprofit making sort of way."

When the house was done they dug a garden and planted corn in it, and bean, pumpkin and tomato seeds, with a splash of marigolds in one corner and hollyhocks along the west wall. Then they enclosed the whole within a picket fence of bamboo sticks, while Scully stood looking at this handiwork.

"At least it will show the local people something. Give them an idea or two even if they burn the house down and root up the garden when we've gone. And if they leave it alone we'll have a house to live in when we come back this way again; and maybe some of the seeds in the garden will grow and give us something to show them in the way of new foods."

In the afternoon a few men came to view the building but stood some way off, none of them coming into the camp except the old man whom they had seen two days ago at the river, by the broken bridge, with the small boy.

He came, now, into the camp with a small bundle under his arm, wrapped in bark, the boy holding onto his hand, and went from man to man speaking quietly to each. But nobody understood his language so he stopped walking about and stood looking around, uncertain, until someone sent for Heli, who brought him to Korbin.

"This man says that the boy is his nephew. His father and mother have been killed in the fighting and the rest of his family have gone away to live with relatives until the raiding is finished.

"The old man has no wife to help him look after the boy, and he asks if we will take him with us so that he can see the world beyond the mountains and become rich enough to buy a wife by the time he is a man."

Korbin, putting his hand on the boy's head, pulled it away quickly, flicking his fingers and muttering that the child was alive with lice and would probably spread typhus through the camp if not cleaned up. Then keeping him at arm's length

**136**

he examined him tentatively and handed him on to the leading orderly, asking him to disinfect the lad, cut his hair and clean him up a bit.

Then Korbin asked Heli to tell the boy's old guardian that he would take him and teach him the trade of a medical man and in three years would send him back here to his own people to work among them. At this the old man grinned and took Korbin's hand, holding it tenderly, like a lover, for some seconds.

But standing there Korbin seemed to sense something familiar about the bundle under the old man's arm, and tugged at it gently. But the old one hung on tightly and would not let it go—until Heli spoke sharply to him and, pulling it away, let the bundle unroll. A grey flannel singlet fell out, such as the carriers wore, with great patches of black blood staining the upper part of it, still sticky.

They all looked at it lying on the ground. Then the orderly walked over and touched it with his foot and stood thinking for a moment. He looked at Korbin and nodded. "Yes, Masta. The Dana man. They killed him."

Heli spoke to the old man for several minutes while Korbin waited.

"He says that the tribesmen back at the last camp did it as a payback for the man that Palau killed. They cut his head off and when we left their land they put it on a stick in the place where we were camped, to warn us not to stay there again."

Marshall, sleeping restlessly, knew nothing of these things that were happening around the camp. He knew only, in his fever, that he was haunted and hedged about with people who were somehow part of him, part of his experience, but would not fit into the framework of his own being, his sense and essence. His completeness. His peace.

What peace? No peace. Who could have peace?

He jerked, and turned over on the bunk, flinging his arms

out, hopelessly seeking to escape the brain chains that tied him to this limited thing. This self: inadequate, alone, unable to share, to let lap over fleshly onto, into another. Not able to admit part ownership with any other person, any sharing, submission, giving. Any shedding of the outer shell, or admitting vulnerability, weakness, dependence, passion.

Sandra.

Ready to submit, to give, to let down her silken defenses. The lovely one. So soft, so smooth, so white, so ready to be taken. Possessed (he moaned in his fever for what he had missed). By him. And he had failed. O Christ. How can such shame be hidden away (with those elegant, slim, slack-mouthed young men in fashionable **pants** yapping like randy little lapdogs, pug-nosed Pekinese, **squatting** on cushions in the lounge room with their vodkas, vermouths, brandy crusters)? Again, O Christ. Sandra is one of them, of their sort. Not of my people. Not of the strong, harsh, savage-smelling, rough, hard flesh, or the taking and the breaking in the dark or in the hot sun without the losing of oneself. Without the giving, the admitting. Yet she too would have done this, would have come this far for me. O the overflowing of unwept tears inside the cavities behind the eyes. The giving of the very guts. The loving. The saying, "Here I am, have me, take me, own me, tell me always what I must do because alone I have nothing. Am nothing but a man who walks on mountains; a shell filled with the moaning of the empty ocean." See (she said), I give you myself. And I was afraid.

Sergeant Sosu.

Save me a place beside you down there by the river's barren bank where you lie alone. Move over, Sosu. Make room for the man who killed you. Yes, it was me. But you knew, and you knew why, though Korbin thought he could take the blame. That it was his lack for not watching that mad carrier. But it was me because I knew it would happen. Foresaw it. I watched you on that raft and my mind cried out to you, "Sosu, save me by dying." Because I had wronged you about

**138**

the rifle in my tent. Because I blamed you for what you didn't do. Because I must always blame somebody. I must never be wrong, must never fail. Why can't I ever be wrong? Not fail? Because if I was wrong I could not go on being God to any of you. Or to myself. And I must be God because there is no other to lean upon.

And you, coming out of the scrub.

Who are you? What is your name? You. Savage man coming at me with your bow and arrow. Pain pointing at me. Yes, I can feel it even now (the fear of it) though you didn't let it go. But died instead. I could have tricked you. Picked you off. Stopped you (I am a perfect shot). Could have flicked the bow-string out of your fingers with my pistol. I, Marshall, the best white bushman in New Guinea. But I let Palau do it for me. And kill you. Why? Because I needed someone to love me so much that he or she would kill another man to keep me alive.

What am I saying? It's not true. I didn't shoot, because I was afraid this skill would also fail. That I would miss your fingers and kill you. And I had not killed a man before. I did not want them to say, "Marshall was jumped by a savage and had to kill him to save his own skin." Better that they should say he was brave. Would rather be killed than break the regulations. Died setting a good example. So Palau fired for me. But it was me killed you. I who had never killed a man before. Never lost a man until I let Sosu drown himself for my shame. Now I am no longer able to boast in the bars of Port Moresby that I can handle natives. That I can cope.

Palau! Is that you, Palau?

What do you want, standing there in the tent door? Palau, you black bastard, why didn't you let me kill him? Why didn't you let him kill me? Me. Better dead. Happier, having no hope of happiness. No longer driven continuously to be me, Marshall, the hollow man who has nothing to give. Afraid to be complete because this means giving, and giving means being less. Afraid to say, I need. Poor Marshall. Poor me. Poor Didimus.

Didimus. My God, what did I do to you?

Didimus. Forgive me. You creep. Twanging away on that bloody Japanese guitar. Hymns in my camp. How I hate you because you are nothing, and I smashed your guitar to splinters and dropped it at your feet and neither you nor the priest nor Korbin nor Scully nor any of them could say Marshall, you miserable cowardly lout, why did you do it? None of them would say this to me. So I had to do it and say it to myself. Hate myself, and so stop hating you for being nothing. Do you understand, Didimus? It was me I slammed against the tent post. Me. Marshall. Forgetting that you would forgive me.

Forgive us our trespasses. Yes, mother, I've said my prayers. And cleaned my teeth. Teacher was pretty. Then the priest came to the school and told us about love.

I don't understand it.

McKerrow, you omniscient prick, why did you send this priest who is determined to love me? I hate love. I hate people who smother me with it, making me helpless. This priest. This pampered Yank. Useless. No stamina. Scared stiff of insects, animals, rivers, rocks, savages. Of me. Wanting me to like him. Jesus. Me. Yes. Me and Jesus. But I do love the stringy, pimply bastard because he is the other half of me. He is the half with the heart in it. The half that is not afraid to love and be loved. The half that understands the subtle joy of suffering. The necessary pain of being hated. Despised. Dependent. Ah, what am I saying? I don't understand. Sandra. My love. Help me. Help me to be me.

Tell me.

What did you and Scully do? No, don't say. I'm not big enough to know. But what did you do? Tell me. Tell me, you sad, suffering, unmitigated bitch so that I may kill him too. Because he is better than me. Is he? Could this boy with the simple, innocent heart make you happy? Complete? News travels, my dear. I heard about you two looking at each other sad and smug. You buggers. O, my darling, get in the queue

**140**

and forgive me so that I may go back again to the beginning, and live.

Constable Palau, coming to Scully's tent, stood in the entrance, looking worried. "Masta Marshall, em i laik dai."

But Scully, writing to his mother, was unworried. "No, he won't die. He's just a little bit sick. Go back to your tent and when Mr. Marshall is feeling better he'll send for you again."

Palau saluted with precise anxiety, turned smartly and marched into the darkness. Then Scully, putting down his pen, excused himself to the priest and went to find Korbin in the medical tent.

He was frowning at Ki's arrow wound and picking neatly with tweezers at the cotton dressing, not pleased with it. He looked up at Scully coming in. "It isn't really deep but the arrow must have had some muck on it and there's an infection here. It'll be a day or two before it clears up and leaves him comfortable." Scully sat on a box.

"Palau just came to me. He was due for a lecture from the boss about the shooting of this savage, and went to get it, but came away without being spoken to and says that the Masta seems pretty sick. I thought I'd let you know in case he needs attention."

Korbin, busy with Ki, answered without looking up. "It's probably the fever coming to a peak. If he's got a touch of typhus with it he could be delirious. I'll have a look at him as soon as I've finished here."

They went together to Marshall's tent and found him restless but asleep. Korbin felt his forehead and his pulse, then woke him and took his temperature.

"Yes, it's pretty well up. You're at the peak of a fever and sleep is what you need more than anything. I'll give you a needle, and by this time tomorrow you should be feeling almost fine." When he had pulled it out and swabbed the spot he tucked the blankets around Marshall tightly. "Stay rugged up if you can. You'll be asleep in ten minutes and won't notice the discomfort. I'll camp in the medical tent tonight so as not to disturb you but Scully will have a policeman on watch all night, just in case you wake up and want something."

Marshall, with his eyes screwed shut against Korbin's flashlight, nodded just perceptibly. They watched him for a few seconds, then left. Korbin said, "That should keep him quiet for about twelve hours. It would take an atom bomb to wake him during the night."

Didimus, sitting on the ground down near the police lines, watched the satellite passing among the stars like a messenger. Then he spoke to those around him. "The new star is higher again tonight. In the morning it will pass right over us and we will know then that God has spoken and the time has come for the Son of Man to die for all sinners."

Garni sat beside him. The little carrier with the bent back (the one who was a ritual killer) sat on his other side. Constable Tau was there, and the wizard from Wanega who could blow away rain and was also a healer. One of Korbin's orderlies was also there, and some other carriers, numbering altogether a dozen.

Then Palau came and sat with them and when they were all quiet he said, "Masta Marshall is dying."

They looked at each other but remained silent until Didimus spoke. "He has devils inside him. We will cast these out and cure him. Then we will be ready."

He got up and they followed him, only one among them knowing what he meant.

They went a little beyond the camp to a place where no one could hear them, and built a rough shelter of sticks and leaves to sit under, and lit a small fire to cook rice which Garni had fetched from the store tent. And some fruit of the mareta palm that Tau had found in the bush, and which takes away a man's sense and frees him from the strings of normal thought. Korbin's orderly brought a plastic container of pure spirit from the medical tent.

142

When they had eaten and drunk together Didimus got up and said, "You are my friends. Wait here while I go and pray." But he went to his tent and slept for more than an hour before going back to join them again.

They sat smoking Father Herschell's cigars and talking quietly until a little before dawn, when Constable Tau was on watch and Korbin and Scully and the priest were still asleep. Then seeing the satellite rise once more above the outline of a high mountain they got up and went silently, like moon shadows moving across the black ground, through the camp to Marshall's tent.

When they reached it Garni stood by the entrance, listening, then stepped aside to let the wizard in. Then three other carriers. Palau with a flashlight. Didimus wearing the priest's violet stole across his shoulders, and carrying a pannikin of water. And the others. Some stood. Some squatted on the ground beside the bed. Watching.

Korbin's orderly leaned over to look at Marshall. He touched him gently, moved his arm slowly from his chest to rest it along the edge of the bed. He waited to see if Marshall stirred. Then he turned him over so that his back was towards them and exposed. He rolled the pajama jacket up over Marshall's shoulders and turned to the others.

The wizard, squatting beside the bed, pulled a short stick of wild sugarcane from the waistband of his lap-lap and began to chew one end of it, crunching at it, crushing the tough fibers into a brush.

Didimus, at the head of the bed, dipped his fingers into the pannikin and let water drip, drop by drop, onto Marshall's forehead. Then he shut his eyes and prayed, making the sign of the Cross on his own breast, then over the sleeper. And prayed again. "Devils, come out of this man."

The wizard came closer and bent over the bed with the sugarcane stick in his hand. The carriers were watching with strained faces, fearful in the presence of mystery and the secret business of the spirits, but fascinated.

They saw the wizard draw the untouched end of the cane brush cautiously across Marshall's back with short strokes, saw Marshall move, sigh, then settle.

The wizard waited. Then he made a swift, sharp cut along the muscle contour of the sick man's shoulders, making him flinch in his sleep. They watched the little red pinheads of blood come, and sucked on their teeth.

Didimus bowed low, beat his breast, straightened again, then dipped his fingers into the tin and sprinkled water around the tent, flicking the droplets with his fingers over all of them. And on Marshall. Whispering the Latin that he didn't understand. "Asperges me domine hyssopo et mundabor . . . sprinkle me with hyssop, O Lord, and I will be clean." As the Bishop did on Sundays in Madang.

Garni kept watch outside with Tau, restless and scared. But inside all were caught up in the mystery, the rituals. They watched without moving while the wizard, using the cane stick symbolically as a tube, sucked the evil out of Marshall's body through the wound in his back, and spat it sacramentally into a tin cup held up by one of the carriers.

With the brush end of the stick he made circles of blood on Marshall's back, then gave the stick to one of the other men, who scraped a shallow hole under the bed and buried it, together with the wizard's crimson spit; blood from the wizard's own tongue, betel nut juice, and the essence of the evil that had made Marshall sick.

Korbin's orderly gently drew the jacket down over Marshall's back and covered him with the blanket.

Then they all went, as quietly as they had come, back into the shadows between the tents. But they were no longer part of the dark now, for the air was beginning to move again, and the sky to turn white along its edges, and men became men again, no longer opaque shadows moving vaguely in the black and insubstantial aquarium of the night.

They came to the middle of the camp. And gradually other carriers appeared, coming from tents and shelters to make

144

their way to where Didimus stood together with his friends.

They came, these others, in the murky, pearl light of early morning, rubbing sleep from their eyes, yawning and showing pink tongues, sniffing and clearing their noses, scratching ribs and armpits irritably. But they gathered with docility, as if rehearsed, in a wide arc on either side of Didimus and his friends, seeming to know why they had come in this unusual fashion to start the day, though Didimus took no notice of them and stood looking at the ground.

He could hear birds stirring, could see smoke rising from the cook's fire. He saw Scully come to the doorway of his tent and look surprised; heard him call for the corporal, and speak sharply at him.

"What's this? What's going on? Who told the men to assemble at this time of the morning?"

Constable Palau was already raising the flag while Gerua and the guard saluted. The carriers, coughing and spitting and whispering, took no notice.

Scully, erupting into sudden anger, shouted at them, "Get to hell out of here and have your breakfasts. I'll tell you when I want you. Garni, get rid of them or there'll be trouble, I'm telling you." He glowered around, confused because none of them moved.

Garni said, "Didimus will do something and everybody must see. Then we can go to Yakanaki and not be afraid any more that other men will die in these empty places, but will come safely back to Wanega again."

"Balls," said Scully shortly. He went back into the tent, then came out again immediately with the priest, who was pulling on his shirt and had bare feet but went straight across the space in front of the tents to Didimus, and spoke to him anxiously.

But Didimus stayed looking at the ground and wouldn't answer, and after some minutes had passed the priest came back and spoke to Scully.

Then Korbin came, in pajamas. "What's happening?

**145**

What's going on?" Getting no answer, he ran across to Marshall's tent and went in. He came out again within a few seconds and said, "He's still asleep."

Then Didimus came forward slowly and stood by himself in the space between the arc of men and the tents where Scully, Korbin and the priest were talking together. Raising his head he began to speak out, strangely and vaguely, while everyone watched him.

"The missionaries have told us about God. Before they came we did not know who made us, but now we know it was God. After that he sent Jesus to show us what to do. He said, 'You must kill my son Jesus and he will save you from your sins.' So the people killed Jesus and he went to heaven and prayed for them.

"God said to me, 'Didimus, go into the bush and I will tell you something.' So I went into the bush and God was in a tree. And I saw him.

"He said, 'Didimus, you know that everyone must suffer many troubles like my son and then they can come to heaven. Now you have had enough troubles and you can come. But first you must die like Jesus and the people will be sorry.'

"When I came out of the bush I saw a new star and I knew that it was time to go with Jesus. So I prayed for Mr. Marshall and sent the devils out of him. Now there will be no more trouble."

Korbin was shouting to Garni, "Don't stand there like a clown. Grab him. Shut him up." Then he stamped about angrily. "God almighty, what's going on around here?"

Then Didimus held up his arms as one about to be crucified, and looked up into the sky. Scully began to run towards him and, coming closer, heard him call loudly, "Papa in heaven, be ready. I am coming to be with you and Jesus."

Nobody was watching the little bent-backed carrier, the executioner. And only a few of those standing close by saw him pull on the bow, his arms quivering.

But everybody saw Didimus suddenly stumble and scream

**146**

almost in Scully's face. Then he collapsed at his feet and lay there, untidily, with an arrow sticking in his back. And they were relieved to see the end of this man who had been a stranger among them, because now the devils would leave them alone and none of them, carriers or police, would die like the Dana man and Sosu, before they got back again to Wanega.

The major in the satellite was saying, "Yeah, that's New Guinea down there. A lot of our boys were around there in the big war. They tell me some of those New Guinea people can be pretty mean. Me, I like it better up here. Nothing much to worry about up here. Everything's going fine. Real fine." He glanced again through the porthole and could see a scythe of sunlight swinging in towards the high spine of the island and smiled, speaking again. "It's kinda pretty, though. Real pretty."

The sun coming up over the mountains washed across the camp and everybody stirred, awake now. The carriers began to walk away as if the death of Didimus had completed something and no longer concerned them; as if his gesture was of itself a satisfactory finality, a rounding off of problems that had involved them all since the patrol first left Wanega.

What he had done this morning seemed to them logical, not requiring further thought or analysis. He had been a man who encouraged trouble and now he was dead. Which was as it should be.

They knew that the white men would see it all quite differently, and were a little sorry for the bent-backed carrier standing patiently between Constables Gerua and Tau while Scully stormed at him, though they knew that no real harm would come to him because of this affair.

They could hear Scully as they walked away. "Fool. Idiot. You're as mad as he was. Haven't we had enough trouble around here? A man ought to beat the ears off you."

He was fuming, not understanding that this little man had

just settled, properly and sensibly, all of their troubles. He turned to Heli, demanding to get the story straight. And in a moment Korbin stepped in and there was more talk.

But the little man couldn't understand a word of it. In any case it was no longer his business. He had done what Didimus had told him to do. What the twelve had agreed to. He felt nothing. No shame. No fear. No responsibility. Every man had his place, and it was his business to kill those who had to be killed when the spirits spoke through the leaders of the people. This was where, as a ritual killer, a tribal executioner, he fitted into the proper order of things. Everybody knew this and accepted him for what he was, the same as they accepted the wizard, and the priest, and acting-Lance Corporal Garni, or Mr. Marshall. And he was quietly pleased that he had done his part cleanly. Now he waited patiently for Mr. Scully to make up his mind what had to be done.

Father Herschell, feeling vaguely worried and responsible, scrabbled in his tin trunk, searching for the violet stole he wore for deaths and burials and muttering prayers of absolution for the dead.

. . . enter not into judgement with thy servant, O Lord, for in thy sight shall no man be justified except you forgive him his sins . . .

He couldn't find it, so went empty-handed to help Didimus on the way to Paradise in spite of the confusion he had caused them all. Didimus was dead when he reached him and for some strange reason had the stole in his pocket: and the fifteen dollars.

A strange lad. Yet he might one day have been a priest. Father Herschell wondered how the Bishop would take it.

Marshall, of course, would be furious.

Extract from the daily diary kept by Assistant District Officer Marshall, on patrol north-northwest of Wanega at the junction of the Ongi and the Yakanaki ranges.
Altitude 8000 feet.                                        29.5.1965

If I were a superstitious man which I am not I would be tempted to label this patrol "ill fated" but the fact is that if one looks deeply enough there is always a root cause for what people loosely describe as bad luck or mischance and looking at the chain of events so far only confirms my belief that I was absolutely right when I warned the District Commissioner that it was tempting providence to attach a priest and a mission native, both without experience of working among primitives, to a patrol of this kind.

This is not a case of being wise after the event because, as I told Mr. McKerrow yesterday when I spoke to him on the radio, of the four deaths so far suffered two (Sosu and Didimus himself) were brought about directly by the actions of the priest's boy, and the other two would probably not have occurred if we had been able to carry out a routine defensive operation instead of being concerned primarily with the security of Father Herschell. If only people at headquarters would take notice of the man on the spot! However, what is done is done and we must make the best of the situation and press on to our destination.

I do not wish to speak ill of the dead but I cannot help feeling that this lad Didimus was a disturbing influence among the police and carriers and we will get on better without him. He seems to have thoroughly undermined Garni and I will have to think seriously as to whether I can honestly recommend the substantiation of his acting rank of lance corporal.

As a result of my inquiries into this ritual suicide of the lad Didimus I get the impression that Garni was absolutely under his thumb and completely unable to prevent a situation that he could see developing under his nose. I personally find this very disappointing as the success of all field work depends largely upon the efficiency of the senior NCO of Police and the reliance that can be placed upon him insofar as control of the carriers and junior police is concerned. Nor do Palau and Tau emerge untarnished from this incident and I shall watch them all very closely from now on and can only hope

**149**

that without the influence of this unfortunate fellow Didimus they will all redeem themselves and restore my confidence in them.

Father Herschell is naturally feeling upset at losing the Bishop's pet lamb but I have given him Pok the Wanega boss boy as his personal assistant and as the priest has apparently picked up quite a smattering of the Wanega language they should get on pretty well together. Pok is both intelligent and keen and likely to prove more useful than the Madang boy as far as Father Herschell's work is concerned. I am not able to do anything about providing a religious assistant but no doubt Mr. Scully will do what he can in this category. In any case Pok is said to be something of a witch doctor so they are more or less in the same line of business.

It is now three days since we left the campsite where the suicide took place—technically I suppose it should be called murder and the carrier Lop Lop will no doubt be charged with that crime in due course. At the moment Constable Gerua has been put in charge of him but he seems quite docile and unlikely to give trouble. However he will need to be closely watched as too many things are going wrong on this patrol and I am not disposed to tolerate any more slackness.

For that matter no one has yet produced a convincing explanation as to how Lop Lop gained possession of the bow and arrow which belonged to the tribesman who was killed in the attack on the camp and which should have been in safe-keeping as exhibit "A" to be produced at the official inquiry into that particular affair and the killing of the tribesman. It is highly unlikely that the District Commissioner will overlook the fact that Mr. Scully was officially responsible for looking after this article.

As for me I feel 100% fit again and recovered from the fever that laid me low during the critical period following the attack on the camp. Mr. Korbin gloomily predicts a recurrence of the trouble in about three days but I feel at the moment that he is being unnecessarily pessimistic but nevertheless am taking pills by the score as insurance. The only after effect of the fever is a peculiar rash on my right shoulder which is quite sore and which Mr. Korbin says could be self-inflicted though I don't remember banging or scratching that shoulder.

Tomorrow we cross the main range and all being well will pitch camp in the Yakanaki Valley so in spite of the handicaps imposed from outside we are not doing so badly.

# PART II

# Chapter 11

I want to be a hero
And bravely take my stand
Wherever duty calls me
Or work awaits my hand

**H**E was not exactly singing, though the old school song was rollicking around in his head, and his whole body moved along lightly with the swing and lift of it; and remembering out of nowhere this tune and these words belonging to boyhood he began to dig in his mind for names that would fit vague faces, and faces that would go with names, and to wonder without worry where they were now.

He looked upward and could see the top of the range a thousand feet above, and a thick filigree of treetips against the sky, and knew that within an hour he would be on the lip of the Yakanaki. He thrust his stick strongly again into the soft, forest-rotten earth and heaved onward with shoulders rolling, feeling strong (no longer sick) and anxious to get to the top to show these ghosts of his classmates this glimpse of his kingdom; to see the wonder and admiration in their faces when they stood there beside him, looking into this great valley never before seen by white men.

> I'd climb the highest hilltop
> Where many dangers lie
> And help a weaker climber
> Life's perils to defy.

The carriers, hurrying to keep pace with him, had no breath for singing but were lively just the same, finding their leader's renewed eagerness contagious. Nor did they mind the hard driving now that they were no longer plagued by the drama and the strangeness of the past days.

Except the two Dana men, who were miserable and could see no future, knowing that the mountain spirits would resent this brash intrusion, this trespass, and would send rain and sleet to wet them all and make them ill. So these two, gloomy, feeling separate from the rest, walked without enthusiasm, staying with the others only because they were afraid to run away—though certain, also, that they would never see their own people again but, like Sosu, would die out here in this unknown land and lie forever lonely.

Then suddenly there was triumphant chanting at the head of the line, and excitement ran back down the slope to flow over all of them coming up; and they knew that their leaders had reached the top and were looking, now, down into the Yakanaki Valley.

They lifted their heads to see how far they had yet to go, knowing that when they reached the top they could rest. Then they hurried, hearts jumping, for this was why they had come and why they had walked so long among so many dangers—to look over the edge of their own world, into the unknown.

They climbed quickly now to the lip of the ridge and saw the staggering, stupendous valley stretching westward widely for twenty miles or more to where another great range rose to block it off bluntly. And after the first instinctive shout of triumph and surprise they were silent, for the enormousness of it overwhelmed them.

Scully, coming last to the summit, pushed his hat back and

154

whistled and, having looked long, following first the north wall, then the south, and after that the open bottom, free of timber, went slowly to where Marshall was sitting on the ground, looking into the valley.

He stood beside his leader and spoke softly.

"It's terrific, isn't it? And beautiful. And too big. There'll be tens of thousands of people living along this length, too many for us to tame and take care of. Too many to face for the first time with so few of us, and so little impression of strength to show. And the priest to be looked after."

He paused, waiting for an answer, and, getting none, looked down. "What will you do?"

He knew that Marshall was thinking; that his thoughts were not only of the practical problems, the realities, the challenge, but of proving something to himself, about himself.

He remembered, then, that this patrol was Marshall's last; that whatever happened in this valley would be definitive, would put the mark on Marshall—make him whatever kind of man he was going to be for the rest of his life. A life spent at a desk. In a little tropical town somewhere in this territory. With no escape, no more unknowns to discover.

Scully watched him take binoculars from his boy, then put them to his eyes and focus on the far side of the valley; and knew that he was looking for a place to aim for.

Suddenly Marshall stood up. "Right, let's get going. I'd like to camp on the other side and it'll take three or four hours to get down and across the bottom even if we don't meet up with anybody. It looks boggy in spots."

He gave the binoculars to the boy to carry and motioned Palau and Tau to come. Then grasping his stick he set out, downward, leaving Scully to get the line going. But when he had gone only a few yards he stopped and called back. "Keep the carriers together, don't let them spread. We don't know what kind of reception we're likely to get." Then he turned again and went on down, setting the pace.

They followed quickly down the mountain though the track

**155**

was no more than a narrow, meandering pad tangled with tree roots, steep, and treacherous with waterworn pebbles hidden under leaves. It led them into a riverbed choked with stones and boulders, and through a funnel of rock into a gully that brought them at last through forest, breathless, to the bottom. And to Marshall waiting impatiently.

They rested briefly and regrouped, then moved out into the open, onto the valley floor, and within ten minutes struck swamp. But they found tracks that went through it, shin-deep in pitch-black ooze, so that their feet were wet and their heads overtopped with tasseled grass that held the heat and flapped at their faces.

They saw nobody; but bamboo spikes were found in the track, under the ooze, put there to lame strangers. One stuck in Marshall's boot and was read as a warning to keep clear of the track and walk parallel to it; and this made progress slower and more difficult, but was safer. And they counted themselves lucky that it was Marshall who had stepped on the first spike with his nailed boots, and not a barefoot carrier or policeman.

Far down the valley mountains were being wrapped in wet cloud, and wide curtains of rain came trailing towards them. Wind, in fits and starts, fluttered the swamp grass, sending flocks of parrots screeching, frantic, towards the shelter of the forest.

The Dana men nodded knowingly but Marshall was resentful.

Not yet three o'clock and the rain already coming. It was a nuisance. They would get wet and cold but would have to keep walking until they found a place on higher ground than this on which to camp. And while it was wet no tribesman would come, so they must wait until tomorrow to make first contact with these Yakanaki people.

He plodded on, set now for a soaking, anxious only to find any rising ground with reasonable protection where they could pitch their tents and shelters and light fires by which the carriers could dry themselves and keep warm through the night; for at this elevation, in a wet valley, they would be ripe for sickness of all kinds.

So, coming to the other side, they camped on a patch of sloping ground in the lee of a limestone cliff that gave shelter from the wind; and got wet putting up tents in a downpour that fell away later to a nightlong, steady rain.

Korbin, humpbacked in a raincape, made the rounds with two orderlies: one with a lamp and packets of antimalarials and aspirin tablets, the other with flasks of hot coffee. Finding carriers already sickening for colds and fevers and needing treatment, he set the police and fit men to keep fires alight all night with wet wood, to warm the sick men and keep swamp spirits away, knowing that fear, more than wet and cold, would make the weak ones droop.

Then, satisfied that he could do no more for them, he came into the store tent and found Father Herschell making coffee on a primus. He sat on a box to watch. "You should get that new boy of yours, Pok, to do something about this weather, Father. They say he's good at getting rid of rain."

Father Herschell found another cup. "Yes, I'll talk to him about it. He's versatile, all right. He says that back in Wanega he handles the weather, medicine, and religion. But they're backward people and follow the ancient system of linking physics, chemistry and religion together, one man being priest as well as doctor and magician. It's only we enlightened people who can figure a division between body and soul, and put barriers between man and the rest of creation."

Korbin said, "I was watching you today. You seem to be getting along well with this Wanega talk. Are you swapping ritualistic secrets with the magician, catching up on each other's mysteries, or merely discussing the relative effectiveness of holy water and wizard's spit?"

The question was put in jest but the priest could have said truthfully, "Well, in matters of religion I find myself closer to this man Pok, the witch doctor, than I was to Didimus,

God rest him. For I have discovered that Pok has no doubts about God, and believes in a supreme being who looks at us through the stars, which are holes in the sky, and sees everything that happens here on earth."

But they were both too weary from the long walk and the weather to make much discussion of such things, and when they had drunk the coffee they separated and went to bed.

Lying in his tent, listening to the rain pattering and splashing on it, and dripping into little pools, the priest thought of Didimus again—of his educated gentleness, the clean, civilized neatness of his khaki shirt and shorts, the sandals and the smattering of Latin. And he compared this with the picture of Pok, who had walked ahead of him on the track these last three days carrying the camera and other small gear on his hairy back, his bowed, tough-muscled legs and lean flanks covered with a dirty grey rag of a lap-lap.

It seemed, somehow, to the priest that this little mountain man, the primitive tribal witch doctor, uncivilized, unlettered, was in many ways more real and more complete a person than poor Didimus had been.

For Pok seemed to have no doubts at all about God. He knew all about Him and understood perfectly the relationship between them. He called him "The Above One" or "The One Who Was Always" and said that the Wanega people believed that everybody, dead or alive, belonged to God without difference, equally and forever, no matter how they behaved.

This is why his people felt the influence of their ancestral spirits so closely and keenly, and depended upon them for help as if they were still living. And God was simply the One who had started it all and kept life going, leaving it to men, alive and dead, to make it good or bad. And it was only when men went gravely against nature that God interfered and showed that he was angry by sending storms, floods, landslides and famines.

But Didimus, although he had lived with a Bishop, had never been sure about God; had never quite known what he had to do to please him or to be certain of getting his help when it was needed. He had never really understood what God wanted of him or expected—had not been sure, in fact, that God was personally interested in him and truly loved him as the Bishop always insisted.

Father Herschell had talked to Pok about these things while they walked, when the way was easy, or when they rested, and found that he had no doubts and confusions.

Pok and the other carriers thought that Didimus had been made mad by the Bishop so that he would always be his servant, and they were sorry for him and so did all that he asked of them. And when he was dead many of them made magic so that the sickness would leave his spirit before it went back to his village, even though they were doubtful if it would be able to find the way back to Wanega by itself.

And Father Herschell, listening to the rain and thinking of Didimus serving Mass for him and wanting to be a priest, wished now that he had taken more trouble with him, had made some greater effort to get to know his heart, his mind, his needs and wishes, what went on inside him. He regretted now that he had not shared more generously with the lad the charity of their common faith, but had treated him instead simply as a servant, a person of no particular significance lent to him by the Bishop, though the boy had served him well and in the end had been willing and ready to die for them all, like his master Christ, though mistakenly and without understanding.

It was all very interesting and made you think, and when he got back to Wanega he might get together with a few of the old men and try to find out more of what they believed. Perhaps he would write something for *Anthropos,* or one of the other academic journals.

But falling asleep he thought that the sound of the rain, dripping in a dozen places, seemed to make music, as though Didimus were somewhere out there in the dark playing his

**159**

sad, meaningless hymns reproachfully; signifying yet another failure to be redeemed somehow, sometime.

At daybreak cloud still covered the camp, closing in upon it so closely that not even the cliff behind them could be seen, so wrapped about was everything with saturated mist; and the carriers, standing in line outside the store tent waiting for Scully's instructions, shivered and looked miserable, clutching at their shoulders to keep out the cold.

"What do you think?" Scully knew that they should stay, but it was proper to ask Marshall to decide; to make up his mind whether to break camp or wait for a weather change, though he was impatient to be moving, eager to explore.

But Marshall was uncertain, not wishing to waste time sitting about damply in discomfort, yet knowing that to move now would be unwise. He said irritably, "We'll see nothing if we walk in this weather, and could go astray, miss something we should see. And none of the local people will get out of their shelters to meet us while this rain keeps up." He begrudged going counter to his eagerness. "I suppose we shouldn't risk carriers getting sick at this stage for the sake of one day saved, though there's little to choose between sitting here and walking in the wet."

Then in the end he gave way and decided to wait.

At midday the sun came out and steam was soon rising from wet tents. Things were spread about to dry, and damp clothes hung along a line.

Scully sent men for wood and water, and had little trenches dug to drain the ground around the tents.

Then Heli went to the edge of the camp and began to call, not knowing if any within earshot would understand what he was saying. But he put his head back and cupped his hands behind his ears and sang out hopefully, calling several times, then waiting to see if he would be answered. But he heard only the echo of his own voice coming back to him from a dozen far places.

**160**

"Yaiu lai bu aah . . . yaiu lai bu aah . . . yaiu lai bu aaaa-
aaah."

But they came later.

Tau saw them first—saw the high grasses sway along the
edges of the swamp though no wind was blowing—and called
to Garni, who told Marshall. In a few moments everybody was
aware, watching, whispering, getting ready, though as yet
there was nobody to be seen.

Marshall slipped cartridges into his pistol and put it in the
canvas holster at his belt, and he sent Palau to the store tent
to break out a pack of twist tobacco. Scully slung his gun onto
his shoulder and moved to where he could overlook the whole
camp. Korbin's orderlies began to set out medical gear for
treatments, and kept an eye on their young recruit, the little
Ongi boy, lest he take fright and run, as the Dana man had
done.

Then a dozen of the valley men broke into the open, out
of arrow range and separate from each other. This was not
the way of Wanega and Dana when facing enemies or strangers, for these bunched together to give each other confidence
and a sense of protection.

Marshall, watching every movement, saw that they were
tall men, a head higher than the Wanega. They were slender
but well-boned, with high hooked noses and fine faces. They
wore their hair long, in thin, stringy ringlets with a headband
of cowrie shells sewn onto bark or lizard skin. Each man had
a pig tusk in his nose and pendants of red seeds hanging from
his ears. For clothing they had only aprons of woven plant
fibers reaching to the knees, and armlets of grass. But each
man was armed with a black-palm bow and arrows, and some
carried a spear.

Father Herschell, keen to see the new people, ran about
the camp with his camera, anxious to get pictures when they
came closer; but he stopped when Marshall called him.

"Father, please take it easy for a while. They're watching
to see what we do and how we behave, trying to find out if

**161**

we're friendly or treacherous. If you run about they will get confused and not know what to make of us. We must all stay quiet and let them see that we are not excited or surprised at their being here. That we have no great interest in them. Remember that they haven't seen white people before, or tents or cameras. Ignore them until they seem to accept us, and make their own approach."

He knew that there were many others in hiding in the long grass. He could see the tassels bobbing and nodding, and birds being disturbed as unseen men moved about the marsh. He watched to see that the camp was not being encircled, and warned Scully to keep the carriers back from the edges of their little settlement.

The dozen Yakanaki men stood still, uncertain, suspicious rather than afraid, ready to turn back into the shelter of the long grass at a flicker of trickery or deceit. And Marshall knew that the other men in hiding would have bows and arrows in hand ready to shoot if anyone from the camp moved towards them.

Only Heli took overt note of them, calling in the trade talk that the Government had come to make friends with them; that there were Wanega, Dana and Ongi men among them, all neighbours from over the mountain; and that the white men were not ghosts but were live, like themselves, and came from beyond the great salt water and had many things to give.

"Sit down with us and we will show you what we have. Bring food for us and we will give shell and white man's salt, and many new things." He was speaking of paper labels, discarded food cans and cartons, tobacco, face powder, bits of rag and bandage, pieces of string, wire, sacking and suchlike. Unimaginable things not seen before by these people.

But it was some time before others came out of hiding, and when these came they, too, stood looking distrustfully and in a while began to talk to each other, to speculate, ask questions, suggest, demur, then finally decide to come closer, all

162

the time keeping their voices down, not knowing whether or not the strangers could speak their language.

They came only a little way; then Marshall went openly towards them, hands held out empty, and sat upon the ground between them and the camp, alone and seemingly defenseless although Palau and Tau had their rifles ready.

Then one stepped out from among them and walked towards Marshall. A tall man of more than middle age with a proud, thin face, who wore as well as those things worn by the others, a phalangar pelt around his neck, and on his head the bunchy tail plumes of a cassowary, worn like a crown. He carried a tall, fire-hardened spear in one hand and a club in the other. Behind him other men were stringing their bows.

When he came to within ten feet he stopped, put down his weapons and took a step forward. Then he sat on the ground to face the white man, seeming unafraid, and waiting.

Marshall thought, this is no savage. This is a real man. If we start right we will go on and do big things in this valley with such people to teach, and leaders like this to work with. He smiled and said the Wanega word for *friend*. "Pijara!"

The man's eyes flickered and he nodded and answered as if he understood. "M'yembo!"

Without rising Marshall edged a little closer and when he was settled pointed to himself. "Government!" He half turned and waved his hands about to take in the camp and the men behind him.

The clan leader came forward as well, and when almost within touch he struck himself roughly on the shoulder. "G'napa." He, too, moved his arms to take in all the land behind him, then pointed farther down the valley and lifted his chin towards the mountaintops beyond them. Then, looking again at Marshall, he laid one hand flat on the ground in front of him to show that he owned the land on which they were sitting.

"G'napa?" Marshall repeated the name, pointing to the

**163**

man, then laid his own hand on the ground and looked at him.

The man nodded.

Marshall, lifting his head a little, called to Heli to bring an ax but to come quietly.

The man made no move but watched with one eye on the camp and the other on Marshall, ready to reach out quickly for his spear at a sign of treachery. So, without looking back, Marshall knew when Heli was coming and held out his hand.

The shadow stopped beside him, black on yellow, gravelly ground, and he felt the ax handle being laid cautiously across his open palm. His fingers closed slowly while G'napa watched. Then he brought the ax round and put it on the ground between them.

He pointed to himself, then to the other man. Then to the ax. There was silence. Nobody moved.

A butterfly fluttered through the sunlight between them and, curious, settled on the ax handle and closed its blue wings while the two men watched. Then, finding nothing, it twitched once or twice and fluttered off again.

G'napa leaned forward and pulled the ax towards him. He looked at it. He picked it up and laid it across his knees and waited.

Marshall, pointing to the other Yakanaki men on the edge of the swamp, made signs that they should come into the camp and when G'napa (for this he took to be the man's name) called to them, and they began to move forward cautiously, he stood up and beckoned Heli to come closer and turn the talk if he could. Remembering Father Herschell's surprising facility with the Wanega and other languages, he called him too, in case he could help. Then when he turned back again he was surprised to see that scores of armed men had emerged from the swamp and were coming into the camp.

He called to G'napa, making signs that his people should leave their weapons on the ground, and although many of them hesitated and some, not trusting the strangers, stayed where they were, refusing, most of the others came on un-

**164**

armed until something like two hundred Yakanaki men were among the tents, looking at everything curiously.

Korbin was speaking to Scully as they watched. "These are bigger men, physically, than any others in the Highlands, and less inhibited, more sure of themselves. They look healthy and intelligent, and if their land is fertile and will grow money crops like coffee and tea, and feed cattle, this could be the beginnings of a magnificent exercise in developing a backward people. A chance for us to show that we really mean it when we say that we have a duty to help these people achieve our level of civilization."

He sounded so much as though he meant it that Scully looked at him surprised, wondering why he had always pretended so much to be a cynic, a man without sentiment. Korbin, sensing this, grinned and struck a pose. "O pioneer, O pioneer! We stand here, you and I and Marshall, in this cradle of creation, this primitive heart of the second biggest island in the world, three heroes (not counting the priest who is a passenger). We are intrepid adventurers. The first white men to set eyes on these stone-age savages who walk peacefully about our camp.

"And looking along this great valley we see a vision. We see it filled with food crops and money crops and village industries. We see roads and airports, schools and churches. Brown people wearing Western clothes, clean and neat, loving each other and no man lording it over his neighbour or coveting his money. And no dirty noses or disease."

He was looking along the valley, a faraway look in his eyes, as if lost in a dream. Then he turned again to Scully.

"Don't worry, son. It won't happen. After me and you and Marshall come the fast-buck boys and the God-is-love-if-you-follow-us chums, and the how-to-be-civilized lads with diplomas to prove that they've read a book and know better than God what's good for his backward savages." He clapped him on the back. "So, my dear Patrol Officer Scully, you've had the very best of it. You have found these people. From now

**165**

on you can only be ashamed of what will happen to them at the hands of the double-talk boys down in the capital."

They could see Marshall, with Heli and Father Herschell, showing the chief a bright red lap-lap, and Heli giggling as he put it on to show how it was worn.

"Look at their leader, that noble savage carrying the two-dollar ax that Marshall just gave him, not knowing that he holds in his hand the price of his people; the thirty pieces. Look at him and weep, for his son will probably be a politician, or a government clerk docking some poor bugger's overtime. A meaningless peanut, instead of a man of some kind.

"See him listen while fat little Heli tries to fill him up with much that Heli himself doesn't understand. Just look at that savage and catch a glimpse of the dignity we white men had once, not so long ago, before worry filled our guts and disgust came between us and those who are leading us to some plush destruction."

There were Yakanaki men all through the camp now, many standing around the medical tent, and already Korbin's orderlies were picking out those with unhealed cuts and sores and beginning to do business.

"They're a good-looking people. It's a pity that our kind of civilization had to catch up with their valley so soon. In another hundred years there might be something better to offer them. As it is we'll take away what they already have of order and logic, and stuff them with irrelevant rubbish and dishonest promises that we won't keep, and make them all, in the end, as mad as little Didimus.

"Then we'll wonder why their children have become spivs and troublemakers and delinquents, who will riot and break into stores, and rape white women. We'll complain that they're ungrateful black bastards who bite the hands that feed them; once a savage always a savage, and it takes a century to civilize an ape."

A Yakanaki came from the medical tent tenderly patting a clean white bandage that the orderly had put around his arm,

**166**

as if it were something marvellous and strange and very valuable. And a little later they saw him again, wearing it on his head with the ends hanging down his back like the twin white feathers of a ribbon-tailed bird of paradise.

At dinnertime Marshall said, "This man G'napa is big time and has connections through marriage and trading arrangements all along the valley. He's going to lead us up to a tribal meeting place tomorrow where we can camp decently for a few days and make contacts. He says there's plenty of food there, and he'll bring in other clan leaders to meet us. It sounds good. Just what we want." And as he went out: "Let's get going early in the morning. It looks as though our luck's changed."

# Chapter 12

"**H**E is talking to God," said Pok, and went on to explain confidentially to G'napa how Marshall's words went through the microphone and into the green box to be turned into silent spirit talk, then went through the wires (which he called K'pu, or threads) up into the aerial and so out into the atmosphere where God was listening. "You will see," said Pok, "that a big bird will come and fly above this man and the place where he lives, and whatever he asks for will fall out of its stomach."

G'napa, too polite to show surprise at anything told him by a visitor, asked quietly, "What kind of bird is able to carry so many things in its stomach?"

And Pok, with the sophistication of six months of patrol-post civilization behind him at Wanega, answered with complete assurance, "When the bird comes you will see that many men could be carried on its back. It will come from somewhere behind the sky and fly through the air faster than an arrow. And its voice will be louder than thunder when black clouds fight, or the river when it falls down a mountainside. But you must not be afraid because this man, who is the Goverment, is its master."

Marshall, speaking into the microphone, was saying, "Yes, we've made a very good contact here with one of the leading

**168**

headmen and should have no trouble from now on. He brought us here yesterday and we're camped on his land, about halfway along the valley. As far as I can figure there could be about ten thousand people on this side and maybe as many on the other side of the valley. But we'll have a clearer picture in a day or two, and an idea of the development potential.

"The bottom of the valley is swampy but perhaps enough of it could be drained to make a first-class airstrip, big enough in the beginning for Dakotas. In any case Scully will take a look to see if it's drier farther up. But if somebody could come today and low-fly the length of the valley to give us a general assessment it would save a bit of time, and maybe make a useful impression on the headmen who are coming to the camp."

They heard McKerrow growling and knew that there would be others with him in the radio room at Kombala to give answers, make notes, fill him in on details as he spoke to the outstations. They could hear the murmuring. Then his flat, cantankerous, voice: "What's your weather like?"

Marshall said, "Clear at the moment. A few stray bits of cumulus but nothing much. But it seems to make up early in the afternoons."

"Okay. I'll come myself in the Cessna and take a look at you. Get a couple of smoke fires going and if you're camped in cover lay a marker out in the open so that I can find you. I don't want to be flying around all day playing at hide-and-seek."

"Will do. We're on a ridge about halfway along on the north side, with forest below us and gardens stretching up behind. Then another belt of forest above with a bare peak rising out of it." He wet a finger and held it up to check what wind was blowing. "We'll light three fires close together, spaced evenly on the lower side of the gardens, with the smoke blowing away from the camp."

There was more murmuring and they heard Rosemary's voice, and an impatient answer from McKerrow. Marshall, looking at his watch, noted that it was not yet nine o'clock.

"All right. I'll be over by eleven. Keep your headmen away from any markers in case we're able to drop your mail."

He closed down abruptly and they heard him calling the young patrol officer at Timbudu.

Marshall took G'napa and two other clansmen to the high peak above the camp, climbing easily for an hour with Korbin for company and Constable Ki, whose wound was healed and the bruised rib no longer paining, together with Heli and other police and carriers. He left Scully in charge of the camp and the priest, with Garni, Palau and other police armed in case of sudden, unexpected trouble.

But there seemed no reason to expect disturbance. The headmen were friendly and the people intrigued with this visit from the outside world. Already women were coming by the dozen with loads of sweet potato, bringing their children so that nobody would think of fighting. And two men had gone to fetch pigs.

So Marshall went off for the morning without worry to look over the landscape and make a rough map, with G'napa and the others to name landmarks for him.

They climbed through the forest freely and at ease, with gaudy birds chattering at them from treetops (not knowing that Ki carried Marshall's shotgun and was watching as he walked, waiting for one to come within range). Then the party came out, within an hour, onto a green slope that swept up smoothly to the green head of the mountain, crowned with outcrops of eroded rock. The sky beyond was blue, clean and clear, an eagle hawk suspended in its emptiness. It was cool and quiet except for the scratch and scrape of Marshall's bootnails on the rocks, and the clicking of insects hopping out of their way.

Again he remembered a phrase belonging to his schooldays. "I will lift up my eyes to the hills from whence comes my

**170**

help." And his heart spoke the words that his lips were not able to frame.

O the peace of these solitary and high places. The vast, unasking tenderness of them dropping as a silk scarf drops across the shoulders. The wrapping up of worry, the easing of all deep-down aches and angers, the smoothing and filling in of furrows, and the hushing of fears that began in the blackness of the womb.

This is what a woman should do for a man. This untying of him. This gentle, imperceptible unknotting. This making him straight and simple and tall like a stick of sugarcane or corn, or a smooth stone lying in the hot sun. A belonging thing with no responsibility. Just once in a while.

This is what he had wanted. Looked for. Hoped for from Sandra. This peace. This not having to "be" all the time.

So they came to the top of the mountain, these dozen men, alone in the middle of an untouched land and looked about them.

They could see the camp, and the sun catching on metal things and mirrors, and knew that Scully had set them out here and there to flash the sun at the pilot's eye, and so guide him. They knew, too, that he would have carriers bringing wood and wet leaves to make the three signal fires; and Marshall felt comfortable because Scully was so splendidly reliable and relieved him of having to do all of the thinking himself.

He turned away from looking at the camp and had Ki set up his little aluminum tripod and theodolite, and with Korbin sitting beside him on the coarse mountain grass began to make a sketch map of the land beyond the Yakanaki, lying out below and beyond them like a model: peak after peak of green, rising in ranges to a huge, slab-sided giant standing at the back with snow on its head (here on the equator). He marked it on his map, then took a photograph while Heli and G'napa fixed upon its native name, which Korbin wrote in a notebook.

171

Two great rivers met in the deep valley at their feet like two silver threads, then flowed westward as one to the far end of their own valley swept with a wide swinging bend southward, away from them. It would flow for three hundred miles through forests, down mountains, into valleys still unseen, go crashing hundreds of feet over huge rockfalls, down through unknown canyons into lowland bogs and swamps; and thence to the fever-filled coast and the Coral Sea.

The eagerness was already creeping into him, the restlessness to be going with the river wherever it went—into secret places away from the world, from people, from the trivial, meaningless, niggling unreality of man-made, imitation truth.

The escaping Marshall, the running-away Marshall, the longing-to-be-free Marshall was saying inside him while he looked along the river through binoculars, they cannot chain me to a table, to a desk and a chair. I will come again, without priests, without anybody but a few police and carriers, and perhaps Scully, and move swiftly. Will follow these huge rivers to the coast, conquer this empty, unknown patch of land that nobody has yet seen. Find a track between here and the sea and be the first man to follow it. I must do this before they call me away from the mountains.

"The Omba?" Korbin had his pencil poised and was looking at Heli, uncertainly. "Did you say Omba or Umba?"

They were naming the rivers, filling in blank spaces on the map, fixing and fitting them into this age, into today. While other men were racing each other in outer space.

They turned their attention to the Yakanaki, and G'napa, standing beside Marshall, showed him all that was in the valley. He pointed out where people lived, named the clans; the passes through which their ancestors first came, where they now met to trade, arrange marriages, feasts, fights, and celebrations; the mountain from which they fetched the greenstone for their axes; the caves where they found the coloured clay for the ritualistic decoration of their faces. Marshall mapped it all, measured, estimated, took pictures,

172

and Korbin wrote down the names of places, clans and population estimates.

They made a strange tableau: a living symbol, timeless though isolated in time; a single and distinct tick in the continuous horology of man's history; a meeting, an overlapping and linking of civilizations; a handing on of the responsibility of continuing and bringing to its ultimate conclusion the unknown destiny of this amazing, unique, limitless thing called Man.

Marshall gave G'napa the binoculars to look through and focused them for him on the camp. And soon he could see and clearly recognize men who were his friends standing closely around the priest (who was showing them a picture book and recording their responses). He saw the astonishment on their faces; the busy, intent and innocent look of men unaware of being watched. And for the first time since the white men came he felt really afraid, knowing now that these strangers were privy to powers beyond his comprehension, that he and his people were ignorant and defenseless against these who could see a man as God sees him, could speak to the great sky spirit as ordinary men speak to each other.

But Korbin was thinking, what can we offer these people that they haven't already got? This man G'napa is better, richer in spirit, bigger than any of us. What can we bring him that won't start a rot? Begin to make him less? That won't plant our own spiritual and mental sicknesses in him: the despair, the emptiness, the pessimism, the uncertainty, the cowardice, the cheating?

He became aware that Ki was murmuring something to him; and when he looked up the policeman was pointing into the east, at the sky, and seeing Korbin unsure said, "Mr. McKerrow!"

"Ah!"

Korbin saw and called to Marshall. "Here's the old man." Then they all looked and soon picked up the yellow Cessna

**173**

slipping down into the valley to fly along it, and in a little while they saw the smoke begin to rise from Scully's fires.

They watched the airplane weave its way along the length of the valley, searching out signs that would say something of the people, give some clue to their way of living. Each family on its own land, in hamlets, in villages? Single gardens or clan cultivation? Living on ridges or hidden on steep hillsides? Few or many?

G'napa, his eyes fixed on the Cessna, showed no sign of what was going on inside his mind but stood there sharp against the sky watching, his hand on the head of the new steel ax stuck in his belt. Seeing this strange thing, more like an insect than a bird, flying on rigid wings, twisting along his valley from one end to the other, he wondered for a moment if his wives and his children would be afraid, would run into the jungle to hide from it.

He saw it rise and turn, then slide down through the air swiftly to fly across the camp, rise and turn and come again and drop something.

"Mail," said Korbin. "And I hope that someone had sense enough to put some fresh meat in with it. I'd give a dollar just for one sawdust sausage."

The Cessna climbed upward and came looking along the edge where they were standing, and passed so closely that they could pick out McKerrow and the pilot side by side, and someone in the back seat looking out eagerly.

"Miss Rosemary," said Korbin. "I think she's laying traps for Scully and the old man is helping her to catch him."

They went back down the mountain and G'napa knew now that however much longer he might live his time was ended; that however peaceful, friendly and generous these white men might be they would change his life, would determine, even without wanting to, its direction and the future of his people; that their coming had set things in motion that they themselves would not be able to control. Even without wishing it they would whittle away, dissolve, obliterate the

174

old authority. They would make senseless and empty the whole pattern and structure of tribal culture and society as it had existed in this valley since the time of the giant snake that had rounded out the Yakanaki to be a nesting place for its mate, and the place of creation.

He felt oppressed. The zest had already gone from this adventure of meeting the white men. Already he was asking himself why he had been chosen to see this change, to be the last real leader of the valley clans. Why couldn't the god up there behind the sky wait until he, G'napa, was dead and safely with his ancestors? Why had he been picked for this day? To see the coming of the big bird?

But in the afternoon he went with Scully, who wished to see how far the swamp stretched westward and what might be required or done without delay to drain a place that would make an airfield in the middle of the valley.

Father Herschell had asked if he might also go but Marshall refused the risk, saying that they were not yet well enough established in friendship with these people to take such chances, especially as the Yakanaki were so many and might muster five hundred bowmen in an hour or less if any misunderstanding or chance offense against tribal custom set them off in anger and antagonism: which was sense enough, remembering how luck had so far run against them.

So Scully took Tau and Palau and two other police, and some boss boy carriers with surveying gear to check lengths and levels; and Heli to ask questions when it came to finding out who owned the land.

When they had gone a little way from the camp they came to a place where dozens of casuarina trees made shade, and thickets of bamboo had been planted to enclose space enough for a thousand men to congregate. Wide pathways lined with bushes of coloured crotons led into it from three sides, one of them coming from a ridge where longhouses had been built low to the ground, enough to hold hundreds of men and their families.

Scully, understanding the place to be a ceremonial meeting ground and so sacred and tabu to strangers, made no move to go inside but followed G'napa into a garden a little lower down the slope where there was a hut with a number of men sitting outside it, smoking twists of green leaf in bamboo tubes and talking.

They approached these men and G'napa spoke to one among them who seemed senior, an elderly and thickset man with little hair left on his head, and that thin and grey, and covered with a flat pad of leaves for protection against the sun. This man sat cross-legged looking up at G'napa, replying curtly to his conversation as if in disagreement, then glancing at Scully and the others without smiling or showing any sign of friendliness.

In a little while they left these men and went into the valley bottom, and when Heli had talked a while with G'napa he told Scully, "The old man in the garden is G'napa's brother. His name is Gunji and he is an elder of the clan and a man of much authority. He is not pleased to see us and will be glad when we go again. But maybe he'll make no trouble unless something bad happens."

G'napa listened and, though not knowing what was said, nodded as if understanding.

Heli went on, "G'napa says that most of the valley bottom belongs to his clan, and that he and his brother Gunji are chief among the headmen. But everybody must agree about how the land is used: how much for gardens, how much fallow for pigs to feed on, how much for hunting land, who may plant areca palms for betel nut, or casuarinas for fencing and firewood. Such things are decided by a meeting of the headmen of every family, so if we want land kept clear for an airfield they must all agree to let it be used.

"Especially Gunji."

Farther on they found a place where Scully and Tau took levels, and Palau ran out the spring-steel measuring tape with the help of carriers, and hammered in temporary markers with the back of an ax while G'napa stood with Heli, watching.

Heli said, "One day the big bird will sit down here in the valley and you will go inside and be carried to Wanega and Kombala, and down to Madang, which is on the edge of the great salt water, and you will see many things."

But G'napa found it difficult to be excited—not even later when, back in the camp, Marshall gave him a gold-lipped pearl shell as big as a plate, though he was grateful and gave a young pig in exchange, and was impressed when Marshall killed it with one shot from his pistol.

Scully went into the tent and the priest looked up from his writing.

"Hi, there, what sort of a day have you had?" And without waiting to be answered, "McKerrow dropped mail this morning. It's on your bed. Marshall just sent it over."

He seemed cheerful, and pleased with himself in spite of being kept in the camp all day while the others went out.

"I did okay myself. A letter from my father with all the family news, and one from my sister who's married to a guy in California. They've got a new baby and it's to be named after me. What d'you know? I'm Uncle Louis for the first time. Korbin's cooking a steak tonight to celebrate."

Scully, happy for him, smiled widely. He was glad to see the priest so pleased at being thought of, remembered, brought back into belonging intimately and simply to a family and other people of his own blood. And he realized how lonely the past month must have been for this man, separate from the rest of them by profession, purpose, background, even nationality: and the lack of any sentimental tie or bond.

"Why, that's fine. Congratulations. Did you get a photograph?"

"Not yet, but they've promised me one. Maybe when we get back to Wanega or Kombala I'll be able to show you the

**177**

brand of baby we breed back in the States." It was pleasant to see him so happy and so gratified.

There were the usual letters for Scully, two from his mother, a couple of others, and a dozen pages from Rosemary. They were gossip, girlish, unaffected, saying nothing much except that here was a girl ready to be wed and bedded, preferably by Patrol Officer Francis Scully.

And one from Sandra, which he read slowly:

. . . I went cold inside, quite dead, sitting here by myself and hearing your names coming from the television set. And the announcer quite disinterested, as if he was speaking of fictitious characters. "Drama in New Guinea," he said, pronouncing it beautifully and putting his tie straight. Then he coughed and told us how a patrol had been attacked by Stone Age savages in the Highlands and some native carriers were killed and a policeman wounded. But he wouldn't tell us your names. You know how they go on saying all but the important thing, the one thing that everybody wants to know—who is it who is it who is it? I could have screamed at the silly little man sitting there neatly with his slips of paper, going on and on about a Government spokesman and reports being received from the District Commissioner, blah blah blah. And I could hear the kettle boiling in the kitchen but still he wouldn't say your names until right at the end when he said, "Our special correspondent in Port Moresby understands that the patrol is being led by"—then came Kenneth's name and yours and Mr. Korbin and the name of the priest who's with you. And you were all safe. I turned the thing off and sat down and could hear my heart beating like a cheap clock. Oh Francis my darling boy take care of yourself, and take care of Kenneth. I worry so much about both of you but mostly about him because he hasn't the special kind of courage and strength that your simplicity gives you. He's too afraid to fail. I know, because when I might have helped him I failed too, and would have gone straight to the bottom if you hadn't just happened to be there. So, strangely, I sit here in Sydney feeling relieved that he has you to lean on. Does this sound silly? That I can think you so wonderful yet love my husband. That I keep you in my heart, secret and O so sweet, yet cry for him when I am alone. Even though he is not yet truly my husband. Not my lover. Look after him for me, Francis, my dear. Help him to believe in himself and to stop running. When you all get back to Wanega he is to be transferred to Madang and I will be there waiting for him though he doesn't know this yet. Perhaps it will be easier for him to deal with me in his own environment, in a place where he is somebody tremendously important and I am only the Assistant District Officer's wife.

He could see her, the white breasts and the long legs lying on Marshall's bed ready to receive him. Then he tried to remember how it was. The anguish and the ecstasy of being in love. And (the priest forgotten) he stood there in the tent waiting for something to happen, waited to feel something, the blood to start thumping, his belly to go hot. But nothing cried out. Nothing inside him leapt up shouting. And just for a moment he felt a sudden, strange and fearful emptiness, a sense of not being, of leaving somebody dead in a bedroom. Then he began to wonder if he, Scully, filled any place in Marshall's mind, in his thinking. To what extent, if any, was he friend or enemy? Or was he just another young patrol officer, a junior assistant of no particular significance whose name he would one day forget?

Because one could, it seemed, forget quite easily, could forget anything, even the fine and exciting things of life—things that had seemed to lift one up when they happened, set one afire, fill one with a blinding white light so that one could never be the same again.

And he knew that his own part in Marshall's little drama was done. He had been no more than a necessary and inevitable but minor character in an intimate and quite private play. And the fact that he had performed with a certain gentle gallantry and grace might some day save him from shame.

When he went to the store tent Korbin was cutting up steak, and saying, "I understand that we're famous. Ken's wife has sent some press clippings about the ding we had with the Ongi people. We made the Sunday papers so you can

**179**

imagine half the people in Sydney sitting up in bed saying, 'Fancy that,' and 'They must be awfully brave' and 'Just imagine living among all those savages.' And we making history."

Marshall came and sat with them, and in a while looked up briefly from his plate and said to Scully, "I didn't know that you knew my wife. She says you have mutual friends. She sounded quite concerned about you being in danger."

Scully blushed.

# Chapter 13

THE sun was well up and the chill gone from the ground when Gunji went past Marshall's tent, scowling to see so many of his clan already in the camp, standing about like children come early to a circus. He went wide of them pretending not to look, but was watching from the corner of his eye and saw Marshall and Scully walking together, talking.

Scully was saying, "It's boggy all the way but seems to get drier as you go farther up the valley, and I'm fairly sure that rubble drains would do the trick. But the aviation people should send somebody in to take a proper look before you commit yourself to recommendations about putting in a patrol post on the assumption that an airstrip can be laid down without much trouble."

Marshall, impatient, said, "I suppose you're right. I'd better take a look myself before we leave here." He waited for Scully to go on.

"They seem to drain the land themselves when they make gardens, because the whole bottom of the valley is scored with a herringbone pattern of ditches, some old, some new, and once we get the headmen on our side there'll be plenty of labour available. It's something they understand." He was trying to be encouraging as well as cautious, wanting things

**181**

to go right for Marshall so that he could go back to Wanega confident, and replete with achievement.

"Yes, that's good. I'll get on to Kombala and ask them to drop a few dozen shovels to us, and a couple of wheelbarrows so that we can give a demonstration of twentieth-century technology; introduce them to the wheel as well as to steel. And we could do with more axes and shell and lap-lap material to show that we're prepared to pay compensation for the land and give aid on a grand scale. We should go as far as we can towards getting the headmen committed before we leave, and make it that much easier for whoever comes in afterwards to get a station going here."

Scully said, "There's a ceremonial meeting place a little way over," and waved his hand towards the valley. "A helicopter could probably land on it in an emergency."

Marshall stopped walking, seemed doubtful for a moment. "They'd probably raise hell if we did land a chopper there though it's worth keeping in mind. We've got this man G'napa on our side but sooner or later some sort of opposition will show up. It's never this easy to settle in a new place."

Gunji, getting near to his garden hut, stopped beside a sapling. After looking round to see that no one was watching he bent down to its butt and scraped away leaves and debris, disclosing a smooth, round stone with a hole in its middle, through which the sapling was growing. He tried the stone to see how tightly it gripped the stick, saw that the springy wood was swollen and overlapping the orifice, making a firm fit, and was satisfied.

He had put the stone there, with the hole in it (chipped laboriously with a flint) nearly three years ago when the sapling was a shoot of no more than six inches and less than a finger thick, and had watched it grow week by week until now it was ready to uproot and trim to make a fighting club for his son—a club in which head and handle were as one, wedded, like a man and a woman in the time of creating. A thing fashioned by nature, combining the living spirit of a tree and

**182**

the deathly strength of a stone. A ritual weapon, to be baptized in blood, according to tradition, so that his young son could attain the status of a man.

Gently he brushed leaves back to cover the stone, and smoothed away all signs of his having been there, then went on past his garden to meet his brother, G'napa, and other headmen in the ceremonial ground.

They were waiting in the shade of a clump of casuarinas close to the longhouses, and nodded at him when he came. One of the men made fire and set a few sticks smoldering to keep their bamboo pipes alight. When they were settled G'napa came to the point.

"For many moons we have heard about the white men and this thing they call the Government. Even when we were children our fathers told stories left by men who came to trade. And they were always afraid that one day the white people would come to this valley.

"Some of you have talked to men of other tribes who said that they had seen white people but we never knew how much of this talk was true. As we became old we forgot our fathers' fears and believed that the white people would never find us. But now they have come and we must decide what to do."

There were nods of agreement, and grunts, and when they saw the G'napa was looking at Gunji, his brother, they waited for the old one to speak.

Gunji said, "My brother carries the white man's ax but I will not carry one. If we make friends with these people as my brother has done, and give them food, and let them go back to their own land and their own people, they will think that we are weak and will come again with many fighting men to drive us from our land, up into the high mountains where we will die.

"They will take our women to be their wives, and will make servants of our sons. Our ancestors will be shamed and our grandchildren will forget to kill pigs for us. And we who

**183**

are headmen will then be less than this smoke that is eaten by the wind."

He puffed at his bamboo tube and let the white smoke drift out slowly while the others watched it thin into wisps and dissipate, leaving no trace. And they felt that he spoke truth.

Then while they watched he put up his hand to straighten his cap of leaves. "If my brother can tell me of the good that will come to us through these strangers, or what they will give us that will make us stronger than we are, then I will listen to him. But if he cannot tell us these things, then I say that we should finish with them while they are few. Kill them, and nobody will know.

"Their own people will wait many moons for them to come home, and then will say among themselves that they were lost, or taken by river spirits, or swallowed up by those who live among the clouds. And they will kill pigs for them and be afraid, and will not try again to find our land to take it from us, but will stay in their own place.

"And we will live in this valley as we have always done, in the way we learned from our fathers who were here in the beginning, and whose spirits still live in these places."

He looked up into the casuarinas, his lips moving silently, and they knew that he was talking to his father, whose spirit lived in these trees.

And those who watched were anxious, for of all the headmen in the valley these brothers were the most respected, and they would have them agree so that everyone would know what should be done about the white men. And while some looked at Gunji others watched G'napa and waited for his answer.

In a while he spoke. "When we were still children I came with my brother to this place to help our father plant these trees where his spirit now lives. And when he was dead we went together to collect his bones from the burial box and put them in his garden. And in all things we have been as one, and have agreed together since we were children.

**184**

"But while my brother has been sitting in his garden with his friends, thinking how to kill the white men, I have been with them. I have seen their leader speak to the spirits and I know by my own eyes that they hear him and send the big bird to bring him whatever he asks.

"I have seen that these men have much strong magic. More than they have yet shown. If we kill them others will come and punish us, and blood will run among our children after we are gone. This is what I have been told by the man Pok who lives with them and understands the Government.

"Already many of our people are filled with wonder at the things the white men carry with them, and soon they will wish to have such things for themselves. So perhaps the time has come for us to change.

"We who are old will soon die, and those who are left will see things that we have not seen. Will know things that we do not know. Many of our young men will leave the valley and other strangers will come to live among us.

"Perhaps my brother is right. Perhaps he sees more truly than we do what will happen. But I say that we should wait a little while to see what our people can gain by living in peace with these white men. Let us watch, and learn what we can from them. If they do no harm let them go. And afterwards we can bring all the clans together and decide what to do if they should come again."

In the camp a dozen Yakanaki were leaning over Father Herschell's shoulder watching while he typed a list of local words and their equivalents. They saw no significance in what he did; did not relate the words he spoke with the marks he made on the paper, but were entertained by the inexplicable magic that made these strange marks flow out through his fingertips onto the paper, for this was how it seemed to them.

Then he showed them a trick. He put a carbon between two sheets of white paper and traced an invisible stick man with his finger on the top sheet, and then, lifting it, disclosed the carbon imprint underneath. They drew breath sharply,

**185**

clicked their tongues and nudged one another, shaking their heads in amazement, murmuring, "Truly this man has great magic."

Constable Gerua, standing guard over the priest, smiled at their simplicity and said to Lop Lop the murderer, also in his charge, "They are very stupid people, these bush Kanakas. It is easy to surprise them."

Having caught an audience Father Herschell used it to help him unravel the Yakanaki system of figuring. He found that it followed in part the way of other Highland tribes, counting digitally. One finger, two fingers, three and four, then a derivative of the local word for "hand" to signify "five." Then one-hand-one to equal six, and two hands to equal ten. One "man" was ten fingers and ten toes and consequently "twenty." But beyond that there were no additional digits: only "many," "a little many," and "a big many," but with tonal nuances refining these general concepts into clear definitions that seemed to the priest to be almost clairvoyant in their accuracy.

So he tapped out a footnote, to be enlarged upon later (perhaps in a special paper for the *International Journal of Linguistics*). Theory: that some primitives seem to make use of senses that are far more delicately perceptive than those of twentieth-century man, especially in terms of communicating concepts, ranging from the mundane (viz. numbers) to the mystical.

Afterwards, finding that his audience soon tired when not continuously interested, he produced his picture book and held them for a while gazing at the illustrations without comprehension of any kind, having no point of reference whatever in which to place any man-made object or material not native to them, not even recognizing as practical objects a clay pot or a wooden effigy, never having seen such things. Only when he showed them pictures of people and told them, in their own language, "man," "woman," "boy," "girl," "baby," did any kind of comprehension dawn. But the mystery of a

186

human face or figure fixed onto this strange substance, paper, was an age and an age and an age beyond them.

He approached the problem, gave them a lead, by using a mirror, so that some saw their own faces for the first time and then could understand, though vaguely, a face on paper; but they were puzzled because the mirror gave each man his own face back to him, while the paper gave everyone back the same face. It was too much to understand. They began to worry and feel uncomfortable. These were things too deep, and made the head ache.

But Marshall came conveniently with two women who were nursing little pigs which, Heli said, had been brought so that one of the white spirits might touch them and so make of them, in due time, great progenitors.

Marshall was smiling, enjoying a joke. "This is your department, Father. You're a priest and the blessing of livestock is a fringe business with you. So, if you don't mind, do your stuff. For the sake of those who come after us I hope it works."

While Marshall stood grinning, Father Herschell made the sign of the cross over the women and their pigs, and asked God to bless them each with increase, and by the power of the Holy Ghost to bring the women and all the other people of the valley into the family of the one true church, and to give them a knowledge of his love, and of the love of Jesus Christ his son who died for these savages as well as for the people of the civilized world.

Then he laid his hand on the head of each of the women separately and blessed them especially, and sent them both away wondering what would happen to them. But his own heart sang a clamorous Te Deum because Marshall had given him this chance to publicly proclaim the Kingship of Christ in this valley, and to speak his name for the first time to these heathen people.

When the women had gone Marshall said, "Well, thanks, Father, you really made a job of it. Now I'm off to do a rather more secular job, or maybe it comes under the heading of the church militant. I've got to show these people what a rifle does apart from making a noise. They have to understand that in a fight the advantage lies with the fellow who has a gun, and once they see what damage a bullet can do they'll be inclined to think twice before getting up to no good."

He signalled to Garni and went away with him, calling out to the priest as he went, "Don't be alarmed when you hear the shots, and don't take fright if hundreds of frantic Kanakas come running through the camp. Just go to the medical tent and stay there until things quieten."

Father Herschell flinched, and thought, God, why did he have to say that? Remembrances of earlier disgrace flashed through him, and he wondered if Marshall had meant deliberately to remind him of that other time when, taking fright, he had hidden in Marshall's tent and to his everlasting shame had made trouble for Sergeant Sosu over the rifle.

Disgusted, he gathered his papers together and took them and the typewriter into his tent while the Yakanaki watched, disappointed that there would be no more magic. But friends were calling them to come away to a slope on the edge of the camp where the other white man, Marshall, was offering new entertainment. They left the priest and hurried after the others.

In an open space six police stood in line to form a firing squad, thirty paces from a newly planted wooden post. Behind them, well back and spread over the slope like fans at a football game, three or four hundred Yakanaki sat waiting and watching, though not yet knowing what would happen. Marshall and Heli stood together, between them and the police, and they saw that Marshall held a bow and arrow in his hand.

Heli shouted, crying out for silence, and when they were quiet Marshall spoke, holding up the bow and arrow. Then Heli turned his talk.

"Men of Yakanaki, you have seen many things in these two days. Many wonders of the Government. Now I will show you a big thing. It will make you afraid, but when you have seen this thing you will know why you must put away your bows and arrows, and your spears, and listen to the words of the Government today, and tomorrow and for all the time that will come. . . . now watch."

They saw Marshall go and stand beside the policemen. Saw him lift the bow, fit an arrow into the string and draw it, aiming at the post. Saw the arrow fly straight, without wavering, and hit the post. Then swing down slowly and drop.

They began whispering together like birds before daylight, shrugging their shoulders and making faces while Marshall went to fetch the arrow. The white man shot well but a child knew that arrows broke against such targets. They were disappointed, even disinterested when Heli held up the arrow and pointed to its splintered tip. They could have told him that would happen. Nonetheless they listened politely.

"Men of Yakanaki. An arrow flies fast and straight but its strength is no more than the strength of a man's arm, and its sharpness is the sharpness of a carved stick made hard in the fire."

Heli threw the arrow down with a quick, dramatic movement and they became interested again.

"The Government has no use for such weak things. Arrows are for children to play with." Contemptuously he kicked the arrow along the ground towards them, and they sat up. "The Government has arrows which fly so fast you cannot see them. They are stronger than the strength of a hundred men and their sharpness is the sharpness of lightning at night."

He nodded towards Marshall and they all turned to look at him. He gave an order, and the six policemen raised their rifles.

They heard him shout and were stunned by the immediate concussion of the guns. They cringed back against the slope instinctively, afraid now but ashamed to run away.

They heard the rattle of rifle bolts, the reload. Saw Marshall tense, then shout again, and again they heard the great crash of sound. And gaped, terrified, not understanding, not

**189**

looking at the post, not knowing what was taking place except the terrible speaking of those sticks that the policemen pointed.

Then Heli called them. "Come now and see what we have done to this piece of wood—this post that is like a tree, so strong and thick that no arrow could hurt it. Come, everyone, and see what the Government does when it is angry." The six policemen walked to one side, leaving the way open, while Heli beckoned insistently. "Come, come everyone, and see."

Heli pointed dramatically at the post.

And suddenly, as one, they rose screaming and brandishing their stone axes, and went running down the slope like lunatics to where the post was leaning. Shouting, they tore at it, pulling and wrenching and wrestling with it hysterically until Marshall fired his pistol at the sky and quietened them. Then he pushed among them and made them stand back from the post while Garni and Palau laid it on the ground like a body. With his fingers Marshall showed them the jagged tears and great gashes and splintered pieces torn away, and the holes drilled clean through it, and he picked up flitches and splinters that had been ripped off by the bullets (thinking, "Thank God some of these police can shoot straight").

Then he walked away, left them to look for themselves, to crowd around, touch, wonder, think this thing out and talk about it.

Later in the afternoon Father Herschell came to him and said, "I'd like very much, if you don't mind, to spend an hour or so inside one of the Yákanaki huts tonight, recording ordinary talk. It's difficult for me to get a line on the domestic vocabulary without working among them in the family environment. I thought that if Francis and some of the others could come with me for the sake of safety, you might arrange with G'napa for me to visit with him."

Marshall went looking for Scully. "The priest wants to go visiting among the locals tonight. I don't suppose I can rea-

sonably refuse him, though God knows I'd like to. I must be
getting jumpy but the fact is I can't help feeling that something's going to happen to this priest before we get him back
to Wanega. It could be the run of rotten luck that's worrying
me subconsciously, or maybe it's the fever still sticking." He
looked around to see if Korbin was within earshot. "To tell
you the truth, George was right when he said that it would
come again, but don't tell him I said so. I feel lousy right now
but I think I can beat it if I stay on my feet."

Scully said, "What about the priest? Are you going to let
him do this job?"

Marshall frowned. "Well, I suppose I should. That's what
he came out here for. But for Christ's sake be careful. We
have no idea how some of the people will react to hearing
themselves on a tape recorder. If you go inside a hut take
Palau and Ki and Heli with you and leave a couple of police
outside. I tell you, I don't like this nursemaid business one
little bit."

When it was dark and they had eaten, two young Yakanaki
lads, who had been waiting, led them into the bush: Palau
following first, then Heli, a policeman, the priest, Scully with
a flashlight, Pok carrying the recorder, the other policeman
and Ki. They walked for fifteen minutes in pewter-coloured
moonlight. Crossed a stream, climbed a ridge and came to a
hidden hollow where there was a low hut built of rough-cut
timber slabs, thickly thatched. Smoke was creeping from under the eaves like steam seeping from a pot.

G'napa met them, rising silently from the shadows as they
came to the edge of the clearing. He led them to one end of
the hut, bent, and rapped the door slats, calling quietly.
There was a rattle of wood and a way made just wide enough
for a man to squeeze through. They stooped, following
G'napa, and went in, finding spaces on the bare earth floor
where they could sit. Three women and six pigs looked up
as they entered.

Scully's flashlight picked them out. First, sitting nearest the door and close to a small fire set on stones, an elderly, spare-fleshed woman with a necklet of dog's teeth hanging between empty breasts. She nodded, tightening her eyes against the unaccustomed light, and went on weaving grass threads into a carrying net, her dignity in no way diminished by almost total nakedness.

Behind her two younger, lustier women with shiny skins tittered and lifted their hands as if to keep the light away from their faces, but when one leaned forward to turn sweet potatoes in the embers, the priest could see that she had circles of clay painted round her eyes and thick white stripes following the contour of her jaw. The other held a young pig across her thighs and was fondling it without thinking, tickling it between the legs while it lay quiet, with its eyes shut.

Bigger pigs, each tethered by a foreleg, were in separate stalls along one wall, some straining towards the food in the fire, the others lying belly-length and heavy, snuffling and grunting and twitching their ears.

Far back in the hut there was another flicker of firelight, and the priest leaned forward trying to penetrate the blackness between, but could not. Then Heli, whispering, said that other women with little children were sleeping there, and that all of these women were G'napa's wives and the old woman chief among them. Through them, and others, he had ties with most of the clans in the valley.

The only utensils Father Herschell could see were digging sticks, lengths of bamboo tube for fetching water, a piece of sharpened cane which was a knife, and a wooden needle used by the older woman in her weaving. There was no furniture of any kind, no bark or wooden dishes, not even sleeping mats —nothing else but a few greasy leaves used for carrying food to the men's huts. He asked for the names of these things, encouraging the women to speak. But the young ones giggled and scampered back into the shadows, where they whispered to the unseen mothers, and the matriarch spoke softly, continuing with her weaving, and was noncommittal.

192

Father Herschell began to be uncomfortable, sensing that he should have known more surely, being a priest and so believing in the divine kinship of all people, that dignity and sensitivity are basic human attributes; that to be primitive is not essentially the same as being brutish; that to be superficially civilized is not necessarily to be superior.

He felt now that he should have approached the women with a little more formality, with more courtesy, instead of treating them as an historical or zoological curiosity. And he realized that it was the same kind of mistake he had made with Didimus. So, when he had done a rough sketch and noted such names as came quickly, he asked G'napa to thank the women.

They left, then, and went to another hut nearby where they sat with men and were more at ease, though Gunji was among them with his young son, a wide-eyed, chubby child of ten or perhaps eleven years.

A thick layer of acrid, suffocating smoke from the fire and the men's pipes hung under the low roof, and the priest's eyes began to smart and his sinuses to run. Then, within minutes, he shuddered to feel lice burrowing under his armpits and scuttling over his buttocks and ribs, making him itch.

Scully, seeing him fidget and wriggle, laughed at him and, when their eyes met, said, "Don't be too long, Father. You need to be conditioned to breathing this kind of atmosphere, and the lice probably carry typhus. But don't worry—George will give us a dusting of DDT as soon as we get back to the camp."

They all watched while the priest set up the recorder, then spoke into the microphone, using what he knew of the trade talk to explain himself and what he was doing.

The Yakanaki were impressed that he should be able to speak with them even haltingly and followed closely what he said, whispering among themselves, seeming pleased that he should be interested in them and their language; and if they looked blankly at him, or in doubt, Heli added explanation,

**193**

and they spoke among themselves excitedly, mending the misunderstanding and putting the words straight.

They watched while he ran the tape back for a replay. Then when they heard his voice come again, though he himself was clearly not speaking, their faces changed, ease giving way to uncertainty and apprehension until Heli explained that this, to the priest, was child's play and no bad magic; that there was nothing in it to make men afraid; and that if they listened longer they would each hear themselves speak as they now heard the priest.

So they were in part prepared, when the priest paused in his speaking, to hear their own voices come through in the background as Heli had said. And astonishment, taking the edge from any fright they may have felt, kept them fascinated, waiting to hear each other, recognizing with shouts of amazement words that had been whispered a few minutes earlier.

But Gunji, who had been silent, stared at the recorder with enmity and growing anger and suddenly spoke out loudly, so that the rest of them stopped and looked at him, listening to what he said while the tape kept turning with the priest explaining.

Scully had stopped smiling. "I'd turn it off if I were you, Father. The old chap is against it and could start trouble. Best we pack up and go quietly."

The priest, leaning forward, switched off, leaving Gunji talking alone, his words beating like blows upon the quiet while all sat still, watching him and listening. He was angry, and the small boy beside him looked frightened and was startled when his father took him roughly by the arm and pulled him back into the far darkness, beyond the sight of those sitting near the priest.

None of the Wanega party had understood what Gunji said, but G'napa, turning to Heli and the priest, using trade talk, told them. "My brother says that it is bad magic if the secrets of a man's mind and the words of his tongue can be taken away from him and put into this box. He says that if

**194**

the white men stay longer nothing will be hidden any more. Women and children will know what only men should know and the whispering of women will fly about like screeching parakeets to make trouble in every hut. No man will be able to keep his talk inside his head or hide it in his belly, and the wise might as well run about shouting like madmen."

They went, the priest thanking the Yakanaki quietly as he bent low to keep his head out of the smoke, and there was quietness behind them. And none of them spoke as they made their way in the moonlight, down the ridge and over the stream, back into their camp.

Marshall had gone to bed but Korbin took them to the medical tent and made them strip, disinfected them and their clothes with powder and sprayed their hair with insecticide.

When they told him about Gunji he laughed. "Good for him. He's got more sense than the rest of us. Can read the writing on the wall. He doesn't want to belong to the kind of society in which a man's personality is whittled down by gimmicks that take charge of him, run his life, make him like everybody else, take away his free will and beat his brains into a useless pulp. Good for Gunji. There should be more like him wherever men are being put upon, pushed around, being told what sort of government they ought to have, what kind of politics they should follow, what god to adopt. Gunji and his kind are good for us. If there are enough of them spread around the world they may save us from the machines that are one day going to kill us. I'd like to meet this man." He went off to bed feeling pleased.

# Chapter 14

ACTING-Lance Corporal Garni, with the help of carriers, was stringing wire from a pole outside Marshall's tent and stretching it to another a little way along the ridge, while Marshall, sitting at a camp table, fiddled with the transceiver set, testing it.

G'napa watched, with Gunji and his small son beside him. "You will see," said G'napa. "Soon he will talk to the spirits. Then the bird will come and bring him food and other things."

Marshall looked at his list, running through quickly to see that he had remembered everything. He needed general stores. Enough rice and cans of meat to feed the carriers on the way back to Wanega without having to stop for another airdrop. Six hundred pounds should be enough, and McKerrow could pack the gold-lipped pearl shell in with the rice to make it safe for dropping. They needed more salt for paying women who brought food. And another small drum of fuel for the benzine lamps. Then he wanted axes as well as the shell to show that the Government would pay for land in the valley when the next white men came to set up a patrol post and make the airstrip. And shovels, which the Yakanaki would love because with them they would be able to dig their new gardens out of the bush in a tenth of the time it usually took.

This, together with the introduction of steel axes, would be as historically significant to these stone-age people as the industrial revolution had been to Western civilization (it was one of his favorite phrases, taken from a folio of speeches made by the minister under the title "Developing a Primitive People"). Then a few knives, judiciously distributed, to make useful allies among the lesser headmen. And the wheelbarrows—if McKerrow would approve anything so extravagantly dramatic.

Korbin came with a paper in his hand. "Here's my list. Tell them, please, to make sure to put in the antibiotics, whatever else they leave out. We've got fifteen carriers sick with septic ulcers and I'm running out of stuff to treat them with." He put the paper on the table alongside Marshall's arm. "I'll be in the medical tent if you need me to speak to anybody at Kombala." Then on the point of leaving he looked down. "Show me your tongue."

Marshall, taken by surprise, did as he was told.

Korbin peered into his mouth. "I thought as much. Still lots of spots. You haven't been taking your dope and the fever's still on you." He took a phial from his pocket and tipped out two tablets. "You're worse than the carriers. They're scared of medicines but you should know better."

He watched Marshall swallow and make a face. Then he went away, muttering, and was busy all morning dealing with patients, making notes, investigating, gathering and adding together fragments of evidence and observation which would indicate, if only in a sketchy way, the health and medical pattern of the Yakanaki.

When they were in Wanega again he would write a report for the Department of Public Health: meanwhile he scribbled in a notebook:

Evidence of malaria here in spite of official insistence that it is not possible above 5000 feet. Possible permanent swamp conditions may explain. Parasite could have been brought in by na-

**197**

tives trading from the coast. Have managed to get only ten blood slides. People too scared of magic to give blood to strangers. But have collected several adult mosquitoes, also larvae. Local people speak of "water sickness," which has symptoms similar to malaria. Spleens fairly evident. Checked on fifty men (no women have yet come forward for treatment) finding fifteen positives. Also fair amount of hookworm, scrub typhus, septic ulcers aggravated by mites, tinea. Evidences that pneumonia is a killer especially among children and old people. Many men suffering effects of old arrow wounds.

A skinny old man was standing there now, pawing at the orderly and pointing at a scar on the backside of his thigh. Then bobbing and nodding and making mouths at Korbin, he tried to get him interested.

"Tell him he's too old for surgery. If I go digging for bits of timber in him we'll have to keep him in bed for a week."

But the old man was persistent even when the priest had been sent for to explain, so they laid him face-down on the operating table made of saplings, and injected a local anaesthetic. Korbin took a scalpel, leaned over him and cut carefully. He felt about until he found the top end of the arrowhead, then slit down gently, separating adhesions (sweat dripping from the tip of his nose and running in trickling rivulets over his ribs). The little Ongi boy, the orphan, learning the business, stood beside him, holding the instruments in a kidney dish while fifty men with stone axes and bone daggers sat watching.

He straightened up, holding in his forceps a fingerlength of arrowhead which, when the wound was cleaned and stitched, the old man took and looked at proudly, remembering again in all its anxious detail that faraway day: the fright, the fear, the pain and the escape; the snapping of the arrow so that he could run without handicap from those who had come from the other end of the valley to settle an old score, steal a woman, or equal out some imaginary insult overgrown with gossip.

Until that day he had been a big man, a fight leader for the clan, but afterwards he became an "old one" of no real account, one to be left at home to mind women and pigs when the young warriors went looking for fight, but respected for what he had been at his best. Now he would be a big man again because, with a courage almost idiotic, he had let himself be cut open and closed up again by the white man; and the wood that had been embedded in his flesh these ten or fifteen years he now held in his hand. His friends, astounded, would look at him with a respect that was almost reverence.

"Give him some aspirin and a sedative and make him lie down for a while." Korbin patted the patient's backside affably, then washed his hands, looking over his shoulder for the next patient.

The orderly nodded at two young men who were waiting with their father, the old man leaning sickly on a stick. Coming forward they said that he had been ill for many moons and although they had killed fifteen pigs for him the spirits would not take away his sickness. They hoped for some miracle from the white man.

Korbin went over the old man with stethoscope, and with his fingers felt for evidence. He took temperature and pulse, asked questions but could find nothing wrong. At which time there was much discussion between the two sons, the priest and Korbin's orderly while the old man lay abjectly on his back, embarrassed to hear himself discussed so thoroughly.

Eventually the priest said, "The old man insists that a wizard has done this because of some dispute about a piece of land belonging to his sister, who is a widow. But there seems to be some other story going around that the old fellow went with a woman to her garden at the time of her tabu, and is suffering the inevitable consequence of bleeding to death through his penis, in spite of all the pigs that his sons have sacrificed for him."

"Passing blood, is he?" Korbin scratched his head. "That's a growth in the bladder, I suppose, but the only way to be sure is for us to take him into Kombala and let Dr. Hovas look at him. He won't trust us that far and come; and I don't have the equipment here to make any tests, so there's nothing I can do. It's the trouble with masquerading as a magician. You either have to work a miracle every time or lose face."

He looked around among the others waiting for attention and picked upon a small boy with yaws, and swobbed a spot on the lad's back to make ready for an injection.

"These are the easy ones. Two shots of penicillin and you've made a reputation."

But he sounded frustrated and discouraged.

Men were all about the camp now and more coming continuously, many of them headmen from other parts of the valley, here because G'napa had sent word that the white men had much to show and many things to say that all should hear.

A little before midday, Heli began to shepherd them all towards the slope at the edge of the camp where Marshall had shown them the rifle fire and its effect upon the log. It was still lying there, and local men, speaking quietly, standing beside it with their visitors, told how he had caused it to be splintered and gashed about and shattered in this way simply by shouting loudly while the policemen pointed their sticks. Although a few of the visitors were sceptical most of them were impressed.

Others were saying that Marshall had sent for the big bird, that it would come soon, that it was already on its way. They could see carriers cutting long grass on an open patch of land down below the camp, and police spreading the calico marker and getting smoke fires ready to light, while Scully watched to see that all was done properly.

Gunji stood, restless and sullen, among the men gathering on the slope, looking about to see who had come, counting those who might be relied upon to line with him in opposition to the white men and so convince his brother that the Yakanaki clans had strength enough between them to act like men: not to wriggle and whimper like timid dogs, nor to run into the bush to hide like women whenever the white men did

**200**

their tricks, but to resist this strange invasion of their territory. He saw the priest come, then Pok follow with the recorder; and began to be angry again. But the others round about him were interested and watched while the priest set up his machine and tested it, getting ready to record the speech that Marshall would soon make; and G'napa's translation of it into the Yakanaki language.

Father Herschell was keen on this. He had spoken earnestly to Marshall about it all through breakfast. "It would be great if we could do this, not just as part of my work and research but to get an historical record of the event, this meeting between you, a twentieth-century man, and the leaders of a primitive civilization. It's the kind of history that will be written into schoolbooks and read in their lessons by the great-grandchildren of these men when you and they are legendary characters." As an extravagant afterthought he had added, "Just think what would be offered today for a genuine transcript of the first conversation between Christopher Columbus and the primitives of North America."

The enthusiasm was contagious and Marshall, smiling quietly at the conceit that aligned him with Columbus but liking the analogy, had agreed, thinking it a pity that he would not be able to take this tape to Suva, to the annual meeting of the Pacific Islands Historical Society, and play it to the delegates. Perhaps next year.

Now he came and stood with Heli, facing these four hundred or more stone-age men. Looking at them, he thought, they seem much like any other crowd of men in spite of their dusty colour and ringlets of stringy hair thick with grease, and the slips of cane or bamboo or pig tusks stuck through their noses. Otherwise their faces are much the same as those seen wherever men collect: in a bar or barrack room, at a ball game, a meeting, anywhere. Men with dignity in the way they look, men with intelligence and strength. Some stupid, some cruel, some timid and some humorous.

Sitting now, on the slope, they watched him while he took some pictures of them to go with his report.

Only two among them were standing—G'napa, tall, grave, graceful though aging, and Gunji, solid, square and strong, hunched up and scowling. These two, a little apart, stood among their people as guardians or teachers stand among children.

They waited for Marshall to speak.

He nodded. Father Herschell switched on the recorder and gave a thumbs-up sign. Marshall turned to face the people.

"Headmen of the Yakanaki clans and families, I am happy because you have let us camp here on your land, and have shown that we can be friends together. We have stayed with you for three days and in this time no man among you has had cause to complain or to be afraid of anything we have done. No one has stolen food from your gardens. No man has killed your pigs or taken your women, or fought with any one of you about anything. We have paid for everything you have brought to us and given you many presents. We have shown you our magic and made many of your sick people well. By these things you know that we have come to you as friends.

"Soon we will go away to tell the Government all about you; but afterwards, when some moons have passed by, other white men will come here to live with you and teach you the ways of the Government.

"They will bring many things. A steel ax for every man. Things that will help you to make better gardens and to grow more food. Build bigger houses. Raise bigger pigs. Everything that you have seen here in this camp you can also have if you help the Government when it comes, and do whatever it asks you to do."

"Then the Government will keep peace among you so that no man will be afraid to walk anywhere in the valley, or beyond. Every man will be free to go where he will. The Government will look after your sick people and make them

202

well again. The Government will teach your children and your young men the ways of the white men."

He spoke in short sentences, waiting between phrases while Heli gave G'napa a meaning to match the words, and G'napa, standing among his people, made sense of them in the common language of the valley.

"When the Government comes it will buy land from you and will build houses for itself and for its own people. It will find a place where the big bird may sit down to rest."

There was a stirring among them and many men looked into the sky expectantly though as yet there was neither sound nor sight of the airplane. And before Marshall could grip hold of their attention again, Gunji's voice rose above the murmuring and took charge. All eyes went his way, for he was speaking forcefully.

Marshall, rigid, listened for a little while, then turned impatiently to Heli. "What's he saying?" Getting no answer, he looked to the priest for help, but Father Herschell was busily letting out lead, urging Pok to go closer to Gunji with the microphone.

The old man was shouting now, calling out his wrath, his hurt, his anger and his fear, flinging words over them, onto their heads and shoulders and bare brown backs, as a priest flings holy water over a congregation.

"Men of Yakanaki: why do you sit listening to this white man as women sit listening to gossip in the gardens?

"Have our ancestors sent him to us with messages?

"Does he come from the place of the dead?

"Is he your mother's brother?

"Or your brother's friend?

"Or is he not a stranger from no place who stands on our land saying that we must change our ways and forget what our fathers have told us; leave what we have, and take up new things which the white people will bring?"

He paused and looked round.

"O men of Yakanaki, why are you without speech? Why

**203**

have you no words for this stranger who says that he will send the Government to live on our land? Ask him, what is this Government that will come to tell us what we must do; that will show our young men and our children the ways of the white men so that they will forget their ancestors."

He was working himself into a frenzy now, almost screaming, beating his breast with one fist, and with the other holding his stone ax by its blade and stabbing at the air.

"What will you do, O men of the valley, when they bring these new things that you do not want and cannot understand? When no man among you has his proper place among the people any more, old or young, wise or stupid, but each must do as the Government says?

"Must I, Gunji, a headman in this valley, be glad when my son has learned to look at me as he looks now at a stranger, or at a pig?"

He could see Pok edging towards him cautiously with the microphone, and his anger began to boil into blind rage. For he hated this thing, seeing in it a symbol of all the evil, all the creeping, secret, sly malevolence that threatened to bring an end to the Yakanaki people and their way of life. He was sure, now, that if the white men came back again and stayed nothing would ever be the same. Nothing would be simple and real and complete as it was now and had been from the beginning.

He could sense an end. A coming apart of the threads that held them all together; that made life in the valley an interweaving of all men's lives and minds, a single cloak to cover all of them. A whole thing. It made him almost weep to feel, in the cleavage between himself and his brother, that the pattern of Yakanaki life was already beginning to disintegrate and break apart, leaving each man alone and unprotected.

He snatched at his cap of leaves and flung it to the ground and spat on it, then tore at the hair on his chest and belly with crooked fingers. He rolled his eyes upward and looked into the sky, crying loudly to his ancestors.

**204**

"If I let these strangers stay here in your place, take away my apron and leave me naked. Make me sick and let me stink like a woman, or like a man who is five days dead. And if these who sit here listening to me are afraid when these men point their sticks, make them ashamed and let me go alone against the strangers even though I am old. Better to die now while I am still a man, than to live until I have no teeth left, and nothing inside me but sweet potatoes without salt: a man without ancestors or gods. A nothing man. Empty. Of no account."

Three police with rifles ready were watching him, and others stood quietly between the clansmen and the camp in case of trouble. Their eyes followed as Gunji walked down now, a lonely man, threading his way between the others, knowing that this was the one moment of his long life from which he could not turn away. The moment that would give final meaning to his being the headman, Gunji, and not just one of these four hundred following men sitting on the slope.

He came down from among them and stood alone in a clear space midway between Marshall and the clansmen, an elderly savage with a stone ax in his hand.

One blow with it would smash the white man's head; and then the other clansmen would rise up, come to life, and run through the camp killing, killing, killing, until all the strangers were dead. Not one would escape. Not a breath would be left in any one of them. There would be dead men everywhere with nobody to bury them.

Then he and G'napa would sit once more under the casuarina trees in the ceremonial ground—two old men content, ready to go to their ancestors, knowing that life in the valley would go on as it had always done, from the beginning, in the time of the snake.

And G'napa, watching from among the men on the slope, understood the anger and the anguish that ran about inside his brother; knew what he was about to do, and how these others from the outside would simply point their sticks at him before he could do it. They would tear and rip his old body to pieces as they had torn and ripped the solid bush log lying there as rubbish where they had left it.

Marshall, aware that the climax was approaching, waited, tense. Ready for anything, he glanced from Gunji to G'napa and back again, looking for a clue to what was in the old man's mind.

The silence was stupendous.

Huge clouds, and the mighty mountains hung with light, were asleep in the heat.

Then a shout from down on the clear patch where Scully was.

"Balus i kam!"

"The big bird. The big bird is coming."

Smoke was already climbing out of the signal fires, and the clansmen on the slope, seeming uncertain, got up and began to edge away, hearing the airplane but not knowing yet what it was and what would happen now, nor how far they could trust these people.

Suddenly some saw it and were pointing.

As it turned itself towards the smoke signals, canting at an angle, sunlight splashed extravagantly along its wing and there were sharp cries of pleasure and excitement.

They watched.

Watched the big bird circling and turning and the sun flashing and catching at its wing—every head bent back and neck stretched; faces like flowers turned up to the sun; eyes following flight.

No one now listened to Gunji, or looked to where he stood by himself at the bottom of the slope cursing the white men and their big bird. Only the priest, through his headphones, could hear him above the babble of carriers and clansmen, and the sound of the airplane gunning for its dummy run, swooping and scooping low across the drop site four hundred yards away where Scully was, then straight at them, screaming up and over the camp, dragging its shadow across their upturned, following faces.

Marshall admiring, in his mind praising the pilot (fine fellow), watched it, not taking his eyes away. He saw it sweep well off in a wide arc, stretching out its sound to a whisper; then turn in and slant down again (he dropped his eyes fractionally to the drop site and checked that it was clear). He saw the airplane come towards the camp and its cargo begin to dollop down (a little late, he thought; whoever was kicking out was fumbling). Seeing one pack jam in the open door, he clucked his tongue, hating such inefficiency and, accustomed to giving instructions, spoke out loudly, "Idiot. Leave it for the next time round."

Then he looked away again. He could see Yakanaki men in clusters pressed distrustfully against the slope; saw the priest twisting the controls of his recorder; saw him look up at Pok, who was losing concentration and moving with the microphone away from Gunji. He heard Father Herschell shout, "Stay where you are, Pok. Stay there, this is fabulous."

And Gunji: like a prophet in a wild, high place arguing with God, looking up, legs apart, head back, haranguing, cursing the big bird, spitting at it, thrusting upward with the ax, almost weeping with despair and the completeness of his anger.

All seen quickly.

Then looking up again he saw that the pack was still stuck in the open doorway of the airplane, with someone kicking at it. He saw it jerk, catch, sag, hang for a moment by a corner, then free itself and fall.

"Christ," said Marshall, "what bloody imbecile is up there doing that?"

He watched it sliding slantwise through the sky, coming at him; and running away from its line of flight, he could hear the shouts, the panic of the clansmen scrambling up the slope, stumbling over one another to safety.

Heard, then, the thud and crunch, and a fearful grunt, and after that heard Pok cry out. And looking back saw Gunji lying on the ground quite still, and Pok falling, and the pack bouncing along the ground a little beyond them both and coming to rest—split open and showing the smooth metal heart shape of shovels.

Scully, down at the drop site, heard the shouts; could see them all running about; then a policeman hurrying down with a piece of paper. Ki came, looking dolorous, and gave him a page ripped from Marshall's scratch pad and scribbled on: "Pick up cargo quickly and get back. One pack landed in camp area and hit old man Gunji. Badly damaged. Also carrier Pok. Situation sticky."

The airplane, making its third run now, dropped cleanly, then climbed to come again, but higher this time, and let loose a little parachute.

Scully, looking up, laughed to see a wheelbarrow swinging in space above the Yakanaki Valley, and the airplane heading back over the mountains wagging its wing as if embarrassed at being party to such fantasy. But he had the note in his hand and began to give orders, sending the carriers quickly to pick up the packs, wondering about Gunji.

"How is he?"

Marshall was at the door of the medical tent watching Korbin at work. He was anxious but not wanting to waste time with talking.

"I've got Heli and G'napa explaining to the clansmen that it was an accident and that we'll pay plenty of compensation. I must say they seem to be taking it better than I expected."

There was a burst of shouting and he looked back over his shoulder but it was only a group of Yakanaki running away into the bush waving their axes.

"G'napa says most of his own clan go along with the notion that the old man brought it upon himself, talking out too loudly against things he doesn't understand. They seem to have adopted the idea that the airplane took his opposition to the Government as a personal insult and so cracked down to teach him a lesson. So we don't seem to be getting the collective blame for it. At least, not yet."

Korbin went on working, listening without looking away from what he was doing: cleaning filth from the mess of torn flesh and shattered bone that had been the old man's leg. He glanced at Gunji's face and spoke to him motherly, seeming to overlook Marshall.

"Poor old chap, you're certainly being civilized the hard way."

"Will he live?" Marshall tried not to seem impatient.

"I don't know. He's pretty badly knocked about. The main force of the blow caught him here, from halfway down the thigh to well below the knee. You can see, it's all smashed about—femur, knee, tibia, fibula. Then part of the pack seems to have wrapped itself around him or swung up and caught him a whack across the lower lumbar region. There's a big patch that's lacerated and chopped about as if the sharp edge of some shovels had gashed him; and maybe there's some damage to the spine. I don't know at this stage. It's too soon to be sure of everything. He's suffering massively from shock."

He was working all the time, carefully, gently, intent; conscious, now, of being a man who was needed, who mattered much, who could do something for somebody and had no need at this moment to put up a defensive screen of smart talk and cynicism.

"I can only patch him up. We'll have to get him to Kombala and into hospital if we want him to stay alive."

He spoke without emotion, almost casually, but they both understood the implications of what he had said. They knew that the Yakanaki would resist, probably stage a mass attack if they attempted to take Gunji out of the valley, whatever they might think about his culpability. They knew, too, that even if they got him away the old man would probably die before they could patch him up and bring him back. And the hope of establishing good relations between the Government and the people of the valley would be set back a generation.

So Marshall hesitated, then changed the subject. "What's the situation with Pok?"

"He's pretty badly knocked about but with luck we'll save him. He seemed to get hit after the pack had cannoned off Gunji and lost a lot of its velocity. But he's bad enough. Concussion, and maybe a fractured skull, and his face is knocked about a bit. But I doubt if his condition is as critical as this old chap."

Marshall began to move. "Sing out if you need help of any kind. I'm leaving Ki and Gerua right here outside the door in case anything blows up suddenly, and there'll be a guard on watch all night. I must try to raise McKerrow and then go and keep an eye on the priest. This is the kind of situation he could foul up without thinking."

He went back through the camp. Scully was coming up with the carriers in a tight line. And over to one side, on the edge of the bush, a patch of white parachute and a wheelbarrow hung from a tree.

# Chapter 15

**P**ALAU, on night guard, watched the clouds hurrying in front of the moon, one following fast upon another, changing the contour and the colour of the landscape continuously, silver to black and back again to silver. He was thinking that the moon, now full, had a worried look like Mr. Marshall; that the atmosphere was damp and rain would be falling soon.

He could hear women wailing in Gunji's hamlet half a mile away, as if the old man were already dead. Behind him, talking in low, droning voices, two dozen Yakanaki men, including G'napa, were sitting in a circle not far from the medical tent, keeping vigil.

Palau was restless, needing Maileeta, wishing that he was back with her at Wanega, and wondering if Garni would keep to the agreement they had made, seeing that Didimus would not be at Madang now to arrange with the Bishop about a new wife for Garni. Though the way things were going it was not so certain that any of them would ever get back to Wanega or Madang or anywhere.

Every little while, away in the bush, there was the sound of shouting as if groups of men were arguing violently or working up to something, though neither Mr. Marshall nor Mr. Scully seemed to think much of it.

He walked along his beat again, his big bare feet brushing

quietly through the grass; and as the moon looked through once more he saw Gerua at the other corner of the camp, and noticed that he was smoking on duty, though surreptitiously, knowing that Mr. Marshall would put a black mark against his name if he caught him.

There were lights in Mr. Marshall's tent, and Mr. Scully was with him. Palau was glad that they had to make the decisions and work things out; not him. All he had to do was to spring to it promptly when they gave their orders; to be gentle but firm if that was the tactic, or tough, as instructed. When a man carries another's gun his own conscience has no troublesome function.

In the tent they were drinking black coffee out of pannikins.

Marshall said, "I explained the position to Dr. Hovas and he'll do his best to get some action under way, but he's inclined to follow the book a bit. I wish to God that old man McKerrow hadn't chosen today to go chasing off to Yelaki, even if that young idiot down there is getting into a mess with his airstrip and the local labour problem.

"There are times when I'd be glad if McKerrow would go to hell and stay there indefinitely, but when it comes to getting things done in a hurry he has the edge on most men I know, and if there's a helicopter in the area he'd lay hands on it by fair means or foul and have it here in the morning.

"And that's the whole point of this situation. If George wants to move Gunji to Kombala we must do it while there's still a chance that the old chap will survive the journey, and while the people here are uncertain what to do about this situation, and are not violently against us.

"But there's nothing more sure than that if we try to carry Gunji out over these mountains on a stretcher he will die before we get very far, and we'll have to carry him back again. On the other hand if we leave it much longer they'll have clan meetings and break into factions and work up a rare old hate against us, so that we'll be in real trouble getting our

212

own crowd out of this valley intact, without being handicapped with stretcher cases; for there's Pok as well to keep in mind.

"We need a helicopter, tomorrow. And the next question is Where will it sit down? The valley bottom is a swamp and the drop site is rough and uneven: it would take a full day to straighten out enough of it to make a completely safe landing pad, and the way things are we can't settle for anything less. So it looks as if we use the ceremonial ground, and God knows what sort of rumpus that will raise.

"To sum up, Scully, my young friend, we're in a bit of a fix and you'll need all your luck and simple charm to get us out of this one."

Scully glanced at Marshall, wondering if there was more than surface meaning in the words, but there was nothing in Marshall's face to say that his mind was elsewhere than in the Yakanaki, dealing with immediate problems. He seemed not altogether well, though, and was frowning overmuch as if suffering a headache or sore eyes, the usual overhang of dengue.

They both took a sip of coffee, and Marshall went on with his summary of the situation.

"I can see George's point of view. It's his job to get Gunji better, and mine to see that he gets every chance to do just this. Of course, if we can get him out without much fuss and the doctors manage to patch him up and bring him back alive and well again, the propaganda value will be terrific. But with a man of Gunji's age, so badly knocked about, the odds against this gamble coming off are astronomical.

"The practical thing to do would be simply to call the clan leaders together and pay out a spectacular amount of compensation, and then bow out amid general acclamation and rejoicing, leaving the old boy to die quietly in his own garden as he would wish to do, with all his family around him to do the proper ritual things, and ourselves safely on the way home and no ill feelings.

"This would be considered logical by the Yakanaki because

it is precisely what they'd do themselves if they were in our place. It's what they hope we will do. It's what they would understand as proper conduct.

"They'll never believe that we want to take Gunji away for his own sake and not for ours, nor will they be able to understand that George has to do everything he can to save Gunji's life even at the risk of losing his own. In their eyes this kind of reasoning, based on personal ethics and pride, is the mark of an egocentric idiot, dangerous to the tribe."

Scully could see that there was still something troubling Marshall, and waited for him to speak again.

"Then there's the priest."

Scully said, "Yes, the priest. He's due back in Kombala within the next two weeks. He has lecture dates in America pretty soon." But he knew that this was not what was worrying Marshall. It was not how much time was left, but the growing possibility that there would be trouble getting out of the valley. The priest would be better out of the way: better for himself and better for everybody else.

"Yes." Marshall was thoughtful. "Yes. I think it might be worth suggesting. Get him out to Kombala on the helicopter. If it comes. The idea might appeal to the District Commissioner. After all, it'll be a load off his mind to have Father Herschell back in one piece, and happy."

Scully said deferentially, "So long as G'napa stays friendly we should be all right. Maybe you can get him to agree to go along with Gunji in the chopper and pay a state call on the District Commissioner, with the priest going as interpreter. If you can raise Mr. McKerrow in the morning you might be able to get something like this arranged, and the whole operation completed before nightfall. Then we could pull out next day. If George agrees."

In the medical tent Korbin was cleaning up and talking to the priest. "The situation is clear enough, Father. It looks as though Gunji is going to die whatever we do. If we were simple primitives like these people intelligence would now

**214**

take over from sentiment and we'd come to some arrangement with his clan to assess the extent of our culpability; then buy forgiveness and absolution with suitable presents.

"But my personal responsibility, apart from considerations of government policy, or our immediate predicament and our collective safety, is to give him every chance to live.

"So here we have the twentieth-century predicament. The dilemma of an age which holds firmly to the material principle of 'win at any price' while making, at the same time, vague and conciliatory gestures in the direction of a religious teaching that it abandoned long ago. As yet we haven't figured how to rationalize our behaviour to comfortably accommodate these two opposite philosophies."

He called an orderly and told him to take the instruments away and wash them, and to bring more clean water, and to have morphia ready for injections.

"We should admit that we are still as basically primitive as the Yakanaki. That we haven't advanced far enough yet to be able to actually practice a religion which sees material defeat as essential to spiritual victory. God sprang Christianity upon us too soon. He should stop torturing us into trying hopelessly to follow a way of perfection for which we are not ready, either as individuals or communities.

"Then we wouldn't need to be hypocrites. Wouldn't have to make anxious decisions like this one, or analyze all the overlapping aspects of collective well-being and personal pride in order to discover why we are justified in deciding the proper way to behave."

He went across to Gunji, drying his hands, and stood looking down at him, his face softening. The old man seemed to be awake but confined within a private framework of limited consciousness bounded by the numbing effects of shock and drugs.

"How can I deny this sick old man and let him die? He is me. Without him I would have no meaning, no purpose. As you, Father Herschell, a priest, would have no meaning if you

**215**

denied your god. I need Gunji more than he needs me, for without him I am unnecessary."

They both looked up as Ki pushed back the flap of the tent and waited to be asked to speak.

"What is it, Ki?"

"G'napa. He would like to look at his brother."

"Of course. Let him in."

Korbin went toward the tent door, and when G'napa came led him in and stood with him for a moment beside the table on which Gunji lay. Then he turned to Father Herschell and said quietly, "Explain to G'napa, if you can, that I want to take his brother to Kombala because this will be best for Gunji and for the clan. Say that we may be able to save his life and bring him back to live more years here with G'napa in the valley, helping him to share the problems that will come with the Government."

He walked away, then, and sat on a box looking angry and dissatisfied. "How can we explain? How can we expect them to understand our behaviour and our kind of civilization when we don't understand it ourselves or believe in it any more?

"How can we come here and preach peace between the tribes, and lecture them about fighting each other with bows and arrows when, in a few more years, we'll be forcing their children to fight in our wars against strangers, using our kind of weapons; bombs and gas and napalm and every other soulless obscenity devised by this civilization?

"Why don't we admit that we don't know where we're going? That we're obviously wrong and way off the track. That our savagery makes theirs seem as trivial and innocent as the mischief of children?"

G'napa, not understanding, wondered if this was some sort of funeral oration, and turned to the priest. "Is he dead?"

"No, he is asleep. Mr. Korbin has given him medicine to take away the pain. Perhaps he will get better."

The priest spoke briefly, knowing that he must not antici-

**216**

pate any decision that the others might make about moving Gunji; that it was not in his province to say what was in their minds.

There was quietness for a while, only the tiny sounds of night scribbled on the silence. The hiss of the benzine lamp hanging from the ridge stick. The clicking of insects, and the susurration of restless feet through stiff grass as the police on watch fidgeted about outside. And over this thin instrumentation the steady, rasping rhythm of Gunji's breathing.

G'napa stood looking down at his brother, watching his face as if looking for some message, some instruction, whispering a few words tentatively, asking questions with his eyes, waiting for some sign, some kind of answer. Then he turned to the priest and said "I will take my brother's things and keep them until he is well again." He nodded to where Korbin's orderlies had left Gunji's net bag lying, together with his pipe and fire-lighting things, the necklet of shells, the stone ax and a bone dagger.

He went alone into the bush, went down by the gully and over the stream, carrying Gunji's things. He climbed the ridge and came in time to the hollow where the huts were. The moon swooned over it, making shadows.

He bent by his brother's hut, asking to be let in, and when the boards were moved away went inside and gave the net bag and pipe and other things to young men who were sitting around the fire, Gunji's unmarried sons and some nephews. He spoke briefly to them.

Then he called to the small boy who was the youngest of Gunji's children, and when the lad looked up, puzzled and a little timid, he beckoned to him with a movement of his head.

They went together through the bush, the boy hurrying close at G'napa's heels, terrified to be out at night, afraid of being separated and left unprotected among numberless unseen spirits; and his father newly dead or dying (he knew not which, although the women were wailing).

They came close to Gunji's garden and G'napa stopped,

waiting for the moon to light the landscape, and when, for a moment, it showed its face again he tugged at the boy's hand, gently, and took him a little way into the bush. He stopped beside a sapling.

He cleared away the leaves and debris as his brother had done earlier, uncovering the stone. He took his bone dagger and dug away the ground from around and under it so that the taproot of the sapling was exposed. Then with the steel ax that Marshall had given him he cut it and lifted it out of the ground. A sapling growing through a stone. A natural thing. A thing of the earth, belonging to this valley. The club that Gunji had made for the day when his young son would become a man.

They went back onto the track and soon, as they came close to the ceremonial ground, the way widened into a pathway. G'napa reached back to take the boy's hand, and they continued side by side until the casuarinas stood up in front of them like fingers reaching for the moon.

They stopped then, G'napa holding the boy by one hand. In his other hand he held the club. A bat flickered in and out of the blackness that crowded about them. He looked up into the trees and in a little while began a quavering, plaintive, tuneless lamentation.

> Gunji went against the strangers;
> Those who have great magic.
> And the bird was angry with Gunji.
> The bird is their father and mother.
> It comes with the sun sitting on its wings
> To feed the white men.
> The bird was angry with Gunji
> And the women already sing his death song,
> They put mud on themselves
> And cut off their fingers.
> They will destroy his garden,
> No one will sit in it;
> His sons will break his smokepipe.

**218**

The bird killed Gunji
And now one of Gunji's blood
Must kill one among the strangers;
It is our custom.
When this is done
The spirit of my brother can go
To the place of our ancestors.

I am getting old and my belly is empty
And no more sons will come from me;
So I take this boy,
Who is Gunji's son,
And do what his father has not yet done
To make him a man.
Then he will have a name,
And a place among his people.

He stood for a little while longer, looking up into the
casuarina trees, whispering. Then he went with the boy to
Gunji's garden and sat in his hut. And G'napa made a small
fire and cooked a sweet potato for the boy, talking all the
while of the clan and its ancestors: how they came into the
valley; of the battles and marriages that made their own clan
bigger and stronger than any other among the Yakanaki
people.

He touched him on secret parts, whispering words of ritual.
He made marks on his body with charcoal and dust, and when
the wood in the fire had burned to ash but was still warm, he
made the boy stand in it, then scatter it with his feet. Afterwards he beat him across the shoulders and stomach with a
whip of twigs. Then he gave him the club. And they stayed
there until daylight.

# Chapter 16

By morning the mountains were hidden in thick mist and the air in the valley was wet with drizzle. Marshall stood inside the doorway of his tent, looking out at the weather and watching Korbin talk on the transceiver to Dr. Hovas at Kombala.

"He's in a mess, Doc. I've aligned the bones as best I can and have repaired the external damage, but what I've been able to do is superficial. There can be no proper assessment of the damage without an X ray, though even without it I'd say that there's not a great deal of hope if we don't get him out of here and into hospital pretty soon.

"From the medical point of view there could be a chance of saving the man in spite of his age, and from the administrative point of view I think it's worth making a special effort to put him on his feet again. A spectacular medical success at this stage might make a difference to the way things go here in the future. Could save the Native Affairs people a lot of trouble later on."

The doctor's voice came back to them, foreign and thick, and flustered. "Port Moresby gives the permission to bring you a helicopter from the coast but she is stuck in Madang with this bad weather. Maybe she comes later. You must prepare the patients for evacuation early tomorrow morning.

That is all, please. I come myself, early in the morning, if the weather is okay."

They could visualize him in the radio hut at Kombala; anxious, concerned. The tubby little doctor with the soft heart, and a manner so mild and shy that any clerk with an ounce of power could confuse and frighten him. He would fuss and become excited, would worry that when McKerrow came back to Kombala he would shout at him and call him an idiot for overstepping his authority. He would weep with frustration and shame as he always did when things went wrong, or those in authority hindered, or were rude to him. But he was professionally resolute, had courage, and would do his duty heroically. He would come and collect the injured men himself, even though he hated flying and had trouble with his stomach whenever he went up.

They signed off and Marshall said, "It's probably as much as he can do with the weather the way it is. We must leave it at that, and gamble that Gunji will stay alive until tomorrow morning. In any case the radio batteries are getting weak and we can't keep making off-schedule calls to Kombala just to chat to Dr. Hovas."

He sent for Garni to come and dismantle the radio; and sent Tau to find Heli.

"I'll get hold of G'napa now and explain what we have in mind. I might even pay out some compensation to Gunji's family this morning to let them see that we mean to play fair in this business. And I'll have a word with Father Herschell and see how he feels about flying out to Kombala with the patients. It might suit him to do this if he's finished the work he set out to do. It would save him the long walk back to Wanega."

Korbin thought, He's more concerned with getting the priest safely off his hands than he is about Gunji. But, walking across the camp with Marshall, he agreed that it might, indeed, be sensible to suggest this; that it would ease the strain all round if it could be done decently and without giving the priest to think that they wished to be rid of him.

Father Herschell, in his tent, changed the batteries in his recorder, then checked the amount of tape so far used, and what was left. He entered these details in his diary, then ran back over the recording of Marshall's last speech, listening through the headphones.

It was a remarkably good recording. In fact, dramatic. He not only had an excellent record of what Marshall had said, together with translations by Heli and G'napa, but the whole or Gunji's interpolated outburst as well, up to the point where they first heard the airplane coming, and the crescendo of sound as it went thundering across the camp to drown out Gunji's shouting. Even then his voice could still be heard quite clearly above the row, just as the sound of sea birds, wildly complaining, overrides the uproar of a storm.

Then the airplane coming again and the frightened, violent excitement of the Yakanaki men when Gunji was hit. Marshall shouting orders; sending somebody for Korbin and cursing the unknown person in the airplane who had blundered so disastrously. The whole thing sounded tremendously exciting.

He switched off, enormously pleased, hoping that Marshall would take time to listen to it; that he would be equally pleased and see it as an effective centerpiece for any talk he might give to the Historical Society when he went on leave.

The priest looked up and saw G'napa standing in the doorway of the tent, with Gunji's solemn young son beside him holding the club on his shoulder. And immediately he was ashamed because already he had forgotten the tragedy and the great suffering contained in what had happened; was already more concerned with the superficial value of his recording than with the mutilation and the pain of Gunji and Pok (who was, after all, his personal servant).

"M'yembo."

He gave the greeting of the valley. But in his heart he was

222

asking: What kind of priest am I who can feel no pain but my own? Can have no part in the sufferings of others but must stand aside, unconnected and detached, not sharing their troubles or mixing mine with theirs. What and where is the compassion of Christ that I'm supposed to preach in word and deed? This love that once flowed from the wounds in his hands and feet and side and now runs like a river in flood to wash away the sorrows of all mankind (so the saints said) bringing universal comfort and consolation. Why can't I, a priest of this same Christ, feel Gunji's pain and weep for poor Pok, or grieve for Sosu and Didimus and the others who have suffered and died on this trip, this journey into the unknown that we have made in each other's company? Why am I so separate, so private in a world, among people, I wish to love and to save?

He sighed, and looked at G'napa. "Have you been to see Gunji?"

G'napa drew in his lips, signifying, "No."

Then Marshall came with Korbin, Heli beside them.

Marshall said, "I'd like to talk to you, Father, about our plans." Then to Korbin, "George, why don't you and Heli take G'napa along to look at his brother? You can let me know how he seems before we tell G'napa what we have in mind to do with him. I'll come across to the medical tent when Father Herschell and I have had our talk." And looking at Gunji's son, "That's a pretty warlike weapon for a small boy to be carrying. A good specimen too. Quite a museum piece. You don't see the oldtime fighting clubs any more except in the most remote of these uncontrolled areas."

He took the club and looked at it closely, speaking to the priest. "It's new. No blood on it yet, which means that the boy is not fully initiated into manhood. Maybe we've come just in time to save some unsuspecting character from collecting a nasty headache." He looked up at Father Herschell. "You should try to buy it from him as a souvenir of your visit. He'd probably swop it for a steel ax."

He handed the club back to the boy, patting his head. "By the time you get to be big enough to swing that thing you won't need it. You'll be going to school."

He took Father Herschell by the arm. "Let's go inside, Father, and talk for a while."

When they were settled he said, "I've asked for a helicopter to come in for Pok and Gunji so that we can get them to Kombala and hospital. It's likely to be a tricky operation and I think that you could help, though you may feel that what I'm going to ask is a bit too much. If so, just shake your head and I'll shut up."

He spoke casually, his face averted, trying to keep out of his voice any trace of ambiguity or overtone of hopefulness. But the priest knew what was coming, and prayed quietly that Marshall would so frame his request that there could be no doubt of its sincerity, no excuse for his overscrupulous conscience to refuse the escape that Marshall was about to offer him.

"There's no chance that the clan will agree to let Gunji leave the valley unless they can send a guardian with him, and I'm going to ask G'napa if he'll go with his brother to Kombala. This will kill two birds with one stone. It'll get Gunji into hospital where Doc Hovas can give him proper care and treatment, and maybe save his life. And it will give G'napa a chance to see the outside world and be a more effective liaison between his people and the Government.

"But here's my problem. We must send one of our own party with them in the helicopter as a kind of guarantee that the game is straight. That we're not going to play any tricks. And whoever goes must also be able to act as interpreter between G'napa and our own people at Kombala.

"Of course, I could send Heli, but this would raise problems in the day-to-day running of the patrol. We'll be out for another two weeks yet—perhaps longer if we have to wait around here for G'napa to get back."

**224**

Marshall looked up now, knowing that he had done his best to make it easy for the priest. "You see what I'm getting at? I'm about to ask a big favour of you."

Father Herschell tried to stay calm, to keep his mind quiet, wanting Marshall to take possession of it. As with a respectable woman wanting to be seduced, the decision would have to be forced upon him so that he could not possibly refuse and so, later, would not need to feel ashamed. He said, as evenly as he could, "I have the feeling that you're asking me to make a decision of some kind that affects all of us. But you're the boss around here and you can lay it on the line. It would be my duty to do anything you figured necessary for the safety and success of this whole outfit and the total operation."

Marshall pressed his lips together, thought for a moment, then spoke decisively. "Yes, that's true, but you're also a guest, and on my level a V.I.P. I can't give you orders without checking with my own boss, District Commissioner McKerrow, who's taken himself off to Yelaki, out of range. So you and I must make our own emergency decisions on the basis of mutual agreement."

The priest knew, then, that Marshall was offering him a chance that he couldn't, without shame, take. Knew that there was no honest way to escape the discomfort, the continuous danger, being the odd man out, the stranger not pulling his weight.

"I guess you'd like me to offer to pack up and go out in the helicopter with Gunji and G'napa. I see your point of view quite well. But I don't know that I could do this and feel good about it later."

They were both discouraged, wondering where they had gone wrong, not seeing clearly that every man must make his own decisions and live by them; must learn to get along honestly with the person he knows himself to be, admitting the limitations of his nature, strong or weak, timid, bold, brave, belligerent, or frightened inside.

**225**

Marshall turned away. "Well, think about it and if you change your mind we can talk again later. We don't need to decide anything before tonight."

He went back through the camp, past the stores tent where Scully had carriers and constables busy fitting the new shovel blades with long handles cut from the bush. He had retrieved the wheelbarrow from the tree and was hammering at its dents while an audience of Yakanaki squatted around him, mystified by these new wonders, waiting to see the worth of them. (Scully, thank God, was uncomplicated. Could be relied upon to do the direct and sensible thing in any situation).

He went across and asked Scully to take some gold-lip shell and small axes from the store and put them together with two or three shovels and the barrow. "I'm going to make a token payment to Gunji's family. Show them what they'll get if he dies; and also give the rest of them an idea of the good things that will come later if they all behave."

In the medical tent he looked at Pok and Gunji, then at Korbin. "How are they both?"

Korbin shrugged. "Pok might make it if we can get them out in the morning, but I wouldn't bet heavily on Gunji. He's holding his own. Breathing not too badly and his pulse is good considering all things, though a few pints of blood would do him the world of good. I can only keep them quiet and ease the pain, and hope that Dr. Hovas can get here in time to do something more practical."

Marshall patted Korbin's arm, then went outside and, calling for Heli, sat down with G'napa and began to talk.

Gunji's wives came at midday; five of them, brought by their brothers and other male relations together with Gunji's sons and unmarried daughters—in all, some fifty-seven people. Waiting to see what Marshall would give them and what he would promise to pay should Gunji die, they stayed together in a group close to the medical tent.

And because Heli had been calling all morning hundreds

of other clansmen were scattered about the camp, but remembering the coming of the big bird and Gunji's trouble they had lookouts posted on the nearby hills and ridges, watching in case it should suddenly come again.

So when they heard the clatter and rattle of the wheelbarrow those who could not see it were startled and looked up and about anxiously until they saw Scully pushing it between the tents. Then they came running and made a corridor through which he passed, smiling widely, while they drew breath in amazement and, peering over each other's shoulders, were speechless, never having seen a wheel before.

Marshall collected them together, with Gunji's family a little to one side, and when they were settled told acting-Lance Corporal Garni to put down on the ground three fine gold-lip pearl shells as big as a dinner plates (which brought a gasp), a small ax, a shovel, two knives, two mirrors and a double handful of cowrie shells in a tin pannikin.

When these were set out neatly he came and stood close by and spoke to the family, and to the Yakanaki people all around, speaking earnestly, anxious to impress with his sincerity. "These things we now give to Gunji's family to show that the Government will look after them and all of you Yakanaki people. And if, because of the big bird, Gunji dies, we will give many more things to his women and children and to the men of his family. For the Government is sorry that this thing has happened between us when we wish to be friends and want to come and live among you in peace."

Then he pointed at the barrow and the things that Scully had put in it.

"All of these things we will give to Gunji's people if, because of this trouble, he must die. And afterwards, when the Government comes, it will bring many such things for the people of this valley." He turned to Garni. "Corporal, show these people how quickly a man can dig a new garden with a government shovel."

Again they were amazed, wonderstruck; could not believe

their eyes when Garni stuck the shovel into the earth and soon turned a deep spit bigger and quicker than six men together might do it with digging sticks, and no strength given to it—only a downward thrust, a pressing with the foot, a twist.

"Ahaaa! How many such wonders would these men have yet to show?"

Marshall looked at G'napa. "Who among Gunji's sons will be first to own such a shovel?"

Heli repeated the question rhetorically and there was quiet while all waited to see who would take this prize. Then there was a whispering among the men and women of Gunji's family, with wives urging husbands to be bold, to make claim, while the sons struggled with shyness.

The small boy, feeling G'napa's touch on his shoulder, looked up at his uncle for encouragement, which he saw in the faintest flicker of his eyelid, and went forward while all watched; but when he had taken only a few steps he turned back to G'napa and with both hands held out the stone club. Then, when G'napa took it from him, the boy ran and snatched up the shovel and stood with it clutched close as something wonderful and loved, and very precious: and was uncertain until one of the women called to him. Then he went to her bearing his prize proudly—leaving the club with G'napa.

Marshall, relaxed now and smiling, asked G'napa to nominate one among Gunji's family to share out the rest of the presents; and when this was done (G'napa standing quite apart from the transaction) he told them of his plan to send Gunji to Kombala.

Straightway the excitement of the share-out died and they were quiet. Suspicious. Taken unawares.

Those of Gunji's family standing with their new possessions in their hands were now uncertain, wondering if these things were gifts after all, or wily, extravagant bribes; proper payment for wrongs acknowledged, or a crafty prelude to some other unimaginable trickery.

**228**

Clansmen, looking to G'napa for a lead, saw nothing in the straight, grave face to give them guidance; nothing to assure them that Marshall could be trusted this time more than before. They began to edge away, feeling for the axes in their belts, their eyes flickering suspiciously from G'napa to Marshall and then to Heli who, with head lifted, called out, urging them to listen and consider.

"Gunji is on the edge of death and will die if nothing is done to help him. But if these white men take him away for a little while to the place where they make great magic, Gunji may find new life and strength, and will take his place among you again."

But they would not listen, nor did G'napa give them any help; and the women of Gunji's family, fearing trouble, broke away from the gathering and ran with their gains into the bush, led by the little boy, who was running with his shovel as if afraid that someone would follow after to take it from him.

Father Herschell, in his tent, away from all this, switched on the tape recorder and, starting a stopwatch, laid it alongside. Then he took up his notebook and pencil and began to play right through the tape of Marshall's speech once more, making note of any Yakanaki words or phrases to be checked with G'napa before they left the valley.

He sat back in a canvas chair listening critically to the first few sentences coming through the speaker.

"Headmen of the Yakanaki clans and families, I am happy because you have let us camp here on your land . . ." He leaned forward and increased the volume.

Close by, at the medical tent, Marshall was talking to Scully. "I don't know what's got into G'napa. He's been a tower of strength from the day we came, and now suddenly he seems to have gone sour. Doesn't give us any help. I can understand that he feels badly about his brother but surely he appreciates that we're doing all we can to make amends. If he doesn't come out clearly in favour of taking Gunji to Kombala we'll have to rethink our plans. With G'napa against us we'd have to fight to get the old man into a helicopter and out of the valley."

But Scully seemed to be listening to something else. He began to look around. And Marshall, turning sharply to see what it was that took his attention, saw that most of the Yakanaki roundabout were standing still. Fixed. Some looking puzzled and some afraid. Uncertain. Looking for something.

He listened, and could hear himself making a speech, then Heli interpreting, and after that, G'napa. Then Gunji shouting, cursing the white men. Crying out that they and those with them should be killed before they could take hold of and change the minds of the young men and set them against the old ways followed by their fathers and all who had lived in the valley since the days of the snake. Before they could poison and spoil and destroy all that was familiar and customary and understood.

It was uncanny. Gunji's voice calling all over the camp. Spreading. Every word coming clearly as though he were still standing on the slope making his speech instead of lying in the tent, senseless, a finger's length from death.

Now he seemed to be screaming at the priest, railing furiously and with fanatic anger against the magic that was catching at his voice and locking it in the little box. One could almost see him shaking his fist at Pok, who had been holding the microphone, but now lay beside him carrying his own weight of pain, and facing death in a strange place.

Then the distant cry came again, as it had come yesterday, from down at the dropsite.

"Balus i kam."

The sound of the airplane.

Marshall started, looked round, alarmed now.

"Jesus, what is that bloody fool doing? Does he want to get us all butchered? Go stop him. Go turn that stinking thing off before these people go berserk."

He was looking around for Scully. But Scully was already

**230**

running the other way, towards the medical tent to warn Korbin, yelling, at Ki and Gerua on guard, that the Yakanaki might come for Gunji.

The priest, listening to his tape, heard the roar of the airplane followed by the shouting of the crowd, but was confused because it seemed to have changed. He switched off and found that the shouting was real, was happening now. Scores of Yakanaki men were running through the camp brandishing axes, the carriers standing, looking at them in amazement.

And he was not afraid!

Not afraid.

Waited: and no fear came. No steely fingers fumbling, clutching at his heart. No sudden running of the stomach. No dry tongue.

"O my God, I thank thee."

He crossed himself swiftly and began to run towards the medical tent, to Pok who might need him. And he prayed as he ran.

"Jesus, Mary and Joseph, give me grace."

And felt brave and grateful and ready to save.

There seemed to be hundreds of Yakanaki around the medical tent, struggling and buffeting and plunging about. He could see the canvas sag and sway, and a forest of uplifted hands and axes waving all around it like branches swishing and dipping in a high wind, amid the shouting and screaming. Scully boring his way through the crowd with Ki and Gerua; Scully cuffing and the two constables thrusting and shoving men back with their rifle butts.

He ran towards all this. Glad. Happy. Almost laughing. Remembering that he had felt this kind of excitement when a lad. He didn't hear Marshall calling to him, "For Christ's sake, keep back." But Constable Tau came hurrying and stood in his way.

It was vexing but sensible to stop and watch, and wait awhile to see what he could usefully contribute besides this newborn bravery.

He saw the tent lurch and lean, then the crowd make way for men who came out carrying Gunji on his stretcher, and Korbin beside them hitting out viciously with his walking stick to keep the excited men from bumping and clutching at it; for though he might be losing Gunji as a patient he would save him all the pain he could until the old man was out of his hands and taken beyond range of any aid that he could give.

The priest stood looking.

He saw Marshall hurrying about, instructing the constables: some to clear the crowd away from the medical tent; others to protect Gunji from the exuberance of his own clansmen though he knew now that the old man would die.

They would take him to his garden hut and let him lie there while the women wailed and the men beat the ground with sticks. They would hang his apron, his cap of leaves, his ornaments and weapons in a tree so that his ghost could reach them; and his pigs and women would be shared among his sons.

Perhaps it was better this way—better than taking him to die in some strange place among foreigners. For the likelihood of saving his life had been slim from the beginning.

Korbin would be disappointed, would feel that he had failed, though God knew he could have done no more for the man. Even now he seemed determined to go along with Gunji and see that he was treated easily; that death was let come gently as might be. Without pain.

For a moment he felt impatient of such scrupulosity, seeing in it too much risk to give any semblance of sense or virtue. But George had his own set of values and was able to look after himself pretty well, and had police with him, armed. They were going only a short way, to Gunji's garden, in any case.

But one man seemed to have gone mad. He was running about wildly, leaping and screaming, waving his ax. He came at Marshall from behind and might have smashed his head in if Scully hadn't slipped between them and tripped the man and, as he stumbled, thumped him behind the ear with his fist so that he dropped like a poleaxed pig.

Marshall turned and saw the man lying there.

"One way and another I seem to be always in your debt these days. I'm sure that my wife will be grateful to you for saving my life. It seems, almost, that you're becoming one of the family."

Scully blushed and grinned self-consciously.

"No need to tell her anything. She's probably forgotten me by now and I doubt if we'll meet again. No point in worrying her with tales of narrow escapes. Let's forget it."

Then he broke away.

"I'd better go see if the priest is all right. He started this barney. And whether he intended it or not he's solved our problem with Gunji."

They found him in the medical tent holding Pok's hand and speaking to him quietly in the Wanega language while Korbin's orderlies cleaned up and made things straight again, picking up bottles and boxes knocked down and trampled upon by the men who had come for Gunji.

"How is he?"

The priest looked up. "He seems okay. They didn't touch him, though he got bumped about a bit and has some pain. George left instructions, and the boys have just given him an injection. He'll sleep soon." He looked at Pok as if he loved him. "Poor kid. I hope he makes it."

They left the tent together and walked back through the camp, quiet now, with only the carriers standing about, still bewildered. Garni was placing his men strategically about in case of other trouble, though most of the police were away with Korbin.

They came, the three of them, to the middle of the camp and were about to separate, Marshall to his tent, Scully and the priest to theirs.

The priest said, "What started all that, anyway? Why did they suddenly decide to take Gunji away?"

Scully watched Marshall, waited for his reply, and was relieved when he simply shrugged and said, "I don't know. You never can tell how they're going to behave or what they'll do next. You need to be either very smart or very simple to stay on their wave length."

Father Herschell thought for a moment, then spoke again. "I wonder if you'd like to hear the recording of your speech. It's very good."

Again Marshall hesitated. "Well, yes. Maybe now is as good a time as any. I'm glad that you're pleased with it."

They walked together to the other tent and, going in, saw the recorder lying on the ground. Smashed flat. Bits and pieces were scattered about as if someone had battered it in anger with a mallet. Or a club. And all the tape was tangled among bits of broken components.

Marshall spoke flatly. "Well, that's that. Doesn't look as though you'll be doing any more recording on this trip."

Then he looked up.

"I'm sorry about that."

# Chapter 17

THE valley was full of shadow when Korbin came back. Only on the highest peaks, away to the west, did the last light of day linger as he came, leaning on his stick like a man who has walked a long way, though he had been no farther than to Gunji's garden. Ki and Gerua and the other police were strung out behind him untidily, one carrying the empty stretcher.

Back in the bush behind them women were wailing while Gunji's sons went gathering wood to make a box for his body. They would truss him like a chicken and put him in it, then set it up in his garden on stilts to keep him from the pigs. When the flesh was rotted they would wash his bones and distribute them among the relations, and each would bury something of Gunji under the floor of his hut. And the chief wife would keep his skull.

As Korbin came into the camp acting-Lance Corporal Garni was pulling down the flag while the bugle blew Retreat, and Marshall stood saluting.

During dinner Heli came with one of Gunji's sons to ask when the rest of the death payment might be made, for the family was impatient to lay hands on this much wealth.

"In the morning," said Marshall, "after the helicopter has

**235**

come and we've got Pok away safely, and any other sick man who should be got rid of before we start back."

When the son had gone gladly with the good news, he went on.

"They're rum buggers. Don't really give a damn who dies so long as the proper compensation is paid and they all get their cut.

"Here's poor old Gunji peacefully minding his own business and we come and drop a load of shovels on him and almost start a war. And if we had tried to take him out and save his life they would have wanted to stop us, and a few more might have died. But now he's gone, and not even cold, they have no interest except in the settlement. In fact they seem highly delighted that it's worked out this way."

Korbin snapped back crossly. "You'd better keep close watch in the morning if Doc Hovas comes with the helicopter, or there'll be a few families getting together to push their old men under it, hoping for a payoff like the one you're giving Gunji's people. It's a new and easy way to get rich and they catch on quickly. A simple and direct introduction to the economics of civilization." Then scowling, he spoke almost angrily to Marshall. "I wish you'd take some tablets and go to bed. You look lousy. As sure as God made little apples you're heading for another bout of dengue fever if you don't rest up and take a bit of medical advice when it's given."

But they overlooked the brusqueness, knowing that he felt cheated by the way things had gone with Gunji, and were not surprised when he stood abruptly and spoke again, this time as if to himself.

"I must go and look at Pok, get him ready to be moved in the morning. There's a chance we might save this one."

Marshall, to ease off the tension, said, "Good. You go. And I'll take your advice and get to bed right now with a couple of your pills. Now that you remind me I do feel pretty much done in." And to the priest: "You'd best rest up, too, Father. Now that Gunji's gone we can clean up here tomorrow and pull out next day before dawn, heading back to Wanega. Unless you change your mind and decide to fly!"

The priest was hesitant. "Yes, I guess you're right. We all need a rest. But there's a few things I'd like to check with G'napa before we go. The tape that was on the machine isn't too badly damaged and I can patch it. And I've got notes on it all. But I'd just like to get a few things straight. Some odd words and phrases. Then I think I'll be satisfied with the work I've done on this trip." He looked at Marshall seriously. "You know how it is, Ken. You know how you feel when you've done a job as well as it can be done. And you know the other feeling. The feeling that you haven't reached your limit. That there's part of you still unused. A bit that you haven't given. You've all put a lot into this patrol and I'd be cheating the three of you, and the police and carriers too, as well as myself, if, for my part, I gave less than all I've got to give." He looked sheepish. "Sorry to be making speeches but I want you to know how much I appreciate what you've done for me, and the way I've been treated."

There was a moment of embarrassment, then Marshall got up. "Okay, we'll fix something tomorrow with G'napa. Right now I must take to my bed or George will get mad at me. He's had a bad day and we should humour him." He turned to Scully. "See if he needs any help, and make sure that everything's ready to mark out the ceremonial ground in the morning. We don't want any hitches getting rid of Pok. Good night now. Don't stay up late."

He went out and they heard him speak to the constable on watch. "See that I'm called by five o'clock."

Korbin was glad when young Scully came to the medical tent to help him; without the priest.

"He's a fine fellow and I like him, but he seems to be a natural-born catalyst. A fellow who can trigger off confusion simply by being present."

They made a list: Two teams of four men each, to carry Pok. A medical orderly to go out with him in the helicopter to help Dr. Hovas. Two sick carriers to be evacuated at the same time. An escort of four armed police to take them all down to the ceremonial ground.

They called the constable on watch and told him to notify the four concerned; otherwise they might sit up all night gossiping and playing cards, which they did when camped in any one place for several days, and would be dopey in the morning.

It was then that Father Herschell left the camp, hurrying through the scrub and down into the gully, out of sight, wondering if the tight ache round his ribs, and the pulse thumping like a slack drum inside his head, were signs of excitement or reflexes of fear still not completely overcome; yet knowing that, although he still might be afraid, and could never be audacious, he was no longer terrified by the mere idea of violence or the thought of pain.

He stumbled in the gully but would not flash a light in case it could be seen by someone in the camp.

He murmured to himself, smiling, "The Lord is my light and my salvation. Whom, then, need I fear? The Lord is the strength of my life, of whom shall I be afraid?"

He thought of G'napa. How surprised he would be by this visit! And pleased that the priest had come to discuss these finer points of the Yakanaki language with him. It was something all primitive people appreciated. Someone from the outside world who would show genuine interest in them and their customs and the language. Who didn't want to boss them about or change their ways but simply wanted to know and understand them and help them if possible. On their own terms.

An animal scurried in the branches of a tree, and his heart skipped a beat, but recovered quickly.

"Thou shalt not be afraid of the terror by night, nor for the arrow that flieth in daytime . . . for he shall give his angels charge over thee, to keep thee in all thy ways."

He remembered where the path branched, going one way

238

to the ceremonial ground and Gunji's garden, and the other way to the huts. The hamlet where G'napa lived. It was where the women were wailing and chanting death songs. The men, more likely, would be in Gunji's gardening hut, talking and smoking, to keep the ghost company.

Father Herschell hesitated, wondering which way to take.

Scully was saying to George Korbin, "If Doc Hovas comes in the morning he can take some mail out, so I think I'll write a few lines to Mother before I turn in. I'll do it here if you don't mind, then I won't disturb the priest if he's asleep."

He wrote for fifteen minutes while Korbin and an orderly changed the dressing on Pok, made him clean and comfortable for the night.

Then he went to his tent. But five minutes later he was back again.

"Don't panic yet but I can't find the priest. He's not in the tent or the usual offices. I've walked all round the camp and have spoken to the watch."

Korbin, leaning over his patient, spoke without looking up. "Give him five minutes. He may be praying in some quiet place. It's the sort of caper he goes on with. Might even be saying Mass. I believe he's teaching Lop Lop, on the quiet, to be an acolyte."

Gunji's young son was asleep beside his uncle under the casuarina trees, at the edge of the ceremonial ground. He stirred when G'napa rested a hand on his stomach, and as the pressure gently increased he woke and opened his eyes. He could see the black columns of the trees reaching into the sky, could see the stars and the pale flat face of the moon diffused behind a thin veil of cloud. He felt his uncle's hand find his own, take and lay it on the smooth shaft of the club lying beside him.

Gunji's club.

He heard him call quietly to someone standing in the

shadows and was surprised to see a white man come towards them across the ceremonial ground and sit with G'napa; the one who had come before to the men's hut and had made his father angry.

"M'yembo!"

The priest took a notebook from his pocket, switched on his flashlight and gave it to the boy to hold, showing him where to shine the light so that he could write by it. Then he talked to G'napa, asking him questions and writing the answers, repeating the words until he could say them exactly as G'napa said them.

He seemed to forget where he was.

G'napa, seeing the clouds slide slowly across the sky, knew that the moon would be obscured soon. That what he must do should be done quickly, before the other white men came looking for this one.

Father Herschell stopped scribbling, turned a page and leaned across to Gunji's son to correct the direction of the light beam from the lamp. Like a curtain being drawn, cloud shadow came sweeping across the ceremonial ground to cover them. G'napa, watching it, pulled the dagger from his girdle. He waited for the priest to leave himself wide open. And as he turned back from the boy, G'napa lunged.

"Ugh." Father Herschell grunted and fell forward, clutching at his stomach. Then he cried aloud with horror and the fiery surprise of pain as his own fingers closed on G'napa's hand and he could feel the clumsy bone dagger twist inside him like a piece of stick. He fainted.

Surprised, the boy sat holding the flashlight until G'napa snatched it from him and threw it to the ground. Then, standing up, he took Gunji's club, thrust it into the boy's hands and spoke to him sharply, pointing at the priest doubled up as if asleep or dead.

Still the boy hesitated, until G'napa took him roughly by the shoulders and pushed him forward, speaking quickly, almost hysterically, lifting the lad's arms up so that he held the

240

club above Father Herschell's head. Then G'napa shouted at him to hit the priest and kill him so that his father, Gunji, might rest in peace among his ancestors, knowing that his son had become a man.

They found him: Korbin and Scully and some police.

"It's this wound in his stomach that's the trouble. Could be anything. The head wound isn't so bad. Bad enough, mind you, but not fatal. Bones broken, but it seems to have been a light blow and there's no evident damage to the brain."

Scully, waiting for Korbin's instructions, said, "Poor Ken. This is really going to set him up. Just what we needed to complete the expedition."

Korbin gave quick orders to the police. "Okay. Let's get going. Take him back to the camp where I can do something useful. If we can keep him alive until Doc Hovas gets here everything may be all right."

They pushed sticks through the sleeves of their tunics to make a litter and carried him back quickly, but he came to before they reached the camp.

"What happened?"

Korbin, walking beside him, heard the whisper and took hold of his fingers. "Don't talk. You were jumped by some local boys but you're safe now. We've got you. Me and Scully."

He was quiet for a while, then.

"Will I die?"

"I shouldn't think so. But we haven't really looked at you yet so I don't know what the damage is. But as soon as we get you back to camp we'll have a good look."

Again there was quiet except for the swishing of bushes as they brushed by, and the thud and rustle of creepers being slashed at and dragged away from the track as Palau and Ki went ahead to make the way wider with their bush knives.

After a while the priest said, almost complaining, "I can't see, and I have a terrible headache. Am I blind?"

Korbin said gently, "No, but you've had a pretty nasty blow

**241**

on the head and maybe have a little concussion. I'll give you something to stop the pain as soon as we get back to camp."

The priest sighed. "I wasn't afraid. And now Kenneth will hate me."

He began to cry quietly.

Marshall was very angry. Buckling on his pistol, he snapped at Scully, "This priest is my responsibility. You should have woken me as soon as you knew he had left the camp. You had no right whatever to go off looking for him without letting me know."

Scully was embarrassed. "We were hoping he wouldn't be far away. Perhaps at the hamlet with G'napa. And we'd have him back and in bed and no harm done without having to worry you."

(Korbin had said, "Don't wake the boss. He's pretty sick if he'd only admit it, and what he doesn't know he won't grieve over.")

"Dammit, Scully, I'm in charge of this outfit. I make those kind of decisions, and I take the blame. I have to take the blame. It's my job."

"Sorry, boss, I didn't see it that way."

"That's the trouble, none of you ever see it my way. But that's the way McKerrow will see it. It's my head that's going to be offered on a platter when our Government has to apologize for a dead American priest. You and George Korbin and this holy halfwit can play at being heroes. Can enjoy the luxury of being lovable characters. Galahads. While I get my bloody head lopped off for being inefficient.

"I can hear them. 'Poor Marshall, a good bushman but no good with people.' That's what they'll say. They'll blame me because I want to be decent. To be nice to people instead of bossing them about for their own protection.

"What d'you think it will sound like at the inquiry? 'This important priest, distinguished visitor and academician, was

242

killed because the leader of the expedition has a bit of a head-ache and the junior patrol officer and a medical assistant were afraid to wake him up.' "

He paused and glared self-consciously, knowing that he had already said too much, more than he really felt or meant. But he was unable to stop.

"Mr. Scully. I'm getting a bit sick of you running my life."

Before daylight Marshall left with Heli and Garni and a strong posse of police to begin his investigations.

They searched the ceremonial ground and its longhouses, looking for weapons that might have been used against the priest, but found nothing. Then they went to G'napa's hamlet, but nobody was there, not even a pig.

"They've cleared out." Marshall spoke to himself, but loudly. "They'll move off and hide with other clans in the valley, the whole lot of them, and it'll take months to find them."

But women were sitting in Gunji's garden whimpering and covering themselves with mud for his mourning, spreading it thickly over their shoulders, arms and breasts, and on the insides of their thighs. There were no men to be seen anywhere.

"Bastards," Marshall muttered, and was immediately sorry. Loving these uncouth, unsubtle people. Not blaming them for what they had done, nor for their running away. Blaming his own people, rather, for muddling what had promised to be a highly successful operation.

He went over to question the women, not expecting to get any useful information but knowing that it had to be done according to the book. As everything should be done. Then there would be no muddling.

Korbin, at the door of the medical tent, watched weather signs, hoping to see the morning mist lift quickly and leave a clear sky.

Behind him the priest lay, barely conscious, with his head bound and his stomach wound dressed, an orderly sitting alongside to keep flies away.

Korbin turned back into the tent. "I'd pray for you if I could, Father, but I found out long ago that one must never expect anything of God, and it's no good asking for what you won't get. Maybe he loves us, I don't know. And if he does he has his own way of showing it. But I love you in my own limited way and I'll look after you until Dr. Hovas comes. Then he will be your god.

"Perhaps that's how it goes. Maybe we are God. All of us combined. Not only the churchgoers and the holy men and women but all of us. Hoboes, bums and phonies, and the ordinarily puzzled people like me. Maybe together we are one god. The god of love. The operative god. Maybe without us the Father god is only a voice talking backwards in emptiness."

He went to the door of the tent again.

"Hey, you, up there. Do you know about this fellow in here? He's one of yours. A priest. And he loves you. But he's suffering and he's going to die because he trusted in you to look after him, instead of listening to one who knows. Ken Marshall. Do you care? Is it anything to you? I guess not. You let Christ die, so why should you save this priest?"

He listened, as if expecting to be answered.

"Okay, I give up. We all give up. Have it your own way. But why do we have to run about like blind mice bumping into one another all the time? Give us a clue. You started it all and you should tell us what we have to do to make it work. It's your world. You made it. Why do we have to suffer?

"If you ever had a message for us the churches have confused it. Send someone down again and let's have it new. Tell us once more what we must do to be saved. But this time keep it simple."

He came back to look at the priest again and, seeing that he was trying to speak, though his eyes were closed, sat beside

**244**

him, leaning towards his lips. And could hear him, so softly and slowly, stopping every few seconds for breath.

"You're right, George. God is nothing without people but people are nothing without God. He needs us as we need him. He even needs you, George." The merest flicker of a smile crossed the priest's face. "Your love for people is not your love but His love being spread around by you.

"He doesn't exist to do things for us. We exist to do His will in the world. And His will is love, and love is human equality, and the only true equality is at the bottom, not the top. We have to reach downwards to lift others up."

Korbin laid his hand on Fathers Herschell's arm, trying to stop him, bothered because he was using strength that might otherwise keep him going until the helicopter came. But when he had rested he went on.

"This is the meaning of Christ's dying. It was God saying that to gain Him you must be prepared to give up all else. No good praying to be spared any sacrifice or pain. No good asking God to give us handouts. The truth is so simple to see, yet so difficult to reach. Until men are ready to give everything to God they will go on dying to save what little they have." He was quiet for a while, then asked, "How's Pok?"

Korbin spoke more brightly. "He's not too bad. I think he'll go on patrol again some day." He looked outside. "It's getting lighter. The sky is almost clear in the east and that's the way the doctor will come. I think we'll have you comfortably in Kombala in a little while.

"And don't worry about your things. Scully's putting them together and they'll go with you. All your books and papers and photographs and tapes. You'll be able to work on them once you can sit up."

Then Scully came, and Korbin left them.

"How do you feel, Father?"

Father Herschell opened his eyes and tried to smile. "Hullo, Francis. Sorry to do this to you."

"It's nothing, Father. These things happen all the time."

He hesitated. "I wonder if you feel strong enough to do a job for me." And before the priest could answer: "It's quite a time since I went to confession."

The priest knew, then, that the question of whether he died or lived a little longer was of no real consequence; that his own personality, his mind and body were of little account except as God made use of them.

And whatever one thought of St. Paul, his legalism and periods of misanthropy and the ferocity of his intolerance, he had the knack of catching at the facts: not me, but Christ in me! That was it. That was all that mattered. Being a channel and an avenue through which God's grace could reach all other people.

Scully saw him nodding, so knelt beside the stretcher, blessed himself and bent his head. "Bless me, Father, for I have sinned."

And afterwards (Sandra settled) getting up, he said, "Thank you, Father. And do what you can for me with Rosemary when you see her in Kombala."

"I will, Francis. And thank you for letting me be a priest. Now, please, will you do something for me?"

He spoke a little more strongly now.

"From the beginning I was afraid, and ashamed of being afraid.

"Soon after leaving Wanega I hid in Kenneth's tent one day, and later, when he complained that somebody had tampered with his gun, I kept silent and let Sergeant Sosu take the blame.

"Then, when Sosu was drowned, I felt responsible and wanted more than anything to make amends; to overcome my fear so that none of you would have to suffer the consequences of it again."

He was breathing with difficulty and Scully wished that he would stay quiet. But when he had rested a little while he went on.

"Yesterday, for the first time, I wasn't afraid. But it was too

**246**

late, because Kenneth had already asked me to leave in the helicopter with Gunji."

There was pain in his grey face.

"I would have gone, but first I wanted to prove to myself that I had won my little victory. That I could be a hero to myself if to nobody else. But I am not a hero. Only stupid, and a nuisance. And Kenneth can send me out now, in the helicopter, with a clear conscience.

"Tell him I'm sorry, especially about Sosu. And ask him to forgive me."

He closed his eyes.

G'napa saw the helicopter come into the valley, and the smoke rise from the ceremonial ground to guide it. He saw it veer, then stop and hover and slowly descend, and he shook his head in wonderment.

The small boy beside him shifted the weight of the club on his shoulder, and G'napa glanced down at him. With uncertain satisfaction he noted the black stain of blood on it. He thought of his brother and was content, though sorry for the priest, who was a good man and might have been a friend.

They saw a great whirling cloud of brown dust rise from the ceremonial ground, blotting out the tops of the casuarina trees; and out of the dust the helicopter coming like some magic thing.

They watched it go back over the mountains.

Extract from the daily diary kept by Assistant District Officer Marshall, officer-in-charge of the Wanega Patrol Post.
16.6.1965.

Home again! At 1425 hours having made the distance from our Yakanaki base camp in 10 days 0175 hours or a shade under six days quicker than the outward journey though understandable on account of having no supernumeraries or sick carriers to hold us back. Even so Mr. Korbin (medical assistant) was able to consolidate much of the good work done on the way out especially among the Ongi who seemed pleased to see us again and full of questions about the Yakanaki people.

No radio communication on the way back owing to spare batteries being lost in the river-crossing incident on the outward journey so no news until I spoke to Kombala this afternoon.

Regret to hear that Father Herschell passed away. Somebody must now go back to Yakanaki to round up suspects and witnesses and bring them in for interrogation, coronial proceedings and possible trial—a time-consuming and costly business that will tie up dozens of people for months all of which might have been avoided.

Could say much on this subject but will keep silent now that the matter is subjudice reserving my opinions for the official inquiry and able to face same with a clear conscience having done everything possible to protect the deceased from the consequences of what must surely be regarded by any fair-minded person as an ill-advised and unwise undertaking from the beginning (see diary entries for 18.5.65 and 25.5.65).

But least said soonest mended and must admit that apart from the irritations and inconveniences brought about by his inexperience I found Father Herschell a likeable chap and very interesting when demonstrating and explaining techniques used in this linguistic business which I must look into a bit further when time permits. Bad luck he could not complete this particular project which will no doubt be allowed to lapse. NOTE: must check on procedures necessary to obtain temporary possession of the Yakanaki tape (my speech etc.) and permission to copy and use this for approved purposes such as Historical Society meetings.

Apart from the unfortunate series of incidents can say that this patrol has been a success. Our basic objective of establishing closer ties with Ongi people and making good first contact with Yakanaki clans and headmen was accomplished and foundations laid for future good relations. In this respect the preliminary payout to Gunji's family created excellent impression and the prospect of a final payment should provide starting point for co-operation when the next patrol goes in to investigate Father Herschell's murder.

So taking things all round can congratulate ourselves on a successful expedition.

248

Have formally charged carrier Lop Lop with the murder of Ngo Ningin (known as Didimus) and will send him to Kombala under escort as soon as the carriers are paid off. Will recommend that he be placed in a corrective institute and taught carpentry which will be most useful here once the place begins to go ahead and new government buildings are needed.

Will also suggest that a young Yakanaki (perhaps Gunji's son) be brought out by the next patrol and put to school at Kombala it being essential to begin training new and young leaders from the moment of first contact.

Have instructed Patrol Officer Scully to arrange repatriation of the two Dana men and negotiate payment of compensation to relatives of the third man, killed during the Ongi incident. Otherwise will have trouble with these difficult people.

Acting-Lance Corporal Garni complains that his wife has gone off to the coast with a surveying team which was through here in our absence. Also he has heard of my transfer to Madang and wishes to go with me. Am annoyed that this information received from District Commissioner McKerrow by radio no more than an hour ago should already be common gossip on the station but appreciate this evidence of Garni's personal loyalty and have promised to see what I can do for him.

Will be sorry to leave the Highlands with so much still to be accomplished but such is the nature and tradition of the service that one must be prepared to accept without question and regardless of personal convenience what authority in its wisdom dictates for the general benefit.

P.S. The wheelbarrow brought back from Yakanaki has been returned to general stores on Credit Voucher C193.

## A Note About the Author

Maslyn Williams was born in England in 1911 of Irish parents. Orphaned early, he was reared in Australia on sheep ranches. After moving to Sydney, he became a film editor-writer for the Commonwealth documentary unit, filling in spare time as a radio script-writer and repertory theater director. In 1940 he was appointed producer-writer to the official film and photo unit attached to the Australian Combined Services. In that capacity, he travelled around the world. He is the author of two works of non-fiction, *Stone Age Island,* and *Five Journeys From Jakarta.* Mr. Williams lives with his wife in Sydney, Australia.